GW00496616

Unbound by Payton E. Carrigan
An imprint of Heartworks Ink

First edition August 2022 Meridian, Idaho

Edited by Rachel Rant at Bluebird Writing and Editing Solutions
Translations Edited by Agata Dueck
Cover Art by Stephanie Jemphrey

Back Cover Quotation
*The Four Loves* by CS Lewis © 1960 CS Lewis Pte Ltd.

ISBN 979-8-9864658-0-7
Library of Congress Control Number: 2022913080

Visit the author's Instagram @author.paytonecarrigan

This book is dedicated to God, the true author of all stories, and to everyone he has used to unbind my own heart.

# PAYTON E. CARRIGAN

# 1

I'm teetering back and forth. Heel toe, heel toe, heel toe. My passport shakes at my side as I wait in line for TSA. The boarding pass tucked in its front cover reads: Adelina McCall Kit; From: Boise (BOI) To: Seattle (SEA); Flight: DL1948; Gate: B6; Boarding Time: 06:00 May 26.

I'm practically jumping out of my clothes in all of my excitement. Well, not quite; I'd never actually just go full-on nude in the middle of an airport. There's a time and place for that, of course, but the security line in an airport is certainly not the right time. Though streaking would certainly be a cap on this adrenaline rush I'm feeling. I'm exhilarated, and nervousness floods my veins.

Seriously, I am currently fourteen hours away from being in the beautiful and exotic Costa Rica. I'll land in the capital and drive another two hours before arriving in Puntarenas where I'll be living. In the midst of finishing my third year of college I decided it'd be best to complete my internship early. I will have school to finish when I go back but I'm glad to have the chance to leave now. I'm not very good with staying at home and figured this was a good way to head out early.

Unfortunately, I'll go back to finish my last semester of school before the biggest day of my life: graduation. Just kidding, I don't even really care about the official stuff; it's just one of those things we all have to do—one that's more for the people coming than anything else.

Right now, none of these future details matter because I'm trying to focus on this moment. Passport, boarding pass, cell phone—check, check, and check. Hopefully everything else I'll need is in my overstuffed backpack.

The bodies rustle around me as I start to strip everything down for those fancy machines. Weapons, drugs, flammable substances—they're checking for all of it, because who knows where people could be stashing this stuff.

As I make my way through this mess we call "security" and out toward my terminal, my nerves calm down and I begin to think. I have two layovers, the first in Seattle and the latter in LA, and lots of time to kill on the planes. I still can't believe I'm about to spend so much time in a country I've never been to before—by myself.

It makes sense though; I mean, I've pretty much tried to live my life as independently as possible. In fact, that's probably one of my greatest goals in life: If I stick with God, I won't need anyone else. At least, that's what I tell myself.

Now this mentality hasn't really worked out the greatest all the time, but hey, I'm fine. My objective is to take on as little damage as possible by interacting deeply with as few people as possible. For the most part, I'd say I've succeeded. There have certainly been a few people who have slipped by my defenses and I guess it's been for the better; yet, I still resist because I know everything is temporary and loss is painful.

Anyway, I'm ready to go and ready to experience who knows what in Costa Rica. For some reason I've always felt drawn to Latin America, and by some miracle I'm actually headed there to live.

Here in the airport I see everyone keeping to themselves. They're worrying about their own hopes, dreams, and plans, concentrating on one thing: what they want and need. In Costa Rica it's different. I know, I know, reality will not meet my expectations, but I do know that in many ways the people there are more open, caring, and alive. It conforms to Latin American culture, which focuses on bringing people together. The ironic thing is that I keep trying to reject this value, to flee any form of life together. My excuse now is that I'm tired of where I live; I'm bored. I hate staying in one place because well, like I said, everything is temporary and eventually the good things will fade, so why not move on before that happens?

Costa Rica may not be different but at least it's a new experience, and I guess I'm leaving after anyway, so I've already got my escape situated. Maybe someday I'll finally be content enough to stay committed to somewhere, something, even someone. I know in my head that all this running and all this isolation and self-reliance is not what God wants for me. In his design we're all unique building blocks meant to create something beautiful together. But 'together' just happens to scare me. So, for now, I'm flying solo.

I politely make eye contact with the passengers in each seat next to me, but who am I kidding? I'm not the type to actually strike up conversation with people, so unless they try to engage with me, I stick to reading a few of the books I downloaded earlier.

As the hours pass by I gaze out my window, peering down toward the mountains, which turn to deserts until I spot the iridescent blue of the ocean, a luscious tropical rainforest, and finally the multitude of metal roofs and concentrated buildings of San Jose.

As I wait for the passengers ahead of me to exit the plane, my legs bounce incessantly. I still can't tell if the adrenaline is from nerves or excitement.

3

As I get farther from my seat, I find myself surrounded by the familiar and still somewhat confusing sound of people speaking Spanish. This is real. I'm here. No more familiarity or certainty.

As I wait in the immigration line, I make a mental checklist of all the things I need to do next. I follow the thinning masses of people and try to read the signs in the airport terminals. I easily get through the line and checkpoint at customs and finally see the busses and taxis lined up.

It's a madhouse as people yell and try to get my attention. "Taxi, lady, taxi." *Don't take the yellow taxis.* I remind myself. They're the ones scammers supposedly use to trap Americans and rob them. The authentic, governmentally approved taxis are all red with a yellow triangle highlighting the doors. Definitely different.

I walk down the sidewalk and immediately notice the heat and humidity adding an extra weight to my skin. A man outside of a taxi waves me over with a brilliant smile and while I'm freaking out, I'm also feeling fairly confident—plus he seems gentler and less obnoxious, so my nerves calm a bit.

As I slide in, I tell him the address I've recited to myself a multitude of times since receiving it. Until I leave, I will be staying with the Espinola family. My intern program worked to set me up in a host home, and the Espinolas are being extra gracious in allowing me to arrive a little early.

As the pavement and gravel shift under our tires, I grow closer to meeting them. The traffic is hectic, certainly less organized than in the States, but we pass through without issues and pull up to a gated garage area. The yellow stucco walls and metal roof of the home are fused alongside the simple and similar home next door. I like it immediately.

Suddenly, the driver honks to alert my host family that we're out here. A petite, middle-aged woman peeks her head out of the door hesitantly but swings it wide energetically once she sees me standing out front. "¿Adelina? ¡Pura vida! ¡Bienvenida a nuestra casa!" This must be Isabel, my host mom. She greets me with a warm welcome and the common slang of the country, which means 'pure life.' It seems like she's normally fairly quiet, but right now her hospitality and energy are showing.

She quickly opens the gate and thanks the driver, who waits patiently for me to hand him the decorative and colorful money to cover the trip. He speeds off and I watch him for a moment, taking a deep breath to remind myself of where I am and to encourage myself to speak.

As we enter the house, a boy standing in the kitchen immediately rushes to greet me. He tells me his name is Axel. I remember from my pre-trip information packet that he's thirteen.

A younger boy comes running from a room in the adjoining hallway. His image reflects that of his older brother's but he is smaller and scrawnier. He stops abruptly behind Axel and looks at me curiously but shyly. "Manuel, dile hola," a girl's voice says from the couch in the room beside us. He obeys quickly, saying hello with more confidence than he is showing.

I watch as the teenager gets up and comes over, introducing herself as Elena. She's the oldest of the kids in the family, eighteen. Manuel is only nine. There are four kids, so that only leaves Luciana, the 16-year-old daughter whom Isabel quickly informs me is with a friend and apologizes for her absence. Honestly, it's not a problem because I'm feeling a bit overwhelmed with just the four of them.

When Axel leads me down the hallway we pass by three small rooms. The first has two small beds in it along with a tall dresser and one long mirror. The walls have a few posters plastered up, one of which displays a group of guys on it that could be the equivalent of a Hispanic One Direction. I imagine this is the girls' room. The door across from theirs opens into a room of similar size with only one bed and minimal décor; the walls contain only a few photos of the family. The simplicity and cleanliness indicate that it probably belongs to Isabel.

The next door on the left, the one Manuel came from a few minutes ago, has two beds similar to those in the girls' room. There are a few play trucks and cars scattered on the floor, and some folded clothes lie stacked atop one of the beds.

Axel points to the small bathroom that's directly in front of us and then leads me into the room across from theirs. I immediately regret that they're giving me a room to myself. It seems larger than the others, and as I look around I see a few trinkets on shelves, which make the room appear occupied. They look like they belong to a boy; the homestay info didn't mention another kid.

I scan my eyes across the bed with deep navy green sheets, and Axel starts speaking behind me. "Esta era la habitación de mi hermano." That makes sense, that this room would belong to his brother, but the drawings by the small desk look much better than what a nine-year-old could produce.

I stay quiet and Axel keeps talking. I deflate onto the bed as he tells me what happened. Their father, Leo, and eldest brother, Gabriel, passed away in a car crash four years ago while on their way into the capital. It's this brother whose room I'll now occupy. Axel says Gabriel would've been nineteen now, only a year younger than I am currently.

From what I can tell, it's definitely left a hole in their family and it may explain Isabel's reservations, but they seem friendly and kind nonetheless. I thank Axel and he exits quickly and quietly so I can unpack my things into the small dresser nestled beside the bed.

I remove my few articles of clothing from my backpack and place them in the drawers. The sound of their foreign language comes down the hallway and floats into my room. I reflect on all I've seen so far. This is what I'll have to get used to. This, and so many other things that are new and uncomfortable—yet so alluring. I don't really know what will happen, but I hope I'm ready for whatever God decides to throw my way. The best way to learn and grow is to just dive in, right? Well, here goes nothing!

The next few days pass in a blur as I'm shown around and introduced to the family's way of life. So far, they've all been more than generous with their time and home and they're patient with my Spanish. I don't know what I was expecting, but this is definitely a different dynamic than what I'd anticipated.

Axel is by far the most social with me, and a little too flirtatious sometimes for the age gap, but he reminds me of my younger brother Trace who is seventeen, so it'll be fun to have another little brother to tease and joke around with. I met Luciana later the first night and she seemed more boisterous than her sister. All of them seem less soft-spoken than their mother.

Most nights as we watch movies, or as they laugh and joke over my mispronunciation and funny accent, I can see the vibrancy and joy in all of them. It's certainly a fun and interesting change from my fully introverted family at home.

Since I arrived, the girls have taken me out most afternoons to explore the peninsula. It certainly isn't large by any means but they're helping me to find all of the cutest cafes and the best—and cheapest—ice cream stands, books, and anything else I could possibly want.

Puntarenas is small but it is the largest city, and the capital, of this province in Costa Rica. The specific area where I'm centralized is the main peninsula, which only extends a few miles and is quite compact. Most people wouldn't really enjoy the small atmosphere, but I love it. I've taken a few mornings or early evenings to run through the city and have found it to be bustling with various buildings and homes.

Isabel tells me that the area is mostly used as a fishing port and for tourists to pass through while on cruises. The beach is also the closest to San Jose, so it's occupied by city dwellers fairly often on weekends.

Things are fairly busy around the city each afternoon as well when I wander around, though the surprise rain storms that come in this summer season catch us all off guard and keep the streets fairly clear.

Most evenings Isabel fixes us all some of the delicacies of the area after she gets back from work. Tonight, the girls and I are trying to help her as usual, but I don't really know what I'm doing so mostly I just watch in awe as they flutter here and there, grabbing spices and flicking things in various pots and pans. I am getting more comfortable, though, and soon Isabel begins directing me toward ingredients. There are still many spices and specific food items that are not yet part of my vocabulary, so I just point while she nods.

The boys are playing fútbol outside with some of the other kids in the neighborhood like they usually do during this time. Luckily, there aren't a bunch of other steps left for the meal and Isabel can see that I'm not of much use, so she urges me out of the house. The gate in front of the garage provides me with only momentary protection. Once I emerge, the boys and other kids scurry around me.

"Lena, ayúdame," Manny shouts for help. I smile at his use of the nickname he's given me. My full name still proves to be a mouthful for him.

I run to an open spot in the street so he can pass to me but fail to make a connection as one of the older opponents rushes toward me. I was never very coordinated, unlike my brother; he's the soccer player. "Perdón, Manny," I try to apologize but he just shakes his head a bit and laughs. I've been out here a few other nights with them and they all know I'm no good. They just include me as a matter of principle, but sometimes we can pass successfully if the other team isn't watching.

I run around with them for the next hour until Isabel calls us all in. Turns out my team won, though I didn't see a lot of success after I joined. I'm pretty positive that wasn't totally my fault.

We quickly eat our soup accompanied by beans and rice, then

Luciana runs to get the speaker from their room. As soon as she connects it, we turn up the music and they try to teach me some of the classical dances from the area. Of course I suck, but they're patient and just laugh at my stiff movements and awkward steps. "More hips," they all tell me, thinking it should come naturally—it doesn't.

I'd imagine that the whole family thinks I'm leaving next week by the rate at which they're throwing me into all of this, but I love it. It's wild and random and crazy.

I should probably start venturing out on my own more so I can meet people and work on improving my Spanish, but it's hard not having a set group of people I can turn to. And I'm not keen on starting conversations with random strangers.

If I don't, there's no point in half of this; I won't grow or get better at the language. I have to be bold and make friends. It shouldn't be too bad, right? Plus, more friends means I can see more of the area, and that wouldn't be too bad at all.

# 2

I'm sitting in the sand with my back along the short cement wall of the boardwalk, watching the lull of the ocean and the few early surfers pack up their boards from the morning's ride.

There is one boy, young man I guess, who is seated like I am, observing the crowd. In his hands rests a book, half open, ready to be read again at any minute.

He's wearing black jeans and a light gray button-down shirt he's folded up to the middle of his forearms. A thin silver chain hangs from his neck, tucking neatly into his collar, and a faint hint of black and blue ink appears to swirl up from beneath his shirt on the right side of his neck.

His feet are not bare as I would've imagined for sitting in the sand. Rather, halfway digging into the grains of sediment below, are a completely overused pair of skate shoes resembling knock-off Vans.

I see others notice him, too. It's certainly not the most normal thing to just sit and read in public, especially not when the sun has hardly risen and it's barely six in the morning.

He doesn't notice. He's turned back to his book and appears to be quite entranced by what he's reading. His face is so at peace as his eyes trail the page, though it's partially masked by the wispy waves of dark brown, almost black hair that trail down from under his dark gray beanie. I must admit—he's cute. I hope he doesn't catch me gawking.

It's quite endearing that he's out here reading. His look matches an almost punk-skater vibe, but his actions seem 'nerdy,' and I find the juxtaposition intriguing.

School has ended for the year and he seems to be about my age, so he likely isn't reading for any sort of assignment. Maybe the book was a gift or a recommendation from a friend. I'm not sure why he's reading it, but I am sure he's quite enjoying it because one side of his mouth twists up in a lopsided smirk and his eyes crinkle a bit as though he's just read something amusing.

If I wasn't such an awkward introvert, I'd probably go ask him about the book. Instead, I'm distracted from my vain attempts at getting out of my shell and startle when someone shouts toward his direction. "¡Ey, Dash! ¿Todavía estás leyendo? Que aburrido mae." Another boy, roughly the same age, ridicules him for reading as he runs across the sand with his surfboard trapped under his arm. He fumbles a bit as the tail end of his board begins to slip from his grasp but quickly regains his footing and keeps his stride.

The other boy now beams up at him as he approaches, no doubt also enjoying the fact that his friend almost just tripped and ate sand.

The boy on the wall, I think he was called Dash or something, takes a bright green sucker out of his mouth before giving a response followed by a joyous laugh. I can't quite make out their conversation now that the shouting has stopped, and the fact that they're both speaking rapid-fire Spanish doesn't exactly help either.

My Bible lies open to where I'd started reading this morning in Hosea. My journal is open too, although I haven't written more than a few lines thanks to the boys distracting me.

Every morning I've been trying to have my devotional time somewhere new so I can experience more of the city God's brought me to. This morning, I thought the fresh, though still somewhat humid air mingling with the sound of the ocean tracing up the sand a mere thirty feet away would be perfect.

I didn't notice Dash when I arrived, but he and the new surfer boy have drawn my attention for probably twenty minutes. The new kid has stopped teasing Dash about reading his dumb book when he should have been out enjoying the waves with the others, but they're definitely still joking around and making fun of each other.

I glance away but quickly refocus on them. When I do, I realize their gaze has shifted away from each other now and… of course, Newcomer is staring straight at me with a look of anticipation on his face. Dash's attention is moving between the two of us.

Did they say something to me?

Dangit. My mother always told me I had selective hearing and well, I was obviously too preoccupied with my own thoughts to realize they'd shifted their attention. Yep, they're definitely looking at me now, but I don't know what they said. Of course.

"Buenas," I reply, hoping that maybe it had just been a simple greeting. "Chau," I mumble as I hop up, collect my things, and start walking away.

I'm not running or anything, I'm not even walking that quickly, but I still feel really awkward. I mean, I know I'm not that bad at Spanish. Hello and goodbye—that's seriously all I could say?

I've reached my bike now and put my stuff in the basket up front. The Espinolas are lending it to me while I'm here, and while it's pretty run-down, it's very efficient.

As I ride away, I catch a glimpse of the two of them. The surfer boy is removing his wetsuit and the other is putting the board into the back of what looks to be an older-style Jeep or truck thing. They're no longer watching me, which is great, but I'm pretty sure I can see the hint of smiles on their faces that lets me know they're still chuckling to themselves. Lovely.

Go me. I've been here less than two weeks and am already entertaining the locals.

In movies and books this happens all the time. Socially awkward girl sees attractive guy, freezes and spills food on herself, or on him, turns firetruck red, then scrambles away. I'm criticizing myself because that doesn't reflect who I am, at least not normally.

I'm not really sure why I left so abruptly. Maybe my six o'clock brain just really wasn't ready for any form of socializing. Plus, it was in Spanish. I get a little slack because of that factor, right? Of course I'll have to get over that road bump soon if I hope to have any semblance of normal conversations while I'm here.

I've come to the conclusion that I was just startled. Why would any sane person try to engage with someone who is minding their own business on the beach journaling and reading so early in the morning?

Except, I wasn't really doing that at the moment, was I? Nope, I was focused totally on them. No excuse; I'm an idiot.

Luckily for me, I don't really care. The likelihood of seeing those guys again isn't the highest; then again, it's not the slimmest either. Regardless of me seeing them—or not, hopefully—it doesn't matter.

I am not the awkward, socially inept, shy girl. So next time— if there is a next time—I'll act normal.

It's been a little less than a week since my awkward run-in with those guys and things are still going well. Generally, when I'm at home, my life is full of stress and the craziness of life. Trying to do everything, be everywhere, engage with everyone.

Other times I shut my brain down completely and read for days on end—engaging in class only when I have to, talking to people only when absolutely necessary, sprinting to the bathroom so I can quickly get back to my story, and eating only when I feel my body start to go into preservation mode. These times are my favorite, probably because they provide a break from the world.

I don't know why I'm always trying to escape. Whether it's from the short conversation with someone I don't know well, the daily life of college, or the country I'm supposed to call home, I'm always running.

I have found that I'm most content when I feel no outside pressures from the world. When I'm living out of the joy I have in God, not because of other people's demands. It's too hard to meet their expectations. But I have to grow in this area somehow to live and love better. I need to learn how to commit, to receive, and also give love.

That's what I'm trying to do now. I'm riding my bike up and down the various streets, winding back and forth like a snake hunting for its next meal. In this case I actually am starving, and I've postponed my touring to find one of the various sodas around the area that I haven't tried yet. I don't know why they're called sodas when they're really just mini restaurants, but I guess it's another part of the culture to embrace.

This morning as Isabel and I ate omelets made of eggs straight from the truck that drives around blasting, "Huevos, huevos," from its speakers, we discussed some of the things I'd been experiencing and hoping to see. She asked me about meeting people and if I'd been able to find anyone to talk to since being here. This means I inevitably told her about the beach and how that was the closest I'd come to conversing with anyone in this country, other than her and the kids.

While I've been maintaining relationships at home, I regretfully told Isabel that interactions here are minimal, and I'm determined to try to step out a bit more.

"Eso está bueno, mija," she encouraged me.

"Si, pero no puedo. No conozco a nadie." Really, like I can't because I actually don't know anyone, so how am I supposed to branch out and engage with them? I'm not exactly in a program with other students, which means I haven't been able to meet anyone that way, and while I saw a few people my age the other morning at church, I didn't talk to anybody. It's fine, I'll start my internship soon enough.

"Pues, tengo una amiga."

"Gracias, pero no pienso que funcionará," I shut her off, not wanting to hang out with one of my host mom's random friends.

"¡Chit! ¡Chit! ¡Chit!" she quieted me. "Ella tiene una hija. Sé que te caería bien." Ohh, whoops, I guess maybe I wouldn't mind meeting someone's daughter. If she's my age then what's the issue?

"Emmm, no, gracias." I changed my mind. What if she's really obnoxious, or she only enjoys sports—sports are most definitely not my thing—or what if….

"Bueno, pues, sí," my mind contradicted itself again, "¿Dónde la puedo conocer?" I guessed it wouldn't hurt to try to find her. I knew I may regret it, but the smile grew across Isabel's face and gave me confidence.

She hurriedly scrawled basic directions on a paper. I snatched it up, hesitated a moment, and then headed to get my bike before I changed my mind. Luckily, the spot Isabel marked wasn't too far down the beach.

As I approach the soda, I can't help but notice the girl who is working as the server. She can't be much older than I am.

Her hair is layered to just above her shoulders and is dyed an extraordinarily vibrant red that would match the color of a parrot's head. It's much more punk than my hair, which is a natural mix of auburn red and light chestnut brown. There's a sparkling black stud on the left side of her nose, which sits in the middle of her delicate and attractive face.

Fascinatingly, from the shredded cuffs of her shirt to her wrists, her sun-kissed arms are lined with an array of black, white, and pastel tattoos. The lightning bolt on the middle finger of her left hand as well as the shirt she wears are what really draw my attention.

Stretched across the front of her shirt it states:

*IF YOU CAN READ THIS*

*MY INVISIBILITY CLOAK ISN'T WORKING*

I smirk up at her and she glowers at me. "You appear to be an American, though British maybe? Well whatever, why are you looking at me like that?" Her Spanish words fire at me quickly.

In my best British accent I proclaim, "Well, I hate to tell you this but…your body is gone!" Annnd I've done it. Her face has lit up in approval at my recognition of her Harry Potter paraphernalia.

"I'm Jo. And while you have obviously wonderful taste in literature, and probably movies as well, you're probably here for food. So, what can I get for you?" I'm entertained by her abruptness.

"Hi, yeah umm Jo?"

"Yes, Jo."

"Alright, well, I know this is really awkward but I'm actually kind of here for more than just food. You see, I've been in the country now for a few weeks and have only managed to befriend my host family and the neighbor's chickens. Well I did sort of meet these—"

"Chica, más rapido. I don't know what you're talking about, but people are going to want food at some point, so I have to serve you before they get here."

I look around and see no one for a few hundred meters. "I think you're going to be fine."

"Well if you haven't noticed…" she pauses and looks at my shirt as though I'm going to have my name embroidered there.

"Adelina, but most of my friends call me Kit."

"Okay Kit, we certainly aren't friends but that's simpler. I actually can't ask you to leave because technically you haven't done anything wrong, and you are a potential customer, but can you please just hurry?" she insists.

"My, my, Isabel told me that you were something, but this is wonderful. Let me get to the point because you seem to appreciate bluntness. I need someone to call my friend while I'm here, at least until I meet some other people. Really, we'll just be more like acquaintances. You seem spunky, quick-witted, and a bit like you want people to think you hate the world while you secretly love it as much, if not more than, everyone else, so I figure that Isabel has pointed me in the right direction. What do you think?" I spit confidently and quickly while her mouth drops and then slowly turns up into a full smile that crinkles up the corner of one of her eyes. I'm as amazed as she is. I swear my Spanish was practically flawless.

"Alright Kit, what exactly does this 'friendship' entail? What's my part?"

"Mostly I just want someone to show me around and provide decent entertainment."

Her laugh is light and airy. "Well I suppose I can deal with that. Do I get to make a few requests of my own?"

"I suppose that'd be alright."

"Hmm maybe I'll just bring them up as we go along. What's our first task as best friends now? Wait, first," her eyes meet mine with a critical stare, "are you a true HP fan or just one of those posers like most everyone else?"

My face sinks, and my mind races backward. Maybe this was a bad idea. I'm about to blow the whole thing and we're only five minutes in. "Well yes and no. Have I read them? No. Have I seen them? Well not fully…"

"I knew you were a phony!" Her face turns to a scowl as she interrupts my attempted explanation.

"Wait hold up, just because I'm not obsessed or not the most knowledgeable in it all doesn't mean that I don't enjoy what I know. You see, my best friend back home also quite enjoys Harry Potter. Like you, she found it detestable that I'd never read or even seen any of them, so she insisted on us watching them together. We only made it through the first three films but still, I quite enjoyed them."

"Ughh you're killing me. Task one: I get off this evening, and we'll start them again."

Yay! Isabel is a genius. Jo actually doesn't seem all that bad and more than likely we'll find our connection somehow. She's a reader, I know that much. And she's a little more edgy than most, so that means that she's fine with going against the status quo. We'll get along stupendously.

I get my food and then spend the afternoon reading and journaling until Jo gets done with work and we walk the few blocks to her house. We have the place to ourselves because her mom and brothers have gone to the capital for something.

It's pretty late when we start, but we grab some snacks to munch on and she makes us watch the first two full movies anyway.

As I grab my bike to head home, Jo looks at me quizzically. After her assessment she nods her head. "This will be good," she tells me as an appreciative smile crosses her face. Because we click so well, I can definitely agree with her statement—but it's almost too good, and it can't last like this.

# 3

I arrive to the beach about an hour earlier than the last time and settle myself on a bench rather than in the sand. Regretfully, the bookworm isn't in sight. I'm left to gawk at the surfers while they skirr on top of the waves as the sun rises to bring in the new day.

Since being here, I've decided this is one of my favorite places, especially in the mornings. The sun rises from behind where I'm sitting and I can tell immediately when it has peeked over the buildings as it begins to dance on top of the waves and brush through the hair of the surfers.

The reflection beams into a brilliant gold that covers everything and makes the ocean sparkle. I never really thought that I could love the ocean more, but sitting here in the fans of warmth, staring at the vast expanse of depth and mystery before me, I've been left baffled again.

I'm not one to appreciate the unknown. I like certainty and stability. I'm comfortable in what I've experienced and what I can have control over. Yet somehow, this all falls void when I enter the ocean. I have no control over the waves or the multitude of creatures below me. I ride adrift on the water as the current goes in and out from the sandy bank. I can look into the skies and feel like I'm floating on the clouds toward space.

I can actually imagine I'm getting to experience a tiny piece of heaven. Just as when one looks at the face of a lake and sees the reflection of trees and mountains and they cannot help but look up at that which is greater and more manifest, I in this moment cannot look out at this grandeur and not acknowledge the hands that made it.

I'm standing on the edge of the tide where the lull of the waves entices me. Before I can stop myself, my toes are being tickled by trails of water. My pants are clinging to the cusp of my calves as I go deeper and deeper.

My breath is gone the moment the first wave rakes hard against my chest, splattering up into my face. I suck it back in as I dive under the next incoming wave. I have no idea what I'm really doing because I brought no towel or swimsuit or clothes for the walk back, but this is where I desire to be and nothing is stopping me.

Well, I guess maybe I'm wrong. I break forth from behind the wave that just rushed over me and peer from the hair that's still sporadically slung across my face to see two surfers gliding toward me. No, not gliding, they're careening full on toward me. Do they not realize that I'm here?

Of course not, no sane person jumps in the ocean this early in the morning if they're not surfing, and right now all of the surfers are back at the lineup.

I'm gonna die. I've been knocked in the ribs by a surfboard before, and I couldn't move right for weeks. So, two boards, one me, and many weeks where I will be incapacitated. I'm stoked.

As they zoom toward me, I notice them zigzagging away from and toward each other jokingly, trying to knock the other off. Until they see me. Now they're both trying to direct each other out of the way, one flying over the front of his board to my right and the other diving smoothly off on my left.

I can't swim away from this catastrophe fast enough. I know you shouldn't casually swim in a surf zone since it's neither safe for you nor the surfers, but I wasn't really thinking about it. I was being serendipitous.

"Gringa estúpida, que tonta. Podríamos haber chocado contra usted." The minute the first sentence is out of his mouth I know he's furious. He calls me an idiot and informs me that they could've crashed into me, as if I hadn't already realized that.

"Eh, Dash, cálmate mae. Mírala." The boy on my other side tries to calm his friend with little luck. Oh wait, did this kid just call his friend Dash?

For the first time, I gather my composure and look to my left side at the guy who had to dive off his board. Oh no. I slowly brush wet hair out of my face so I can see better as I glance to my right at the guy who's still mumbling under his breath.

You have got to be kidding me! I look over to my left again and yep, he's still staring at me. It's the surfer from the first morning. Which of course means the kid on my right really is the one person I both do and don't want him to be at the same time.

While he did just try to chew my head off, he was right. So, despite my desire to fire attitude right back at him, I stammer out an apology. "Hey, Dash is it? I'm so incredibly sorry. I definitely didn't mean to get in your way. I completely forgot about all of you surfers and just dove in. I know I trashed your ride, not that it looked like you were taking it all that seriously but that's beside the point." I silently curse myself for adding this last part, which may only frustrate him more. "I wasn't really thinking. I'm just gonna go and I won't bother you both anymore."

"You're right. You did get in the way and ruin our ride because you weren't thinking," he interjects—in English nonetheless—and pauses as I begin to slowly trudge back through the waves, careful not to lose my footing. How much more embarrassing would it be to fall on the way out?

I look back cautiously when I hear him begin to mutter something again, quieter now, "I'm not worried about those things as much. I'm just frustrated because we could have seriously hurt you."

As I look toward him with confusion, I hear the other boy bark out a laugh. "Are you serious Dash? All of that and you're worried?" He splashes water toward him playfully. "You had her so freaked out. Apologize to the poor girl."

I turn around fully now to look ahead at the two of them. "I don't need an apology from either of you. He was right." I turn back to Dash, "However, kid—"

"Kid?" he questions, and I quickly realize how dumb this probably sounds seeing as 'kid' is a term usually reserved for people under the age of twelve.

I continue, despite the odd choice of words. "Yes, you could've been gentler. Especially if you were really just trying to express concern. I mean, who yells at someone and makes them feel like a horrible person just to be like, 'I was just worried about your safety. I don't care about the rest of it.'?"

"I wasn't worried about your safety."

"Oh really?" I've been walking back toward the beach while talking to them, but I take a step forward now. I clear my throat and lower it as I try to make my face look gentle and peaceful, "We could have seriously hurt you," I mock whisper as I smirk back at him.

I feel kind of rude as my sass comes out extra aggressively, but like I told myself the first time I saw him, I'm not the timid, shy girl and I don't want that to be the image they see.

"Oh dude, she so got you," the friend says in response to my mocking.

"Shut up Luc! So what if I was worried? That could've been a lawsuit or whatever you Americans do to look out for yourselves."

"Ahh I see, you didn't actually care. You were just watching your own butt."

"Watching his butt?" Luc asks, perplexed as one side of his mouth turns up. "Don't you mean that you were watching his butt?" Oh shoot, that's so not what I meant.

"Umm no," I giggle and then begin to laugh as they gawk at me. *I've lost them,* I think as I try to recover. "It's an expression. It means that he was really only thinking about himself." I'm sure my face is quite pink now, so I decide to give up. "Anyway, it was nice seeing you all for a second time," I say, acknowledging that I recognize them from the other day, "Hopefully we won't have to do this again."

I traipse through the last few feet of calf-high waves and run toward the beach to snatch up my sweatshirt and backpack. I quickly try to wring out my hair and shirt but I'm still soaking wet. I can't really make myself much warmer without taking my clothes off, and that's certainly not happening with those two bums still out in the water; instead, I try to use my sweatshirt as a makeshift towel. This works very poorly, so after a few seconds I give up and throw it over my head. Despite the exterior layer, my wet shirt clings too tightly to my torso and causes me to shiver. I curse myself silently as I remember that today I decided to walk to the beach.

"¡Chica, espera!" I hear one of guys shout from behind me.

I turn to see them both swooping to pick up their boards before the waves can catch them and throw them onto the beach.

"You look a little cold there, and we've got some towels in the Jeep if you'd want to use one," Luc offers and then raises his eyebrow in a joking way. "You could change out of your wet clothes if you want to." At this I scoff and turn back around even though the shivering has gotten worse.

"Hey, he's completely kidding. He's not like that," Dash yells out at me as I continue walking.

"Yeah, I'm sure you're both so noble," I reply over my shoulder.

My judgement is overly apparent and not super justified, but I've run into these guys twice and it's been a wreck both times. I'm sure they're not really that bad but this is what I do anyway: use heavy sarcasm and pessimism to keep people from engaging with me. I can't really help it, it's like second nature. Yeah, it keeps me from connecting with people, but it's just easier. Plus, my pride won't let me take it back.

I hear shuffling behind me and glimpse over my shoulder in curiosity.

Dash is walking after me at a quickened pace with a towel in hand. Oh goodness. I know he's not going to let me walk away so I finally stop and turn around.

"You're shivering," he says softly, ignoring my earlier comment as he extends the towel toward me.

I'm sure my cheeks turn pink again so I bow my head and take it a little too eagerly before clumsily wrapping it around my shoulders. "Thank you, and I'm really sorry for my response. I don't really know what I was thinking," I try to reply as an amused smile lingers on his face.

"It seems as though you haven't been thinking much, and it's still early. I'd be curious to see how you survive an entire day."

I'm caught off guard by this snarky comment so I don't respond. It seems as though he's joking and not genuinely insulting my intelligence. My intrigue heightens and my eyebrows instinctively quirk up with my reserved smile.

"Would you like to come back to the Jeep to get warm, or are you in a rush? I promise you won't be asked to take your clothes off." I look at him carefully and begin to walk alongside him. "Although, it may be better for you to warm up," he continues hesitantly.

I'm drawn to a stop again for a second until I realize he's being serious and not gross. "It'd be best to get you into dry clothes, and we have some extra sweats you could use." I take this into consideration when he laughs quietly to himself.

"Who goes into the ocean wearing denim? That's seriously

like the biggest mistake you could've made this morning." His amusement sparkles in his eyes.

"Actually, I think the biggest mistake I made was assuming I could come here for peace when in reality I was bound to humiliate myself again." His eyebrows raise curiously.

"You're telling me what transpired wasn't peaceful enough for you?" he asks as he ignores my comment about being humiliated. "Well okay, but you have to admit it was exciting, right?" He's raising only one eyebrow and I'm not sure if this is a serious question or if he's still somewhat joking about what happened. I think it's both.

"Oh definitely!" I proclaim with feigned agreement. "This morning I thought I'd be coming for some rest, yet what actually occurred is that I spontaneously decided to jump into the ocean with all my clothes on."

I inhale quickly to catch my breath. "This was then made even better when, followed by an abrupt and life-threatening introduction, I met two absolutely charming gentlemen." I now look hard at him for emphasis, "One of whom tried to drown me in guilt as if the pummeling waves and impending surf boards weren't enough, and the other practically offered to help get me out of my now saltwater-infused clothes," I huff in exasperation.

"So it was exciting, no?" He inquires again with a heavy accent lifting the end of his sentence. *He's so annoying it's cute.*

I can't help but quirk a smile as I walk the rest of the way to their Jeep.

"Ey, you got her to come back. I'm sorry, Sirena," Luc replies gently, referring to me as a mermaid to emphasize his point. "My comment was out of line. Nonetheless, here are some clothes you could change into if you'd want and if you can trust us not to look." He says this last bit with what looks to be slight shame that is quickly replaced by a generous smile as he extends a pile of black material to me.

I shift around to see if there are bathrooms in the general area and find some a few hundred yards away. Regrettably, that's farther than I'm willing to walk right now.

I open the back-passenger door to the Jeep and set the clothes on the seat. In the midst of shifting my towel back and forth between my hands I manage to replace my wet clothes with a pair of sweatpants and a hoodie that smells deliciously of guy's cologne.

I look down at the sweatshirt and notice the text that runs along the left side vertically. In white lettering there are the letters PATD. My heart rate raises a bit at the recognition of the simple acronym for one of my favorite bands and the black and white image of its singer. I turn back questioningly at the guys and find them both staring at me with perplexed expressions.

I ignore this and point to the hoodie. Luc immediately directs me to Dash. "It's some weirdo pop punk group he listens to. Don't ask." Luc shrugs as I look at Dash who doesn't say anything. I give a small smile that hopefully demonstrates my approval before I spin back around.

I grab my clothes from the floor mat and wring them out a bit before turning back to the guys who are looking at me expectantly. "Thank you guys. How should I return it all?" I ask meekly. I don't really want to come here in the mornings anymore if there's a chance that I'll run into them and I don't expect that I'll be intentionally meeting with either of them any time soon, so I'm stuck.

"Well, we should be surfing here again Thursday or next Tuesday. That's when we come most often," Luc tells me. Then emphatically he adds, "And my sister has a board you could use! You should definitely come out with us! You know, so then we can keep tabs on you and won't risk crashing into you again."

I'm intrigued by his invitation and kindness, yet I can't accept. "Yeah, I don't think that'll work."

"Why, you don't think you can do it?" Luc's eyebrows dart up with his daring question.

Dash speaks up softly, "We could teach you."

"Oh I'm sure you'd love that, wouldn't you," Luc accuses with a teasing smile, though I don't know if he's directing his comment to me or Dash. "Come on Sirena, you have to."

"The issue isn't a fear of riding, I've done it before, though admittedly I'm not the greatest," I respond without giving many details.

"So what then? What makes you hold back?" Luc asks sincerely.

I ignore his questions, because honestly I can't give a valid reason for avoiding them. Nonetheless, I say the first thing I can to alleviate more probing. "Well, I don't want to keep your clothes forever, so I'll be here. Not sure when, maybe Thursday, maybe Tuesday. Don't go to extra lengths to wait for me."

Honestly, I don't know what I'm doing. This whole morning, while it's been a huge nightmare, has also been beyond entertaining or, as Dash would say, 'Exciting, no.' Plus, I'd totally be down to come surfing since I haven't had the chance for a couple summers.

"We usually get here around five, before the sun has started to rise. Arrive then and we can get you in a wetsuit. Also, I'd advise that you wear a swimsuit next time rather than jeans, and maybe bring your own change of clothes and towel." Luc's jokes make me more eager to join them, but Dash can still see my reservation.

"Come on, Lucas, she clearly does not want to come surfing with us." Dash's irritation causes him to say his friend's whole name in conjunction with a sound of slight exasperation before he turns to me. "Keep the clothes. Whenever you end up here next just bring them with you; and if I'm not here, then bring them the next time. I'm not in a rush to get them back," Dash assures me.

"Yeah, alright, thanks. I guess I'll see you around," I say hesitantly before I turn and walk away.

# 4

The past few days have been exciting as I explore and am introduced to new areas. Yesterday I spent the afternoon wandering San Jose with my host family. There is so much that I didn't capture on my journey from the airport and, while big cities aren't my favorite, it was good quality time with them as they pointed out all the important places.

They also took time to drive me from the bus stop to where I'll have my internship. Isabel was pretty worried that when I finally got to come on my own I'd get lost. As we drove by I told them my hopes about interning with Hogar de la Esperanza. I shared about the burden I gained in high school for human trafficking victims and how this 'House of Hope' is meant to care for and bring restoration to victims through showing them Christ. Honestly, it sounds perfect, and I hope it'll give me an idea of what I'll want to do after I actually graduate.

When we got back the evening was fairly relaxed, but I awoke today to a text from Jo saying she had a fun surprise for me—which I'm now preparing for.

I don't really know what to expect since it couldn't possibly be more exciting than Harry Potter, which we've watched the past two nights, but Jo assured me that what we are going to do is essential to my experience here and that I'd love it.

While she hasn't even known me a full week at this point, I trust her, which is crazy because I can barely trust people I've known for years. I don't know how, but we've clicked so easily. The things I love are the things she loves. The things I laugh at are the things she laughs at. Plus, we try to avoid the same things, which means that if I wouldn't like the surprise, she wouldn't be taking me.

She even thinks she's earned the right to lecture me and give me advice already. When I decided not to go to the beach to meet the guys Thursday morning I didn't hear the end of it. "Que tonta, ¿Por qué tan cobarde?" I don't know exactly what the last part meant but I think she called me what is probably the equivalent of a chicken.

I tried explaining that the issue wasn't a matter of fear but more a matter of not wanting to deal with the frustration of interacting with them again. I mean it was decent, but at the same time I also left with a bit of a ruffle in my skirt. Figuratively, of course.

Surfing would be nice, but at the same time I don't want to look completely incompetent. Maybe I am a pansy. I convinced myself it's fine that I didn't go. They probably didn't miss me or even remember that I was supposed to show up, so there was no real harm done.

To avoid further lecturing, I didn't tell her that I actually did go to the beach Thursday morning, though it was a few hours later. The surfers were all gone by then and a cruise ship was pulling into the port. It's weird to think that technically I'm not really a tourist. Even though I don't fully know the language, culture, or even my way around half of the city, I'm not a tourist. I live here. I actually live in freaking Costa Rica.

After her arrival this evening, Jo tells me, we are going to live more authentically alongside the Ticos. We're experiencing culture, meeting people, and living with no boundaries on our hearts. Well, maybe a few boundaries. We both still have our standards and our morals, and those will definitely be maintained.

My brain raises huge red flags as she tells me that we're going to enjoy ourselves by saying yes to experiences and taking risks.

Maybe I'm crazy, but either we're dressing up for some sort of stylish and cool Harry Potter fandom meeting or we're going dancing. At a club.

When I jokingly accuse her of dragging me to the former, she hits me lightly. "You'd only be so lucky if I took you to such a special event! Alas, no, tonight we are hitting the town and going to Búho's."

She stares at me for a moment, expecting my face to turn up in excitement. "Only THE hottest bar on the entire peninsula, Kit. Get excited!" She proclaims in a mock sorority girl voice, which causes me to burst into pseudo-giddy schoolgirl mode.

"Oh my gosh, Jo!" I say between jumps while clinging to her arm. "How could I ever be so lucky?"

She rolls her eyes at me. We both know neither of us are the prissy schoolgirl, sorority girl type. Not that those girls aren't wonderful people, because many of them are; it's just not our vibe. We tend to veer much more to the edgy, dark side of life rather than the preppy, pink side.

Proving my point, she's thrown on a gray All American Rejects tank top which I'm pretty sure is actually for guys. It's tied at the side of her hip above studded black shorts and combat boots. While heels are generally a must in the clubs for women, we'd maybe collapse. I know I would anyway; I can barely dance, let alone do it in heels. That's why my feet are laced with smooth bottomed, knee-high gladiator sandals partnered with my camo shorts and black halter top.

While I'm excited, I'm also fairly anxious for tonight. I mean, I've taken a few dance classes throughout my time in college but those certainly didn't put me at the level of a local Costa Rican, born with el ritmo in their veins. At a minimum, I don't make boxes with my hips anymore like my cousin and I used to do, but I certainly can't say my movements are fluid or attractive to any extent. To my astonishment, Jo winks and tells me otherwise when I show her some of my practice moves bashfully.

"¡Ten confianza en ti misma!" She lectures me. "Confidence is sexy!" I hear her yell behind me from the bathroom as I turn to head out the door.

"Let's go! The club isn't going to hold off the party for us," I yell back at her as she scurries out, lips now bearing a shade of midnight blue skies. "Aye, chica. ¡Que bonita!" I encourage, showing my approval of this new addition to her outfit. She elbows me in embarrassment before heading down the street toward the club.

After walking down a variety of streets, I can see a line is already flooding out of one of the buildings before us. A door opens to reveal a dark ramp leading upstairs, and a glow of flashing lights and pulsing bass stream out of the doorway. "Here we go," I say with a deep breath as I step reluctantly to the back of the line.

Jo steps in beside me and begins to sway lightly with the music that's fading into the street. It doesn't take long before she's speaking up over the crowd murmurs to tell me again, "We're taking risks tonight Kit...*You* are taking a risk."

My heart races at her words and the pounding around me as we get past the bouncer. As we step inside I think back to how I used to hate the idea of dancing. I always thought there were three options: be really good, look stupid to some degree, or look provocative. So, knowing I wasn't going to be able to do the first and wasn't going to try the third, I never danced.

This was my thought until one night when I found myself at a house party among a group of people from church. Unlike at most other places I'd been, people weren't moving on one another or drunk beyond cognitive thought. Almost everyone was centralized in the room, where the strobe light and blacklights had the greatest effect. As I looked around the room, I saw a few people who seemed good, but most of the others fell into the second category—they looked ridiculous.

After some time, a few girls in particular caught my eye. It wasn't because they danced better than the others, maybe the exact opposite even, but it was because of the joy I could see radiating between them. They were smiling from ear to ear and swayed along to the beats without hesitation. Their movements were nowhere near smooth, and they couldn't really hold a rhythm at all. But they didn't care. They were just enjoying being together and letting the music move them how it wanted to.

In that moment, I decided that in the future I was going to dance. No matter how dumb I looked or what others thought, I wanted to experience the same happiness those girls had displayed that night.

Since then I've grown a strong affinity for dancing, and while my experiences with Latin dancing have all been quite Americanized, I've loved it.

Now, I'm excited to get into the real deal. I can feel the pulse of the music switching the pulse of my heartbeat and it's drawing me in to itself. The cadence of my heart quickens even more at the mere thought of dancing.

On the other hand, my mind races at the thought of dancing with the guys here. In class the guys were always awkward and kept their distance; here I know the guys have no issues with getting up close. While it's authentic, the idea of it freaks me out, like, a lot. I want to dance but my brain is flashing through how many boundaries it may cross. I take one last moment to remind myself to guard my heart and then I look with anticipation at Jo.

She's looking back at me and I can see her eyes are gleaming with a look that asks: *Are you ready for this?*

I smile back at her, but she isn't completely convinced. "Kit, it'll be okay. You can say no when you want, you can dance when you want, you are free to have fun." I find myself starting to relax—

until she winks at me—but then she just laughs lightly and says, "Plus, for a while, we're just going to dance together, and I'll be the best dance partner you're going to get all evening."

I push her shoulder jokingly but inside I'm telling myself that we should just dance together all night.

Honestly, I'm a little overwhelmed by the number of attractive guys in the crowd. For some reason, I've always had an extra appreciation for guys who have a little Latino blood in them, and while God could find me the most attractive pale-faced white boy after I get back, it's certainly not what I'd expect. My inner self is battling as I think of how the guys look and how fun they are, or at least as fun as I envision them to be based on cultural tendencies. I have to center myself, not allowing lust to draw me away from the pure enjoyment that can be had.

The people are gathered along the edges of the dance floor and at tables. Surprisingly, only a handful of couples are dancing with each other. When Jo and I join in among some of them I don't feel awkward at all. It's just fun, and my comfort level grows as more people join us and fill in the empty spaces.

While dancing, I look around the bar and try to take in my surroundings. The girl who is DJ-ing is up on a small stage above the crowd at the back of the room and looks like she's having a blast. It's not usually common for women to be DJs but she's a wonderful exception; the mixes she's playing have most everyone on their feet and she hasn't played a poor track yet.

I can't see the edges of the room very well because I'm packed tightly on each side by too many bodies, but there appear to be a few people standing on the outskirts talking. There's also a bar on the opposite side of the room where all the stools are filled and people sit with drinks at the counter. Others crowd in beside them to talk or order their own beverage.

Above all, my attention is drawn to the far wall, which actually opens up to outside despite us being on the second floor. It's like they just cut out the top half of the wall. It is so hot and humid in here that the open air is extra attractive right now. Plus, I'm dead tired. I don't know how long we've been here; it feels like it's only been a few minutes, but my muscles are telling me it could've been hours.

Alongside me Jo continues swirling as though she hasn't noticed the exhaustion at all. It makes sense, as she's probably used to the high energy and dancing and she likely comes here most every week. While she isn't the most athletic person, she can definitely dance. Sweat has only just barely started to break on the tip of her forehead along her hairline, and she still looks gorgeous even though the layers in her hair are becoming a bit more disheveled.

"I have to go sit at the bar. Or at a table. Or outside. Something. I'm dying babes," I say through labored breathing while she keeps moving. I'm not sure if she can really hear me but she nods anyway. "I'll join you in a little bit. Just a few more songs," she yells back.

I can't help but wonder how she's going to find me again among all the people who are in here, but I'm not all that worried. The bar closes at 2:30, and we decided that we'll stay until then. No exceptions. After that, if I haven't located her I'll call her or just wait around until the place clears out.

Slowly, I trudge my way through the revolving bodies over toward the bar. I don't know what I want but I've got to drink something. Here I can legally drink so I consider if I want alcohol. I've never loved the taste of it when I've tried sips of my parents' drinks or my friends,' but sometimes it isn't bad, like when it's mostly sugar and juice. I do know, however, that I cannot have more than one, maybe two drinks. Because of my size, and tolerance of zero, I'd be drunk in a heartbeat with any more than that. No thanks, that's not on my checklist for tonight, or any night for that matter.

When a friend and I were at a huge dance club in Europe I ordered a 'Sex on the Beach' and it was incredible. Fruity and not overpowered by the burn or flavor of alcohol. I lean over so the girl at the bar can hear me and try to ask if they have anything similar to this. She smiles kindly and whips something up for me quickly. I also ask to make sure they'll throw pineapple in since it's my favorite. I would normally order a piña colada but it's not fitting my mood tonight.

After paying, I grab my drink and slip over to the open-faced wall. Immediately I can feel the cool air from outside and in minutes I'm feeling refreshed. I lean with my back up against the wall and slowly slide down until I'm sitting on the floor. Some people shift their eyes toward me in confusion but I don't really care. I've sat down in the middle of crowded concerts before when I'm tired and I'm probably more exhausted now than I was then. It's not my fault there aren't any chairs over here.

From this level I can only see people's feet, yet this may be more fun than being within the crowd. Feet are flying all over. The men's feet are more precise and calculated it seems, slower. The women's heels are kicking and spinning and sliding across the floor in front of their stable partners. I'm mesmerized by the activity on the dance floor.

I could only hope to be able to move this fast and could only dream of being able to dance so well. I can't stop watching them.

Time passes quickly as the bodies move among one another. Jo hasn't found me, but I don't mind at all. I'm enticed and entranced by each step and twirl. My eyes flick from partner to partner, but then my view is hindered. I see nothing beyond the gray acid wash pants and pair of knockoff vans that align themselves at my toes.

# 5

"Hey, did all of our Latino action wear you out Gringa?" I hear the swirl of Spanish words come down and reach me.

"Just shoot me now."

"I'm not a mobster, honey, and you're not in Colombia," the voice responds.

Oh dang, I didn't realize I'd said that so loudly.

"It's a figure of speech," I respond. "What I was more specifically thinking was 'Wow, I'm so glad it's you again! Or rather, thanks for getting in my way."

"What? You enjoy almost getting stepped on and watching people dance on alcohol covered floors?"

"In fact, yes. I was enjoying watching everyone," I say with the same attitude I'd had before.

I'm shocked a bit by the frustration I'm feeling all of a sudden and feel bad. I lower my voice as I alter my response. "Everyone moves with such a passion. The beat flutters their hearts and runs at the same speed as their feet. The men push and the women pull in perfect synchronicity. No couple hits any other, but they slide in circles around one another smoothly. It's like in the ocean, every life form works perfectly with the others to create a perfectly beautiful harmony that builds on itself."

When I raise my eyes from his feet and look up Dash is no longer looking at me as though I'm a lazy gringa who can't keep up with his way of life. Now he's looking at me with a quizzical look on his face that's furrowing his eyebrows. His attractiveness isn't hindered at all by the asymmetry created.

"Did you just compare our dancing to the ocean?" He questions.

"Yes, as a matter of…" I begin to retort back at his interrogation.

"Woah, hold on." He interrupts me hurriedly, trying to slow down my aggressive words that have been triggered again. "It was a very descriptive image. I've never really thought about it that way. But you're right. It is certainly beautiful."

"Oh," I reply before shutting my mouth and bowing my head to both take a drink and hide my slight shame at being so rude.

"Yeah." He kicks my foot lightly, drawing my attention up. Those dang shoes.

As my eyes travel upward, I catch the rest of his outfit. His pants are not quite skinny jeans but they're also not really baggy. He's wearing a simple button down again but this one is white with dime-sized surfer images on it. What appears to be the same necklace as before hangs around his neck.

Looking at him again in this darker lighting, I have the courage to take in his face a bit more than I was willing to previously. The green, blue, and red lights shift across his strong features. His jawline is lightly shaded with stubble, which he apparently didn't shave this morning, and surprisingly, it doesn't look too bad.

I shift my eyes up a bit farther where his eyes are too shaded by his wavy hair in this dim lighting for me to see them properly. Despite this, I notice he has a few subtle spots of lighter skin around his right eye, which are creating a crescent of birthmarks. They're similar to a few other marks I saw freckling his arms, but they're more concentrated here and it's alluring.

Below that there is a deep dimple beginning to show itself on the corner of his mouth. As he runs his hand back through his hair briefly, I also notice for the first time that he's wearing a pair of black studs in each ear, which only enhance his skater look. Oh my heck, I'm swooning!

My face is certainly flushed from watching him so long and I pull my eyes away, fighting to see around him. I assume I'm too low for him to see the color in my cheeks, and if not, I was dancing not too long ago so he probably just assumes it's from that if anything. Hopefully.

He speaks slower now, as though he's been taking in my presence the way I've just done with his.

"So…were you actually going to dance or are you just going to sit there on the ground staring at people?" I don't know if he's referring to how I was watching the dancers or if he's subtly alluding to the fact that he realized I was gazing at him for way too long.

I lift my drink as if to demonstrate that I'm busy and as such am unable to dance at the moment. I'm hoping he'll take the cue that I'd like to be left alone to rest and just take in the evening, but he doesn't.

"Are you asking me to get you a refill? I'd say that's hardly polite, seeing as you and I don't really know each other. Plus, guys usually only buy drinks for a girl if they're trying to hit on them." Ouch. Is he saying he wouldn't want to hit on me?

He's smirking at me so I don't totally know if he's joking or if he knows he just said something that could be offensive.

Makes sense I guess—he doesn't know me, and I certainly don't look the most inviting from my secluded position on the floor. I give him a hard time about his comment anyway. "You're telling me you didn't come over here to start up a conversation as a means of making a move? How disappointing," I say as I make a tsk sound with my tongue to demonstrate my disapproval. Or it would be, if I were actually serious in my response.

Am I serious? Do I wish he had come over to flirt with me?

Maybe, I mean it's a nice compliment. But then again, he is the guy who kind of yelled at me…and also the guy who followed after me to deliver a towel and a change of clothes. What do I care anyway? Maybe he's nice; maybe he isn't. It isn't likely that this could go anywhere.

I don't know if he's a Christian, and if I were even going to try to risk a relationship, I'd want someone who could lead and encourage me in my faith. Plus, I'm in Costa Rica; it's not like it would be logical to any extent at all to start something with someone. *Holy cow, Adelina! Slow down.* I scold myself. *You've seen this kid three times now. I mean he is most definitely quite attractive, but how am I even considering a relationship? That's taking these interactions way too far.*

When I come back to reality and look at him again, the smirk on his face has grown to reveal his dimple. It's as though he just heard the whole conversation I had in my head and finds it very entertaining.

Oh shoot, was I talking out loud? I'm not that oblivious, am I? Definitely not. I think he's just intrigued by my previous remark. "So you do want me to buy you a drink?" He inquires playfully as though his question completely addresses the underlying idea of my desire to have him hit on me.

"No, there is definitely no need for that. In fact, I'm just finishing and going to find my friend," I explain hurriedly as I stand to my feet. He reaches down to assist me, but I've already stood. I'm not looking for help and I don't need it, not now or in the general aspect of life. I can help myself.

"So watching everyone else has lost its intrigue."

"In all honesty, your interruption has kind of taken the peace away. I wasn't really anticipating some stranger awkwardly trying to hit on me. So now, I'm trying to avoid him by giving the excuse that I want to go dance," I remark as though he isn't the stranger of whom I'm referring.

He catches on without hesitating even a moment. "I'd say that we're most definitely not strangers anymore. I've seen you three times and we've spoken twice. That does not equate to strangers in my book."

"Hmm bummer, it still does in mine. You see, we technically haven't even been introduced to one another."

"You mean to tell me that Sirena isn't your real name? Here I'd been thinking that Luc was a psychic."

"Nope, sorry. Now if you'll excuse me." I walk past him to the bar to set my mostly empty glass down. I grab the lemon from the side and quickly take a bite before tossing it in the trash. I smile at the habit I developed when I was younger thanks to my grandpa who always enjoyed watching my face scrunch up.

"So you're not a mermaid," he retorts from beside me now as I spin around to look out at the dance floor again.

"I didn't say that." He's close at my side, and it's taking much of my attention just to avoid looking at him. "I simply said that wasn't my name."

"So, you are a mermaid, but your name isn't Sirena. Makes sense, it'd be weird if I was named 'Human.'" He responds with a light chuckle that makes me smile slightly.

"Mmhmm," I agree without actually speaking. For some reason I haven't actually gone back out to the dance floor, I'm torn between the desire to hurry away and to see where he's going with this conversation.

Plus, along with his intriguing demeanor and captivating style, I just caught a burst of his cologne.

"Where is this psychic friend of yours?" I ask, switching the subject and attempting to distract myself.

"Luc? He's out there somewhere. Probably trying to find a girl he can buy a drink for." His comment makes me look at him a bit quizzically.

"I thought he wasn't that type of guy?"

"He's not. It was a joke. He's just dancing. You know, that thing you said you were about to go do, Sirena." He calls me Sirena like his friend had and I don't know if I want to correct him and tell him my name. Probably not.

Nicknames are definitely easier. They're less intimate. It's why I ask people to call me Kit, it allows a disconnect.

"Sirena. Hey." He calls me out of my slightly sidetracked line of thinking. "Are you going to dance?"

"Yep. Thanks. Say hi to your friend for me," I reply shortly.

"Wait," he commands though I haven't actually made any motion to leave yet. "We didn't do introductions. I'm Xander," he informs me. I'm immediately confused. Did I seriously hear wrong? Or maybe he has a twin?

He must recognize the question on my face because he adds to his statement quickly. "My name is Xander Dashiell Urraca. My friends usually call me 'Dash.'"

"Good to know," I reply while I think of my opinion on nicknames again. *I like his name. The whole thing.* For the first time I think maybe nicknames aren't so good—his friends are taking the depth and strength from his name. I nod my head to acknowledge my understanding and stand quiet.

"You still haven't told me your name," he says quickly, interrupting my thoughts yet again. I had hoped he'd forget and I could just walk away.

I sigh lightly. "It's Kit."

"Is that short for something?" he asks me—even though I'd rather he hadn't.

"No," I retort back as he just stands looking at me. I sigh again. "It's my last name."

"Wow Sirena." He ignores the name I've just given him. "You weren't even going to tell me your real name."

"It is my real name. It's just my last name," I contradict.

"And?"

"And what?"

"What's your real name?"

41

"I already told you," I respond back, but he just looks at me expectantly. I wait a few moments. "Adelina. Adelina McCall Kit." I retort my full name with emphasis and attitude and then begin to move toward the dance floor.

He catches my hand lightly, in a way that catches my attention but doesn't frighten or disturb me. "Adelina," he replies, too softly and smoothly. His accent makes my name sound more beautiful than it ever has as he rolls through each letter. *And I thought I loved my name before.*

His voice still holds that soft, rich tone. "¿Ven a bailar conmigo? ¿Porfa?" He says this last please as though he is almost pleading for me to join him in a dance. My pulse is pounding in the tips of my fingers as he keeps them held.

I freeze. Oh no. No, no, no. This is the moment. Jo told me I had to take risks. I agreed that I would. Did God do this to me on purpose? Knowing that I wouldn't want to? What in the world?

"Adelina," he says again quickly. "You were already going to dance. Now you don't have to wait for a partner. Would you allow me to dance with you at least for a moment before going to find your friend?" He repeats the question again in English as though I hadn't understood the first time. I had; how could I not?

We're taking risks tonight Kit…You are taking a risk.

Jo's voice from earlier this evening rings so clearly in my head. Why did she have to say that?

The thing about risks is that they're scary. That's why this is a risk. So many factors play into why I wouldn't want to go dance with him. But there are others that make my heart beat faster, already preparing for the music to carry us across the floor.

*It's just a dance.* I hear the voice in my head, though it can't be my own. It's too willing. *Faith is about stepping into the unknown. Faith is built upon taking risks. That's why it's called faith.* Oh, this is definitely not my usual line of thinking. Oh goodness, what am I doing? What am I thinking?

I nod and bite gently on my lower lip in embarrassment. I take a hesitant step forward, my hand still enclosed by his, acknowledging that I'm going to let him walk with me to the dance floor.

He must sense my hesitance as he steps in front and leads me. He speaks above the crowd, "Tranquila, chica. No muerdo." *I don't bite…usually.* I think. I don't bite…*hard.* The two words that kids in junior high jokingly used take his comment one step further into flirtation. Even just the thought makes my heart beat faster and his face, taunting me, escalates that.

"I don't care if you bite. I was just thinking about how I'm going to trash those designer shoes of yours when I step all over 'em."

As soon as I've said it, I realize my first sentence was way more inviting than I'd meant for it to be. His right eyebrow quirks up in interest. *Yuck. What a typical dude!* Of course the idea just enticed him.

"I worked multiple weeks saving money for these shoes. You'd better not trash them," he says in a voice that holds only the slightest bit of seriousness.

Oh, that's not what I was expecting. A comment that'd be intimately accusatory or one that would make me faint in embarrassment—what I expected—didn't come. I stare silently for a second to see if he'll replace his comment or add to it, but he doesn't.

"You'd better lead exceptionally well then, because you're dancing with—" I pause, trying to think of a way to describe my horrible, stereotypical, white girl dancing skills.

"A professional, I'm sure," he chimes in as he begins to spin me away from him before catching me smoothly and pulling me back into his chest.

Discomfort floods through me. While there is still space between us and we aren't dancing bachata or one of the other more intimate styles, we're much too close. I know this is their culture, but I can't dance like this—with a man who looks like him. I try to step back and pull away but we're already moving together around the dance floor.

I can barely imagine what we look like. I've seen a few episodes of *Dancing with the Stars,* and in my mind, he's the divine instructor and I'm the pitiful student—though I'm certainly nowhere near celebrity status. That's not what it feels like, though. Our bodies are moving fluidly and smoothly. As the songs transition and time flies away from us I realize more people are starting to look in our direction. No, no, no. I don't do attention, especially in something as intimate as this style of dancing.

He spins me out and I find Jo's face quickly. A smile glued to her upturned eyes tells me she's incredibly proud. When I see her, I realize how distracted I've been by this boy and our dancing. I immediately start having second thoughts so I try to let go and move toward her. When he pulls me back in, I breathlessly tell him it's probably time for me to leave and that I'd seen the girl I came with signaling to me.

He calls me a liar, softly joking to convince me to stay. Unfortunately I am lying, which means his comment makes me feel slightly guilty. Jo and I said we'd stay until 2:30 and, while Xander and I have probably been dancing an incredibly long while, I'm sure it can't be that time yet.

"I'm serious. I've got to go," I tell him again, feeling like an idiotic, self-imposed version of Cinderella, running from the handsome prince on the dance floor. I pull myself from this analogy and remind myself he's not a prince. He's a flirt and he's one of the many men here who fall at the feet of the exotic white girl.

The media has depicted white women, specifically Americans, as girls who travel to experience it all—the parties, drinking, drugs, and sex are usually the 'highlights.' I am not one of those girls, though, and I should leave sooner rather than later to avoid giving him the wrong idea. At least, that's the excuse I give myself.

Really, I think I'm just terrified by the fact that I'm feeling attracted to him. He seems so sarcastic and annoying, but charming at the same time. Some of the charm seems to have washed away a bit now, though. I don't know if he's annoyed that I've refused to stay or disheartened by my leaving.

His voice pulls me from my thoughts for the first time since we started dancing who knows how long ago. "Alright, I'll let you go. But Tuesday you should definitely come by the beach." Maybe he really is disheartened by my leaving.

"Bring my clothes. I want them back before you forget you have them," he adds on quickly. Maybe he doesn't care. Scratch that. There's no way he cares. Why would he? He only wants his stuff back, and his words clearly display his lack of interest.

Concluding that there's nothing further to say, I walk away swiftly.

"I still cannot believe you left early!" Jo tells me in exasperation. "You couldn't even wait for me? What was the deal with that?"

I don't know how to justify it to her. How do I explain that it was more than just people watching us that freaked me out? It was the idea of possibilities. It was the fear of feeling something. It was me not being willing to let God walk with me through the experiences of life. Even one as simple as dancing with a cute guy.

There literally wasn't even any commitment. I've seen him three times now, and already I had to shut down my feelings as if they were a sin. It isn't wrong for me to find someone attractive, is it? No, of course not. I just can't be consumed with them. Which in its own way I'm doing now by overanalyzing my idiocy.

Why do I trust people so minimally? Scratch that, why don't I trust people at all? I don't even know the answer to that myself, so how can I explain it all to her?

I can't.

I tried to ask God about it in church yesterday. Like I've done a few times before. God, why can't I trust anyone? Why can't I trust you? Shouldn't it be so simple after I see all you've done in my life and in the lives of those around me?

Of course I know, logically, that I can trust God and therefore trust people. This knowledge just hasn't reached my heart. I'd say my heart is broken, but that's what people say when they've been injured by someone. Someone or something had to break it.

That's not me. I just can't help but think that my heart never really worked all that well in the first place.

"Well you are going to go Tuesday morning, aren't you?" she asks, impeding my train of thought.

"Of course not." I'm sure Xander can wait a little while longer, and I'm certainly in no rush to see him again.

"Are you kidding me? You're such a chicken!"

I know.

"I am not. I just don't jump at every guy who tries to dance with me in the club. Patience is a virtue, you know."

"Yeah, yeah. You're just making excuses. You know you want to see him again."

I know.

"You're definitely wrong about that. I don't care." I pause and analyze my words. I'm not just lying to her. "Okay, so maybe he's attractive." Her eyebrows quirk up. "Okay, incredibly attractive." One side of her mouth now quirks up as well. "Jo! Stop looking at me like that! There are like 3,972,000,022 expectations I have for the guy I'd want to be in a relationship with. From what I can see at the moment, he meets like three."

"Mmhmm. Isn't that enough to start?"

"No. He's missing the key."

"Which would be?"

"I want someone with a strong faith, Jo. If I were going to be with someone, which I certainly don't expect at all, I want them to be able to race alongside me in my faith: someone who could lead me in my stubbornness, provide for me when I don't want their provision, and protect me even though I think I can protect myself." She stares at me blankly as I ramble on.

"Lord knows I'm going to need someone who can humble me in my pride and challenge me to learn with my heart rather than my head. Teach me to turn to the Lord before I turn to him and to be anxious about God before I'm anxious about him." I don't know if I should continue but she just keeps watching me.

"I once watched a sermon series on dating. I love learning, you know, and I thought I'd want to have all the information possible ahead of time. Plus, then I could speak into the lives of others if they wanted it.

"Anyway, the pastor spoke about how we first should seek someone who knows the Lord, but then beyond that they should be *actively* pursuing him. To live their life without passivity, giving up their comforts to live in obedience, putting God's will above their own, his mission above their own." She's still staring so I take this as a sign to continue.

"After this he talked about how physical attraction should certainly be there, and chemistry as well. Beyond that he didn't see how much more was necessary." I pause for a second reflecting on all of this. "Essentially, if both parties find one another attractive— hopefully incredibly so—if their personalities get along well and they enjoy spending time together, and if they both put Christ's will above their own and desire to push one another to him first, then that's all one needs. That. That's what I want."

"Sounds like a lot less than three billion whatever you just said to me," Jo proclaims haughtily.

"Yeah, I suppose so. But I think there's so much more to it than all of that." How do I explain that even with the security of knowing he loved God first, I still didn't have enough confidence that things wouldn't end? How could I explain that I doubt? That I lack faith?

"You think too much, Kit."

Gracious, she knows me so well. Am I that transparent? Her

eyes search my heart as she questions me again. "What is faith? It is believing even when you don't know the outcome. It is trusting in the unknown. It is letting God lead your head and your heart."

I hate this. I hate that I know she's right. I hate that I know what she is saying is true, and yet I can't change.

I've asked so many times for God to teach my heart rather than my head, and it never happens. Granted, I'm probably still holding back when I ask.

I tell myself it doesn't matter right now. I don't want anything to happen anyway. I leave in less than six months. Sure, God has his own timing but for all I can see, it's not worth it.

"I'm not going Tuesday," I say with finality.

# 6

I'm kicking myself as I walk toward the beach this morning. I'm thinking I should've come earlier but I'm debating as to whether or not I should even be going at all. Jo has been on me about it since Tuesday, when Dash had originally asked me to meet him.

Last Tuesday.

I'm telling myself that I avoided him for a week and a half because I was busy or tired. Who wants to wake up this early in the morning? I mean, maybe I didn't mind it before, but now I see how ludicrous I was being.

I know I could've probably met him last Thursday, or even this Tuesday, but I didn't. If I let myself be honest, it's probably because I'm annoyed at him for his attitude when I left. And I'm also annoyed at myself. If he didn't care to see me, then he could be patient. The clothes could wait. I knew I wouldn't forget. How could I forget someone like Xander? I mean Dash. I can't use his first name, it's too intimate.

Over the weekend Jo and I traipsed through the jungle-type forests, seeing spiders the size of my palm and brightly colored snakes amidst the vibrant flowers and greenery. We even made our way to a waterfall and found ourselves joining people at the bottom for a quick swim. But then I was reminded of my spontaneous dip into the water, and the guys, and how I've been avoiding Dash.

Now I'm not avoiding him anymore, at least not physically. As I head right toward the beach they've occupied twice since I've been here, I try to collect my thoughts and sporadic emotions.

I'm early enough that hopefully they haven't gone out to the water yet. I just want to give him the clothes and leave. Then, from here on out, I'll avoid Dash and his obnoxious sidekick for good.

I see Luc's navy green Jeep parallel parked beside the paseo as I approach. Two sets of legs poke out from below the open back door. As I raise my head, my stare is met with Luc's. The grin, already plastered on his face, only grows when he connects the dots in recognition of who I am.

"¡Aye! ¡Sirena! Have you finally come to dance across the waves with us?"

Dash turns around to face me as he finishes zipping up his wetsuit. To my amazement, he also has a smile on his face. It fades a bit when I don't respond. I remember to speak up—to stop staring. "Ehm, no. I only came to bring back the clothes."

The hope now fades from Luc's face as well. "That wasn't the deal," he provokes, as his eyes smile with taunting and his lips pout a bit.

"We never made a deal. You told me when I could come back and I'm here."

"I told you my sister had a board you could use."

"And I told you that I didn't think it'd work."

"Right, we went over the fact that you were scared."

"I'm not scared."

"Did you even bring a suit?" Dash questions, throwing both of us off of our little debate.

I can't answer. Yes, I have my suit.

"Of course she does! What kind of idiot would come back

50

without it?" Luc replies for me. I know neither of them can see my suit because of the light jacket I'm wearing, but Luc's comment has made me feel almost exposed.

"¡Sirena!" Luc exclaims as he tosses a smaller wetsuit toward me, snapping me out of my contemplation.

"Lucas, she has a name."

"Well she hasn't been gracious enough to correct me yet so I'm going to stick to what I know."

"It's Adelina…Adelina McCall Kit." He recites my name, exactly as I'd presented it. *He remembers? My middle name even?* My thoughts stall me before I quickly sputter past his comment.

"Just Kit…That's what everyone else calls me."

"Like a baby fox?" Luc speaks up again and it sounds like he may be laughing lightly.

"Yes. Do you have a problem with that?"

"No, of course not." He sputters at my accusatory tone. "Some baby foxes grow up to be quite fierce and vicious." His tone is joking again, and I know he's referring to my sometimes-less-than-pleasant personality.

"Anyway. You can get dressed over there." Dash interjects again, pointing at the bathrooms that are still too far away.

I hand over the bag that has the clothes in it before setting my own on the ground. I then turn as though to leave. Really I just don't want them staring at my chest as I take off my layers to slip into the wetsuit.

"Alright here's the deal guys: I need you to know I'm only doing this with you two right now because I haven't surfed in about two years and I miss it. So, that also means this may be a little rough. Don't make fun of me." I point my stare specifically at Luc as I say this. "And you. Don't yell at me," I remark while glaring at Dash.

They look at each other bashfully before nodding in acceptance of my words.

"Wonderful! Now let's do this!" I say, throwing my clothes in the back of the Jeep.

"Hey, hold up there Sirena."

"Kit." Dash and I both correct him together. That's embarrassing.

After a quick chuckle, Luc collects a few more things and then signals that he's ready.

As I'm paddling out past the lineup of other surfers I'm reminded of my summer in San Diego a few years ago. Almost every Saturday morning I'd hit the beach to use the free boards that a ministry team loaned out. I'd sit out past the breaks watching the waves rolling toward me. As I do this again now, the joy and peace of God rush over me.

I watch the guys race the waves, jumping up at just the right moments, and then yes, they dance on the water. Luc described it perfectly.

I sit, blissfully content, as the guys come in and out until finally I'm knocked out of my trance by a splash of water. As I sputter to get the salt out of my throat, I glare over toward where the water came from. Dash just smiles challengingly at me.

"You're up, Sirena," Luc says from behind me.

"That's alright. I'm fine lying here," I retort calmly.

"We're gonna head back in a little while," he informs me.

"I'll ride back in then."

"You scared?"

"Not really."

"You sure?"

"Yeah. I'm not scared. A little nervous, sure, but I'm content watching."

"Are you watching his butt again?" Luc inquires as he paddles over by me.

"I told you, Luc! It was a figure of speech."

"That doesn't mean you weren't doing it literally," he prods.

"Luc, leave her alone," Dash says from right next to me. I hadn't noticed him paddling over. They're now almost sitting in front of and behind my board, making an 'I' shape with our boards in the water with me in the center.

*I'm trapped.* "Guys. What's up?" I ask, feeling wholly uncomfortable with the way they're looking at each other.

"Nada, hermana."

Luc's language shift also catches me off guard and I'm bracing myself for whatever is about to happen. There's really only one likely solution and I'm not stoked about it. "You know, for being a mermaid I don't think I've seen you get in the water yet," Luc taunts.

"Half of my body has been in the water all morning," I say with a tone of warning.

Dash is staring at me intently when he speaks. "I don't even think your hair has a drop of water in it."

I pull the tip of my braid up and wave it at him. "As it turns out, my hair is just long enough that it reaches the water." I whip it back over my shoulder so it falls again just below the middle of my back.

"Nonetheless, I think I'd like to see if you can swim as well out here as you do near the shore," he responds, the challenge set in his tone and a predatory look in his eyes.

I see the flip coming before they've moved so I begin to inhale a deep breath subtly. *They're gonna regret this.* As soon as I'm under I immediately swim beneath the tip of Luc's board and push it hard, sending him backward into the water.

I thank my swim coach now for all of the drills we did to improve lung capacity. I swim beneath Dash and tug gently on his right foot, just as a tease. His board tips lightly and he starts to kick his feet as I dive deeper for a second to avoid the mess.

As the water above me stills, I can feel a wave coming and I swim hard for the surface. I use the roll of the wave to my advantage and push hard on the side of his board, using the momentum of the wave along with my weight, to send Dash over.

When I surface Luc is still sputtering. I assume Dash is still under his board but then I feel a brush against my legs and he comes up right in front of me. Way too close.

With Dash so near, I can see the green water reflecting off the gold rays in his deep brown eyes. They're astonishingly beautiful, not simple or plain, but like the sun during an eclipse—rays beaming out from behind the pupil.

I'm smacked in the face by a splash of water. Half of it was blocked by Dash's body, still way too close to mine, but Luc definitely meant to hit us both.

*Oh my gosh, thank you.* I want to say this out loud, in gratitude for his distraction, but obviously shouldn't.

I'd been staring. Hardcore staring. Not even subtly staring. Right into Dash's eyes. *Then again, he was staring right back, wasn't he?* "That was uncalled for, don't you think?" Luc remarks as Dash moves out of my direct line of sight.

"I'm sorry, did I ask to be sent into the water? No, but you did it anyway. So I merely thought I'd return the favor!"

"I enjoyed it." Dash smirks at me. *What does that look mean?* He is now holding onto both my board and his own. "Why don't we take the boards in and we can swim around a bit or something?"

"I think I've now had my fair share of swimming," Luc croaks from beside us.

"Come on Luc, don't be such a party pooper," I chastise.

They both laugh and look at me with curiosity. I think it's my phrasing again.

"I've been riding and wiping out all morning. Plus I don't want to splash around with you two kids. I'm about ready to call it a day."

I panic slightly again because I don't want to be left with Dash by myself. I chime in, "I should probably get on with my day also, I guess," I say, looking at Dash for agreement. "You ready to be done?"

His response doesn't leave room for any other option. "Only after we see you catch a wave."

"I'll ride one back in, then we can head out." *Hopefully I'll be able to get up. Hopefully I won't crash.* My mind takes off, thinking of how embarrassing this is about to be, but a question interrupts my thoughts.

Dash looks at me with intrigue, "We?" he questions. *What about 'we'?* "You said we can head out. As in the three of us together?"

*Umm. Did I say that?* "Ehm, I mostly just meant back to the beach and Jeep so I could give the board and wetsuit back." I think that sounds fairly reasonable; I wasn't really trying to insinuate that we'd engage beyond this. Right?

"Let's just ride in already, we'll figure out the rest later," Luc says, reminding the two of us that he's still there. Message received.

I look back to watch the waves rolling in behind me and prepare to take the second one. I paddle hard and feel the water drift under my cupped hands. The wave lifts behind me and I use the momentum to jump up. The water is pretty smooth and my ride is simple. As I approach the beach I half jump, half fall off, but quickly sweep up the board and stride out before the water catches us both and sucks us out.

I turn around to see both boys on the same wave, and I'm transported to the first time I 'met' them. Today, thankfully, they both finish smoothly and smile at me as they scurry out of the water.

When we get back to the Jeep, I place myself in between the front and back passenger side doors this time to give myself an extra barrier in front of their wandering eyes. I also hang a towel over the gap in the two doors to create a type of curtain before quickly changing all of my clothes. The process is much easier than last time.

After taking down my little fort, I go around back to see if I can help with anything and to return the wetsuit. The guys have been busy putting boards away and haven't had time to change yet. Immediately my attention is captured. *Dash's necklace.*

It's a cross, but that could mean anything. Crosses are often worn merely as jewelry. Plus, Catholicism is the most predominant religion in Latin America so he could wear it in that context. *But what if it's different?* I shut down that line of thinking immediately. *Probably not.*

"Would you mind if we gave you a lift back to your place?" *Dang it, I was staring again.* I look up at Dash's face so I can respond. Would I want them to take me home? At the absolute most it would only take me twenty minutes to walk. But I am trying to be more kind. Plus, guys like this chivalrous stuff.

"I guess I wouldn't mind. I mean, if it's not too much trouble—"

"Seriously? Of course it's not. You could live hours from here, like in Jacó, and he'd still be offering you a ride home." Luc grunts as Dash elbows him in the side.

"You stopped helping. Get her board in the car." Dash's comment is neutral but the look in his eyes sends a warning to Luc.

"No worries, I'll take care of it," I say, gesturing to them to change.

"We have a few things to do around this side of town before we head back. Would you mind joining us? I assume you probably live on the other side of the city?" I don't know why he'd just assume that but it's true.

"No problem." The words slip out easily, but I don't know if I want to wait. I don't really know if I want to keep hanging out with them. Yet why would I not? *Why can't I just try to become friends with others like a normal person?*

Luc nods at me and then jumps into the driver's seat. I go around the front and then stop short for a second when I realize there is only one seat rather than a bench. I move to open the back door and realize that they had to fold down the back row of seats to fit the boards, which are tucked at an angle.

"Hey y'all, I think I'm actually just going to head out," I remark nonchalantly.

Luc looks into the back seat and recognition hits his eyes. "Oh shoot. I forgot. Don't worry though, it's no problem, you two can share the front seat." *No. We can't.*

I don't want to be rude and I'm trying to make friends, but I can't do it.

Even beyond dancing, I'm just not that into people being in my space, let alone with them touching me. I can't even remember the last time I was okay with people touching me. I can barely do handshakes. Definitely no massages. No holding hands. Nothing. At all. Not even hugs.

It's all due to the dumb hormone oxytocin. Released in our brains at a simple touch. Interconnecting people and increasing feelings of devotion and trust. Thanks, but no thanks.

So, my obvious solution has been to avoid touch as much as possible. Keep myself from the bonds that would ultimately be broken. It all sounded smart at the time a few years ago when I learned all this in class. Now, when I flinch at the mere brush of a hand, I realize that maybe I took it all too far. In some ways it seems like my brain reacts as though touch is abuse, which I guess is what I've trained it to think.

Logically I know it isn't healthy to completely avoid any forms of bonding to people. A simple caring touch on the arm isn't a bullet, and sitting beside someone isn't going to cause a car crash.

Then my feelings crash in and remind me I'm not just sitting by anyone. I'm sharing a seat with Dash. The bookworm, surfer, and dancer. Who just so happens to have a cross necklace that may or may not mean he loves Jesus. Oh my gosh, I'm overanalyzing everything.

I've been quiet for too long. Luc told me I could share the front seat with Dash. I've got to break this habit. "Yeah sure. I guess if you don't mind," I whisper out, swiveling to Dash who seems to have been lost in thought a bit as well.

"I offered to give you a ride, we'll do that. I'm sorry about the inconvenience." I can't tell with his dark caramel skin, but it seems as though he blushes a bit. It's likely that I am as well, but I quickly scoot into the car and as close to the center console as possible so he won't notice. He slowly slides in next to me and hugs the door a bit more than necessary. Now I can see how ridiculous it is. "Are you alright? There's room, you can move over," he remarks carefully.

"Oh, no, yeah, I'm good." He doesn't need to know I'm squished. "Are you good?"

He gives me a tight-lipped smile. "Yeah, I'm great."

"You're both scrunched together and uncomfortable, we all know it." We both look at Luc now rather than each other. He's right.

We each settle back a little. With us both relaxing, it's put us fairly close. I'm tucked a little bit against his side and he puts his arm up and across to Luc's seat to make more room. I shift over again toward the center. "Adelina, you're honestly fine. Don't worry about squishing me. As long as you're comfortable, I'm comfortable."

I try to analyze his comment but get nowhere. "Yeah, alright, thanks," I finally say, leaning into him a little bit again.

My mind is whirling. I was definitely uncomfortable from not having enough room to sit, but that is nothing compared to right now. I'd even debate that it was actually better before, compared to the emotional discomfort I'm experiencing now.

The possibility that I'm crushing his ribs makes me want to pull away. However, the warmth coming from his side heats my shivering body from the inside out. The chill I was feeling earlier has definitely been replaced and I'm almost even comforted by the rhythm of his chest moving as he breathes. *Hopefully these errands won't take long. I can't keep sitting like this.*

As we pull away from the beach, Luc is trying to apologize while also bragging about his 'baby.' "She's a classic. Jeep Cherokee XJ built in '98. She runs like a stallion still for all the crap she's seen. I snagged her from some horrible man who wanted to use her just for her parts—" I smile as he rambles on.

"Mae, ya cállate. You're boring her." I'm a little surprised by the voice that rumbles from the chest beside me as Dash shushes his friend.

"Oh no Luc, you're totally fine. I like listening." While I don't care much for cars, I do want to try getting to know him. Plus, he's not asking me to share, so it's not a problem.

He looks at me with a tight-lipped smile and his eyes are apologetic. To distract him I quickly ask, "What's on our to-do list for the morning and where are we headed?"

For the next five minutes he shifts into tour guide mode and describes everything we pass, who owns each shop, and how he knows them or their children, and what's going on in their lives. As we get to the port area on the other side of the peninsula, he finally tells me that we really only have one stop because of the fact that nothing else is open.

When we stop, the smell of fish and oil and something else equally horrid fills my nostrils as Dash opens the door. He reaches out his hand to help me from the car and lightly tells me, "You can only trust about 60 percent of what he says. His sister is a gossip and half of what he knows is all thirdhand."

I look up at him questioningly as he places his hand on the middle of my back to usher me out of the way of the door. Great, well I'm only going to be able to pay attention to a quarter of the 60 percent if Dash doesn't remove his hand immediately. Thankfully, he walks away quickly to a small boat.

"Was he whispering to you about how much he loves me?" Luc pries. I nod my head, still stunned, and walk forward with him.

Dash is already conversing with whom I assume is the owner when we approach. They're laughing and joking with one another, but as soon as the man notices me with Luc he stands. "Ahh Lucas. Finalmente has encontrado una novia. ¡Qué bonita!" The older gentleman enthusiastically greets Luc before turning to me. "Un gusto, soy Vicente y este es mi panga."

*Umm nope.* I'm definitely not his girlfriend but I'm too caught off guard by this statement and his compliment to say anything. Plus, it's an effort to keep myself from laughing.

This only gets harder when Luc throws his arm over my shoulder. "¡Sí, verdad! Es tan linda." *Luc, what?* He looks down and beams at me boldly while proclaiming my beauty. "Sin embargo, no es mía, tengo otra. Además, Dash no deja de hablar de ella." I'm surprised to hear him tell the man that he actually has a girlfriend. But wait. *Dash has been talking about me?*

Vicente's attention now shifts from us to the boy in front of him. Dash is wide-eyed, and highlights of pink seem to be creeping into his cheeks. I think it may not be from embarrassment, however, but rather from irritation. "Lucas, no seas tan ridículo, cierra el pico por favor." *Why would it be ridiculous for him to talk about me? Should I be offended? I think I might be.* I'm not sure if he's joking but that's the appearance he seems to be trying to give.

"¿Cómo se llama?" Vicente asks Dash, no longer acknowledging me directly.

"Adelina." He says it gently, just as he has every time before, and I'm surprised by the shift in his demeanor.

"Kit," I correct him, annoyed that he thinks he's my spokesman. Vicente just shakes his head at us and turns away chuckling.

"You see, Puntarenas is now more of a fishing city than a port city since most of the main ports shifted to Caldera. Vicente here is an old family friend and he always gives us some of his catch in the mornings whenever we happen to drop by." Luc tells me this while we wait, and I wrinkle my nose as Vicente returns with a chest that thankfully contains some of the smell.

The boys talk and joke for a minute before turning to leave. When they finally do, Vicente looks right at me intensely before I turn away. "Cuídate, amor," he affectionately warns. *What does he mean by that? Take care of myself?* Is he talking about Dash?

When I get back to the Jeep, I open the door to the back and crawl in beneath the boards on the flattened row of seats. I see Luc and Dash look at each other in confusion and Dash seems to give Luc a look of warning. "Are you going to be comfortable there, Sirena?" Luc peeks back at me from over the seat.

"Much better, thank you." I'm not trying to be rude, but it's true, this makes me feel much safer.

"Ready to head home? I know you're dying to stay with us longer, but we're done with our tasks and headed back. Of course you could join—" I interrupt before he can finish and tell him my address. He navigates his way without any issue and stops in front of my host home.

"Well, thank you. I thoroughly enjoyed my time, so I appreciate you allowing me to tag along."

I jump out of the Jeep and hear what sounds like a door opening as mine is falling closed. "Ade— Kit, I'm sorry if I seemed rude at the port earlier. Sometimes Luc just keeps talking when maybe he shouldn't, or he takes his jokes too far and I get uncomfortable and awkward. What I said wasn't kind." *What part of what Luc said would have made him uncomfortable?* "That's not to say anything against you. I know I just made it sound like that, but really it isn't anything bad about you."

"Yeah, no worries," I say as I turn to walk away because I really don't think it matters that much now.

"Umm, also—" I turn back around at his voice to see Luc avoiding eye contact with me and trying not to smile. "I was wondering if you had WhatsApp," Dash continues.

Of course I have WhatsApp. It's one of the most essential forms of communication used around the world, Latin America included. I've had it almost as long as I've had an iPhone. I don't know why it would matter to him, though.

It takes me a moment to realize that he's asking for my phone number. Why didn't I have a plan for if something like this happened? I don't want to lie right to his face, but I don't want to give him my number, either.

Maybe I'm overreacting. He could be respectful, and maybe the cross around his neck is more than a fashion statement. Actually, who am I kidding? That would probably be worse because that would mean he's more serious, and I know how to handle that even less than horny scumbags.

This'll be a wreck, but I guess honesty is the best policy, right?

"Yeah. I do," I remark, keeping my answer short and simple. I don't reach to give him my phone and I don't start reciting my number. I just start to walk away before briefly pausing and looking back. "Also, I'm sorry for crushing your ribs earlier, in the car," I add the last part as though he wouldn't remember but say it all in a way of creating a distraction. *Wow, I am a complete pansy.*

# 7

"Kit, are you crazy? Now you've probably crushed more than just his ribs. Think about his ego, his pride, even his heart!" I don't care much about the ego or pride—with those I'm probably doing him a favor. And I don't think it'll affect his heart like she seems to think.

"Jo, you're overreacting."

"Overreacting? Don't you think you could've just given him the number and then ignored his messages like most girls do?" Well, actually no. That thought hadn't crossed my mind at all. I was too busy freaking out. "What even was going through your head?"

I don't know what I was thinking. I can't explain my behavior to myself, let alone others, but I try to explain my thoughts from the moment anyway.

She looks at me with a mix of frustration and recognition. "Okay, I understand you not wanting to give your number to a sleazeball, but what if he isn't? You said you don't know his intentions, so what if they were actually respectable? Why would that be bad?"

Here we go. "Well, the most immediate and obvious fact is

63

that he lives here." She just stares at me. "And I live thousands of miles away." No change in her face. "Okay, let's think in the hypothetical and say his intentions are good. Well, first let's presume that he's asking for more reasons than as a friend. And let's say that something did happen romantically between us. Our relationship would only be in person for a few months, tops. Then we'd have to break up and so what's the point?"

She looks at me like she doesn't understand why that's the only reasonable conclusion. "Statistics show that people in long distance relationships should see each other in person at least once a month in order to maintain a strong and healthy relationship. That is obviously completely unrealistic in this case, so it's a moot point," I add to help her see clarity. There's undoubtedly so much more to it, but hopefully this is the simplest way to get her off my back about the whole thing.

Her face finally shifts and she becomes stern as she speaks, "Two things: One, you need to think of the now. Where is God trying to take you at the moment, and what could he be trying to teach you? And secondly, I don't think the idea of distance is the biggest issue here. You're running from something else."

Of course I'm running from something else! The issue isn't the distance, it's the commitment—that would still not be guaranteed. And honestly, I haven't really taken the issue to God because every time I start to, he tells me to stop running also.

It's like when people run marathons. They've trained for a while and so they don't really feel the pain of the run for the most part, it's just a gradual numbing that takes place and at some point, they can't feel any of the exhaustion or pain. Everything goes numb. Due to this, the racer can continue for miles upon miles. Sure, in this analogy they have to finish the race and the pain comes back and they can feel the exhaustion. Maybe the analogy isn't a perfect representation, but then again, maybe it is. Either way, if I keep running then I can remain numb. I avoid the pain. Logic.

I try to explain this theory to Jo. As she sits quietly, I grow confident in the idea that she's going to drop it. Plus, we aren't actually friends so what does it matter to her anyway? As I finish, she stares at me for a moment and inhales, removing all oxygen from the room. She lowers her voice and speaks to me as you would to correct or teach a young child.

"Aye, hermana. Every race has a finish line. Eventually you have to stop running." Even the running is temporary. But it doesn't have to be, right? "But listen, mi amor, what happens at the end of the race? Each racer is met with a team of people who are there solely to support them. They aid their hurting muscles and give them food and water. They nourish them. This is the same team that drives beside them during the race, just waiting for their racer to reach the end, and they're also involved in all the prep work before the race as well."

I begin to think the metaphor of the race is morphing, and I look at her disapprovingly.

She continues. "You're saying the race is you running from and avoiding love because of the pain that comes with it. I get that." Then what is she getting at? "I'm saying that the race is the journey and experience of love." Is she smoking something? What does that mean?

"You see, each racer trains and builds up their endurance and strength before the race starts. Sometimes this process is hard or painful and sometimes breaks are needed to regroup. But then the race starts and adrenaline floods their veins, drowning out some of the stresses for what it will mean to continue and endure. Throughout the race the adrenaline fuels ecstasy, 'the runner's high,' and this sometimes helps them overlook the pain. Sometimes it comes anyway.

"Now, sometimes at the start of a race one runner will stick with another to help pace them and push them. At some point, it may not be enough, so the racer will push forward on their own, even if it's hard to fight the wind by themselves for a bit. In time, they'll get used to it and will become strong enough to race on their own. However, the racer may catch someone else faster and better who will push them again. This may happen many times in a race.

"Sometimes, a racer will find one person along the race—possibly at the start, maybe in the middle, and for some not until the end—and this person pushes them continuously. The two will exchange places off and on, both encouraging and challenging the other farther, and both helping block the wind for one another for the duration of the race. Then at the end they race for the finish, ecstatic for what comes next. In the case of life, they eventually die, sometimes beside another and sometimes on their own, or sometimes with only a support team around them. Nonetheless, the other racer made this racer's run the best it could've been. Together they fought until the finish, pushing through the pain which they undeniably experienced at times, to celebrate in the joy of the completion."

She ends her story there and I'm stunned to silence. She made it sound difficult but beneficial—incredible. "Adelina, the training takes time and the race isn't ever completely perfect. Starting the race takes courage because it isn't easy and because sometimes it's painful. But it is always worth it in the end. Whether a racer runs with five other people or one, each has helped her reach the finish stronger. They are all worth it. It is all worth it."

Maybe we are friends. She is certainly challenging me and encouraging me—fighting for me—as a friend would.

"Okay." With that one word I try to express to her that I will try. I want to run the race. But I'm also afraid. "So let's say he is respectable and godly and he's interested in being more than friends, a running partner so to say. I still don't live here."

"True, but who's to say you couldn't do distance? Forget about statistics, Kit. Think about who you are. Think of the God who sustains you."

"Okay."

"You continue fighting and racing together until your time together ends. God will use all of it from beginning to end, whenever that is."

"Right. But can we slow down, please? Remember, we don't even know what his intentions are. Or more importantly, if he loves God."

I fall silent when Isabel calls out to me, "Adelina, mija." Jo assumes she's included in this summoning too, so we run out to meet her in the kitchen. "Fui a recoger el correo esta mañana y encontré una carta para ti." She retrieved a letter for me this morning? "Perdón, pero no sé cuánto tiempo ha estado ahí. No he revisado desde el miércoles pasado." It could've been there since last Wednesday? That's over a week ago.

Jo's voice startles me, "¡Kit! ¡Ábrela!"

I can't open it. I'm too confused. My mom doesn't know our PO Box number here, which means none of my other friends or family do either. I didn't even think of the fact that our family had a PO Box or a place where we could receive mail. "Kit. Más rapido." I can feel Jo bouncing on her toes behind me.

I study the front of the envelope, trying to gain some insight about what it may be and who it could be from. There's not even a return address. Is that a thing here? I don't know.

I gently slide open the envelope, making sure not to make any crooked tears. Jo is about to just rip the envelope from my fingers, as my precise movements aren't fast enough for her.

Inside there isn't a letter as I'd assumed. Rather, within the envelope, there is a piece of glossy cardstock a little larger than a notecard. Imprinted on the front of the card is an incredibly stunning image of a beach on it, which, upon closer analysis I realize is this beach—the one I've been going to most every week. The image is darkly lit, almost black and white but there is a gold light radiating from behind the buildings that lie behind the ocean and shoreline. The photo must have been taken from out in the water in the early morning. It's stunning, one of my favorite views here by far.

Jo reaches for the card and I stretch my arm away from her, giving a look that tells her she needs to calm down and be patient. Isabel just looks between the two of us with confusion before turning her attention back to the card. Right.

I flip it over and the back is designed like a postcard. I think the whole thing is handmade, but it seems completely authentic. The top doesn't have a stamp so it must have been hand-delivered. Scrawled in a somewhat shaky cursive on the right side is my full name. Below that is a drawing of a petite fox. Holy wow. It's beautiful.

The left side is written in a straighter script. It's clean and mostly straight. Almost too nice to be stereotypical sloppy male handwriting, but looking at the fox again, whoever it is must be artistic, so the gender is undeterminable. It's also not signed by anyone so I'm still a bit confused, though my pulse is beginning to rise as I think of the few possibilities left for who it could be. And how long has it been there? All week? A few days?

Jo's breath on my neck tells me she's looking down at it as well so I shift my position a bit. I want to see what it says first. Then I can share it with her.

As I read, I translate it into English so I can understand it more clearly. It's short and fairly simple:

> *I had to ask around for the family name, but it wasn't too difficult to get the friendly people at the post office to put this in your mailbox.*
>
> *You didn't give me your number. I was a little disappointed. But not disheartened.*
>
> *+506 2629 1417*
>
> *Your move.*

Oh. My. Goodness. My mind is freaking out. I hoped it would be Dash. I also hoped it was some arbitrary person who somehow randomly overheard my name. That would be easier. Now I'm stuck. Jo is at my back again so I pass the card over my shoulder to her without speaking.

I wait a moment for her to read it and it doesn't take long. She doesn't say anything either, but I know exactly what she's thinking when her squeal pierces my eardrum.

No, no, no. Nope. "Jo, I need you to calm down."

I know I said 'okay,' but I lied.

Isabel looks both worried and confused. "Tranquila, no se preocupe." I try to calm her nerves with my few words.

"Es de un chiiico," Jo taunts, stretching out the word 'guy' for emphasis, causing Isabel's eyebrows to raise with intrigue. "¿Quién es, mija? No sabía que tenías otros amigos." I can't help but cringe and laugh as she mentions my lack of friends.

"Nadie. No lo conozco muy bien." I reassure her that it's not really anyone, as I don't know him well anyway.

Jo chimes in unbidden. "Whatever, you so like him."

"I've seen him a total of four times, talked to him only three of those times, and each of those times we didn't exactly have the most positive interactions."

Isabel looks like she's only picked up half of our side conversation with the language shift. "Podemos hablar más en otro momento, mamá. Pura vida." Her curiosity seems to quell as I tell her I'll share more later. She nods meekly before scurrying away.

I turn around and Jo is smiling at me with eagerness and anticipation in her eyes. "What are we gonna do?"

I quirk my eyebrow at her. "We?"

"Well obviously you're emotionally and relationally stunted, so I'm just saying you may need a bit of my help."

I laugh lightly. Who is this girl? "I'm emotionally stunted?"

"And relationally." She bites her bottom lip delicately, nodding her head while trying to contain her laughter.

In seconds we're both laughing and struggling to breathe.

"Emotionally and relationally stunted?" I exclaim again and the laughter picks up once more.

She sucks in a gulp of air. "I can't be around you. My eyes are sweating!" I can't breathe. Lungs are closing. Abs too constricted. "Can you die from laughing? I hope I die from laughing," she exhales between breaths of laughter.

I can't stop, but if I could I'd tell her that actually you can die from laughing. Essentially your body gets to the point where it can't move anymore even though you're conscious. Or you could suffer from a cardiac arrest. Many other symptoms flood into my mind from a quick study I did once over this same question: ruptured aneurysm, collapsed lung, strangulated hernia, seizure, stroke, or asphyxiation.

As I try to recover, I tell her yes, you can die from laughing, so she needs to leave me alone or she'll end up committing manslaughter.

As we grow quiet again, I think of what she said and know she isn't wrong. I definitely have warped views of emotions and relationships. Even if I didn't, I'd probably still want her help. "Alright, so what are we gonna do?"

"Message him of course! You'll hate yourself if you don't. I'll hate you if you don't. And I can't even imagine what it'd do to him!"

"Oh whatever. We'll all be fine."

"You say that as though you're not going to message him."

"Mmhmm," I respond simply, causing her eyes to widen in a fiery frustration.

"He's already waited a week, I'm sure. Do not run away. At a minimum you could pursue a friendship with the guy."

"Jo, I don't know how many times I've told you; I don't make friends."

"Yeah. Yeah. That's also you running. Plus, you have an incredibly twisted definition of the word 'friend.'" Her fingers

70

practically break at the emphasized quotes she puts on the word friend. "Just stop making excuses!"

I roll my eyes in annoyed submission. "I don't even know what I'd say."

"Anything! '¿Qué pasa? ¡Hola! ¿Cómo estás? Thanks for the number. You're gorgeous and I think we should get married!' The options are endless."

"Be serious."

"I am! Well, all except the end, you can wait a few months before throwing that out." She giggles at her own joke and I'm still trying to catch a breath from it all.

I'm freaking out. I don't know how to be casual. I know that most of my friends have always been guys, but dynamics and interactions shift when it's a guy you could possibly like. Do I possibly like him? I definitely don't want to think I do. It's so much easier. I've thrown out all of Jo's ideas so far.

After another extended amount of time I finally decide what I'm going with. I slowly type his number into my contacts and save it there before going into WhatsApp. When I finally search for his name, his profile picture comes up, and I'm floored again. He really is so attractive. He's got his arm around a boy who's maybe a few years younger than him but who is definitely late teens. While the skin color and hair are a bit different, they have the same deep brown eyes. The younger boy doesn't appear as mature, but he definitely has the same prominent jawline that will make girls fall at his feet. I wonder if this is his only sibling, or if he has any others.

I click on the contact to start a new message:

> *Do you by chance know if there are any laws against stalking within Costa Rica? I'm getting random letters from some anonymous sender and I'm certainly not one to let these sorts of things go on unaddressed.*

There, it's sent. I don't know if that was the best thing to go with, but I can't let him off too easily; plus, if he can't handle my sass then he wouldn't be right for me anyway.

Jo looks at me and I just look back wide-eyed as we wait. "At least let's look at his profile. Most people put a brief description of themselves or something." She says this while already reaching for and grabbing the phone out of my hands. She stays silent for a moment while she reads. "Is it just me or does this seem biblical?" What? No way. I lean into her and read:

*Cuando soy débil, entonces soy fuerte.*

"Yeah it's definitely a concept in the Bible. There was one specific time when Paul was struggling and he had a 'thorn' he kept asking God to take away. It isn't fully known what the thorn was, but God never took it away. He told Paul that his grace was enough. The thorn, or suffering, could and likely would continue because God's grace abounded. God told Paul that in Paul's weakness God's power could be made perfect. So essentially Paul then rejoiced in his suffering and weakness because in it he was able to glorify God."

"Well that seems pretty straightforward to me." Jo's eagerness floods through her voice.

"Maybe not. It doesn't have the verse beside it or anything. People often support biblical ideas without even knowing they're from Scripture."

"Well, I guess you can always ask him," she prods.

"Or not."

"Well, you've got to say something because someone just sent you a message, and I'm willing to bet that it's him," she says glancing down at my screen that's lit up again with a new notification.

"Or not." If I don't check it I don't have to respond, right? Jo just glares at me. I think part of me wishes she weren't here. It would be much easier. I wouldn't have her watching over my every move, or lack thereof. "Alright. Alright."

*You know, there aren't actually any explicit laws against stalking. I'm sorry, I guess that's not really very good news for you. It's certainly seems to be good news for your stalker though.*

"He literally doesn't even care that you're joking about him being a stalker. He just embraced it and admitted he wants to talk to you."

"I mean, not exactly, but kind of," I agree in the same eager voice that she used.

"Come on! I have to leave soon. I want to see as much of this convo as possible." I chuckle at her. I think she is more excited about this prospective guy liking me than I am. Actually, she's definitely more excited.

I write back quickly:

*I guess I have to take action into my own hands then. Any suggestions for how to get rid of him?*

*Dash: From my perspective you're probably already out of luck.*

*Me: So what's the solution? He did slyly get me his number, so I could try to talk to him.*

*Dash: I don't know. Messaging people you don't really know can be sketchy sometimes.*

*Me: True. Maybe he'd get the idea that I actually wanted to talk to him.*

*Dash: Well, you could always explicitly tell him to stop stalking you. But then again, what if you told him and he ignored you?*

"You're enjoying this conversation way too much."

"I'm entertained. That doesn't mean I like him."

"Keep telling yourself that. I'm headed home. I'll need an update later."

"You're not even going to tell me that I have to talk to him still?"

"I think you already had your push, now you're too intrigued to stop messaging him." Dang, she's right. Friendship though. I'm just trying to become better friends with him. Right? That's it.

I push her toward the door, "Get out of here. I'll talk to you later." Another message from him pops up on my black screen.

> *Have you ever heard of Stockholm syndrome? Where someone ends up falling in love with the person who kidnaps them. Maybe in a similar manner you'll learn that you really enjoy engaging with this guy.*

Bold move. One, he just referenced falling in love. Two, he assumes that I'll enjoy talking to him.

> *Me: And here I was thinking you wanted me to continue messaging you. But maybe I'll just initiate a conversation with my stalker friend instead. Like you said, maybe I could actually enjoy engaging with him.*

> *Dash: Well what if I told you a secret that would maybe make you want to keep talking to me?*

I'm really just dragging this all on. I don't even know where this is going anymore. Like, what's the point of this? Why are we even engaging in this hypothetical reality?

I reply anyway:

> *I couldn't tell you. Maybe you should just share your secret, and then I'll let you know what I'm thinking.*

> *Dash: That'd be too easy. How do I know that you won't just ditch me after you know the secret?*

> *Me: Trust me?*

> *Dash: Well, let's just say that your stalker and I may be pretty close.*

> *Me: Really, so you could tell him to leave me alone?*

74

*Dash: Yeah, but I don't think I want to do that.*

*Me: You don't want to tell him? Or you don't want to leave me alone?*

The two blue checks showing that he's read my message sit for a few minutes. Now who's being bold? Eek, what am I doing? I need to take it back. I can brush it off right? Just laugh and make a joke? Or maybe just stop responding altogether. Would that make it better or worse?

I mean, from the beginning I insinuated that he was the stalker, obviously. But in that message I addressed him as himself and the stalker. Either he doesn't want to tell the stalker to leave me alone because he is the stalker, so he'd have to leave me alone, or with the second question he flat out admits that he, as himself, doesn't want to leave me alone. As I kick myself and debate how I'm supposed to proceed now, the screen notifies me that he's typing. I pause, waiting to see what he says.

*Both.*

Was it wrong for me to expect another sarcastic response? I can handle that. I didn't need serious and intentional. Now I'm just uncomfortable. I don't know what to do. How do I respond? I'd ask Jo to help, but she's busy with her family. I'm on my own. And I'm wasting time. He can clearly see that I've read his message. Stupid read receipts.

I'm literally stuck. I don't know how to answer, but I feel weird not responding. I led him into it, didn't I? Plus, if I answer, do I just continue with that conversation in the same way or do I respond seriously? I suck at engaging with people. Why do I just throw things out in mock fashion without thinking through the connotation and severity first?

*Thanks? But maybe you both should just take a step back. You don't actually know me at all.*

Ugh. Was that too aggressive? My walls are beyond heightened right now. If he was serious, I don't know how to deal with that. However, we really don't know anything about one another, so that was an accurate and a fair warning. Right?

*Fair point.*

That's it? I didn't think he'd just drop it. Should I message back or just leave it? I didn't say he couldn't message me at all, just that he should be patient. Well honestly, I don't know what I meant to say. I decide against messaging him back. He's the stalker, after all; he started this.

The rest of the evening is really peaceful. I talk to Isabel and in typical mom fashion she gives me support but also doesn't forget to tell me to be cautious. She's now the second person warning me to be careful; that's a sign, right? Or are people just trying to protect me?

For almost an hour she lights up with the story of how she and Leo first met when they worked the long hours serving tourists. They had a whirlwind romance where they each fell head over heels for one another and never looked back.

It's so fascinating, the language we use for love. Like how they fell for one another, implying there's a lack of control. Also, while it's not as commonly used anymore, people say they're smitten with another. Smitten! This word is derived from the word smite, defined as to strike down or attack. So people are struck or attacked by their feelings, which also implies a lack of control.

Who would want that? I can't even imagine it. Isabel and Leo were enamored instantly, smitten by one another. Their hearts took over and they abandoned their brains behind with no way to catch up. Nope. I like my brain, thank you very much. Though I do have to admit her story was sweet. But love is a delusion, the stories never depict all of reality.

"Ay mi amor, tienes un gran muro alrededor de su corazón. Lo más importante es el amor."

Wall around my heart? I'm a little closed off but so is everyone else, right?

My mind circles around this thought when my phone lights up again. "Mija, te llego un mensaje." I thought Jo went to Jacó with her family. They were going to be at the beach all day and she said she wouldn't have time to text or message.

But it isn't from Jo.

> *While I don't know you, I think I'd like to get to know you better. Some friends of mine are getting together tomorrow evening to hang out and watch some movies. Would you want to meet some more people?*

That's casual, and thankfully, not a date. While I'm not really a people person, it could be fun. Also, I would like to get to know him better, too. Possibly.

*Will Lucas be there?*

I emphasize his whole name and add italics to be a little more dramatic. One, Luc is the only other person I know, and it'd be good to have a familiar face; two, I can't make Dash think I'm going just for him.

He replies quickly.

*Will that get you to come?*

*Me: We'll see.*

*Dash: Great! I'll be at your house around 9.*

*Me: I never actually agreed to going.*

The blue check marks highlight my message but I receive no response.

# 8

My knees are bouncing up and down incessantly as I sit on the couch with Axel and Manny flanking either side of me.

This afternoon, us five kids went to the beach and I used the opportunity to talk to the girls about their lives. They've been fairly reserved since I got here, but after gentle probing they began to open up. The boys ran around us, kicking a ball back and forth until they got too exhausted. Before rushing into the water, Manny approached the three of us and asked that we join them. I looked to the girls and they each rolled their eyes, too cool to go swim with their brothers. As I shifted to stand, they looked at me questioningly.

Oh the sad life of a teenage girl: don't be excessively active, don't enjoy spending time with your family, don't mess up your appearance, lay on the beach and look good, invest in the lives of people on social media more than those in reality. We're all guilty of feeling the desire to be little more than a beautiful body, but boy are we missing out.

I knelt back down between them and spoke, addressing the problems that come with only desiring to uphold our image and not being bold enough to show love to their siblings, to get their hair wet and experience the rush of the waves. I told them to be beautiful and brave, following their desires beyond what is only acceptable for picture-perfect women, and with that I turned and ran hard for the water that had been calling to me all afternoon, diving in at the last minute before a wave crashed into me.

Axel, Manny, and I wrestled and fought against each other and the waves, laughing and screaming. Luciana entered first, jumping on Axel and tossing him momentarily into the pull of the waves. Elena stood at the water's edge watching with longing and hesitation; I guess she needed an extra push.

I whispered quick instructions to Manny and immediately the two of us rushed toward her. Clasping onto her arms on either side, we dragged her toward the water. While she resisted lightly, I could see the joy spread across her face as she glanced down to her youngest brother whose smile had stretched beyond his ears. After this we played tag and swam out beyond the breaks, spiraling through the water until our legs turned to jelly.

In that moment all I could think about was Trace and the times we raced across the lake to the buoys or when we jumped into a waterfall together in Hawaii. Boy, do I miss that kid. I began to tear up with gratitude for the family I've been blessed with here and the one I'm missing back home.

The miniscule droplets at the edges of my tear ducts threw me off guard. I never cry. I can't even remember the last time I had a 'good' cry—the kind where you can't control your breathing and the tears roll down your face and off your chin to reach your collarbone like rainfall.

Sitting on the couch now, I begin to embrace the idea that I seriously am emotionally stunted. I can barely tell when I'm actually feeling something positive—everything feels neutral—and I definitely don't feel negative emotions. I've suppressed them too much. I'm realizing that my only indicator for feelings is a physical reaction.

If I laugh or smile, I know I may be happy, or perhaps

condescending, and if I cry then I'm sad or frustrated. Of course it could be some other things, too, but those are the basics. Those I can generally understand with my physical response, but then there are the times when my heart constricts and it hurts, or it constricts and I feel joy; or there are the times when my stomach stirs like the ocean. I don't know how to interpret those; I just know there's some sort of elusive feeling infiltrating my brain and I hate it. I read about a thing called Alexithymia once and as I sit on the couch thinking, I wonder if I'm affected by it. It's more or less the idea that someone can't identify their emotions and it creates a deeper unawareness of self and hinders social relationships. I definitely would say those things are relevant to me.

I hate my lack of feeling. I hate not understanding the emotions I actually do experience. I want to feel. Yet, I hate how feelings take away my control. I don't determine when I'm happy or hurting, I'm just triggered. I don't want that.

Like now, I feel a longing to be home. Yet I see these boys beside me in protective mode and I feel joy.

Shoot, that reminds me.

This morning Axel overheard me talking to Isabel about Dash coming to pick me up to hang out. He immediately started asking me questions, wanting to know if it was a date: do I like him, is he attractive, do I need company… He continued asking random questions every few minutes until we got to the beach and he was distracted. Now, being back home, he's on alert again and has enlisted Manny to join him.

They're both jeering about beating him up or giving him a talking to, which I know probably won't happen. Trace has always been the same. "Are you talking to any boys yet?" he'd pry.

"No, you know that."

"Just checking, I'd have to beat them up."

"You're supposed to talk to them first."

"Nah."

I doubt he'd ever really do anything, just as I doubt these two will do anything, but the idea is comforting anyway.

We all startle when we hear the subtle rattling of the outside gate. I look between the boys, waiting to see if either of them is going to greet him or if they'll allow me to do it. They each look back at me, unsure of what their job as my protectors entails in the moment. I push off the couch and walk to the door.

I don't think he even put forth any effort, but dang he looks good. He's wearing shoes similar to the knock-off Vans from before, but these ones are high-tops and have a white stripe running down the side from the back. I think they are authentic. He's wearing black jeans and a black shirt with a very slight v at the collar where the chain tucks nicely.

I can see a bit of his tattoo from here as well. I can't help but wonder if he has others, I don't remember seeing any, but I got distracted by the chain at his neck last time, so maybe he has a few. I look at his arms, and while they're tucked into his back pockets, it looks like there may be ink on the inside of one of them. That'd make at least two.

I raise my view up and now realize another part of why I failed to notice much about him. His eyes. Still. They're captivating in the glare of the light and even more so in the shadow of the doorway as I let him in. What's more, they're staring right back at me. I feel a shiver run down to my toes.

He's waiting for me to say something I think, but the boys come up from behind and speak for me. *Dang it. I stared too long. Or did I? Maybe time just seemed slower?* They ask his name, where we're going, and what we're doing.

They sound more intrigued than inquisitive and I can't help but remember that they'd have a brother who would probably be a few years younger than Dash is.

They're basking in his presence now as he speaks to them. As I listen, I'm probably not much different. *Dang it.* Manny leads him

81

around the living room and through the kitchen as though he's his new best friend and I'm not even here. While Axel was the most social when I arrived, I quickly realized that Manny is the most outgoing of the family.

Being dragged by his shirt, Dash looks back at me quickly before I give him a quick smirk and wave him off. I pick up a few things in the living room before trailing them into the kitchen. When I arrive, the boys are gone. I hear laughter coming from down the hall and head toward the boys' room.

Axel is pinned beneath Dash, and Manny is clinging to his back with his legs wrapped around his waist. They're all yelling and squirming around one another. In an instant Manny's leg spasms, or maybe kicks, and Dash shifts away quickly and tries to regain his breath. The other two look at each other with guilt in their eyes before cracking up. This makes me laugh as well and when they all turn to face me I realize they hadn't noticed me. Dash looks up with a tad bit of pain still hidden behind the smile that is quickly filling his face. I guess Manny ended up displaying his protective side in the end, even if it was on accident.

"Ya chicos, vamos. Me gusta que disfruten, pero, necesitamos salir." I could let them beat him up a bit more, but I suppose I should save him. Then again, I'm not really in a rush to go with him. *And yet I am.*

I head out of the room and they follow me with Dash not a moment behind them. They crash down on the couch when we reach the living room, and suddenly the protective mode comes back. They look at him with curiosity and warning as we walk to the front door.

"Sorry about that," I tell him as we leave the house and he shuts the door behind him.

"Are you?" He asks with a tone of challenge and sass.

"You're right, I'm not. It was so entertaining."

"I'm glad you enjoyed it," he smirks to himself, "but the night's only just getting started."

I quickly lock the gate after us and am stunned to silence when he walks me around the corner. *Oh no. No, no, no, no, no. Yes?* He has a bike. Not a dinky bicycle like mine. A motorcycle. They're popular all over the country due to their efficiency, but it didn't cross my mind that he'd have one, let alone that he'd use it to pick me up.

The motorcycle itself isn't a problem. I've ridden since I was a child, and before I had my own I rode between my parents or grandparents when I was a baby. Heck, I even jumped on the back of a scooter with a kid in Italy just for a photo op once.

To my dismay, it's not a sportster or a cruiser, which would've possibly had an extra seat on the back. It's more like a dirt bike, which means there's really only one seat, and nothing to hold on to except the person in front of you—that means Dash. Maybe he would let me drive? I think somehow being in front would make me feel more comfortable because I could ignore that he was behind me.

I still don't speak. He's looking at me with an expression of concern, trying to read my face. I'm sure he'd see a mix of anxiousness, fear, and discomfort. But I'm also positive that my eyes are reflecting excitement, anticipation, and thrill, so he doesn't know how to react. "Is this alright? We can walk if you'd like, it'll just take about a half hour because she lives toward the inland part of the peninsula."

I know his offer is genuine, but it's also ludicrous. I shake my head and he looks at me for a second quizzically, still not sure how to proceed. "You wouldn't be open to letting me drive, would you?" I say as a smirk tugs up the right side of my mouth.

He looks at me for only a moment before a smile breaks across his face. "Not likely," he chuckles as he gets on the front and passes a helmet to me.

I figured, but now I'm not as excited to get on and I hesitate. Reluctantly I pull the helmet on my head, and I notice Dash watching me intently as I thread the strap and buckle it underneath before swinging a leg over the bike. His face still expresses curiosity when he kicks it to life.

The whole ride I try to hold delicately onto the back of his jacket, leaving a slight space between my thighs and his, and my chest and his back. He peers over his shoulder now and then, specifically after I tug his jacket a few times going around the corners to keep my balance on the lean. *Ugh, why is this so horrible? And so perfect?* It's horribly perfect and my mind is reeling.

The drive isn't even ten minutes, and yet when I get off the bike my legs shake with adrenaline. This happens sometimes after things like rock climbing and cliff jumping, so I'm not worried. It's only happened maybe a couple times after dirt bike riding though, so I can only presume that it has more to do with Dash than with the ride.

As we approach the door I can already hear the noise, and I become immediately overwhelmed when we enter the house. The door enters right into the living room and there are probably thirty people in here. Normally thirty people wouldn't be that big of a deal, but the space isn't very big.

Dash smiles down at me and he looks like he's totally in his element. "Can I introduce you to people?" he asks, gently placing his hand on my arm to guide me farther into the room. While I'm very hesitant, I nod my head and follow him around to the various groups of people hanging out. I immediately start logging names away in my head but don't get much further than that with remembering details.

From out of nowhere I feel someone come up and hug me from behind. Immediately I freeze. Dash notices my shift in posture. "Lucas, get off her." I exhale in relief, grateful it's just Luc. That makes it better, though I'm still a bit uncomfortable.

"It's okay, sorry, I didn't know it was you," I say to him, plastering a smile on my face and trying to play it off as though I wouldn't have reacted the same way if I'd known who it was, which I definitely still would have.

I think I'm successful because they both just smile back at me. "Well, what do you think?" Luc asks. "Has she met Violetta? She has to meet my Violetta." I look at Dash with confusion because I'm pretty sure I haven't met her. "You'll know when you meet her. She lights up the whole room." I don't know how I feel about that, I'm already fairly overwhelmed. "¡Violetta! Venga, Bonita."

The girl walking toward us is stunning. Her smile itself illuminates the room and she hasn't even spoken yet. "¡Hola, hola, hola! You must be the mermaid! Lucas has told me about you." I'm not sure what that means but she seems pretty stoked to be meeting me, so it can't be all that bad. The boys smile at us before excusing themselves.

This girl is darling. I swear she radiates the sun with all the joy that emanates from her. She asks me question after question. First they're about my home and family, then about school and my internship here and what I want to do with my future. While I try to evade them, she is persistent. I speak most about what I hope to do at Hogar de la Esperanza and how I want to connect with girls who have been trafficked to show them the restoration they could experience through God. After about half an hour she seems content in the collection of information she's gotten and saunters off to greet some other newcomers. I take the opportunity to gather myself and breathe.

I didn't notice, but while I was talking to Violetta the others have prepared to watch a movie. Most of the lights are shut off and people are quieting down, snuggling next to each other on couches and lined along the floor.

I make my way to one of the walls of the room that opens into a hallway and sit just inside the doorway. This spot makes me feel like I have an escape route. It also saves me the discomfort of being squished beside all of the bodies.

After a few previews, I feel someone sit down beside me. Without turning I know it's Dash. While Violetta kept me busy and engaged, I kept a keen eye on him in case I needed to break away and have him take me home.

He's been meandering around since he left with Luc. It was entertaining to watch them move from group to group every once in a while. They were charming and endearing with the groups of women, and more boisterous and loud with the groups of men.

I shiver in response to the whisper on my cheek as he leans over to ask if I'd like anything to eat or drink. When I ensure him that I'm totally fine he nods and then quietly comments on my time with Violetta. "She and Luc have been together for about five years now. I think she really liked you, not that there are many people she doesn't like, but despite your hard outer shell you seem to have made a nice impression on her." I elbow him gently in the side. *Was he joking? He seems to switch between endearing and borderline rude so often I can barely tell.*

As the movie begins, he averts his eyes from me and his face is illuminated by the screen. It takes me a moment to realize that he'd been staring at me, and then another to realize that I'd been doing the same. I turn back to the screen and see that we're watching a movie called *Puerto Padre.*

I'm not sure what the whole message is, but as I keep watching I realize there's a deep subtext to it. The plot line follows a teenage boy, Daniel, who is looking for his godfather. When Daniel shows up where his godfather used to have a job, he finds out he's dead, but he stays on this specific peninsula to work anyway. He meets a girl while working at the hotel and a romance begins to bloom. It's interesting, but as I watch more, my heart twists, my body goes stiff, and I shrink toward the wall in discomfort.

This is one of the biggest issues in Costa Rica and the movie casts it aside because it's a way of life. They could make a whole movie just out of this theme, but this isn't the plot, it's only a part of it. This is the type of ministry that I want to become involved in here.

The hotel manager is selling the girl to guests. The boy wants her to leave, and she wants to, but she can't. I tune out a good portion of the movie because my mind is reeling. She's being prostituted and they portray it as no big deal. I knew this was a problem here but sitting in the country itself, in a home on the same peninsula, and watching a movie that depicts these realities is making it so much more real.

Dash must have noticed my change in posture because he delicately slides a little closer to me. "Are you alright, Adelina?" He asks it so tenderly that part of me wants to just tell him everything I'm thinking and feeling, but I don't.

"Yes, yeah sorry, it's kind of a sensitive topic, just, this is what my internship here is for," I whisper back casually.

A look of worry flashes quickly across his face but then disappears as he stands up and returns shortly thereafter with a cup of water and a napkin. I won't need the tissue, but I understand why he'd expect me to cry. Nonetheless, it's a sweet gesture, so I thank him quietly.

Part of me curses myself for letting him see that I'm feeling anything at all. The other part of me chastises myself for thinking this. It's okay to care, especially about this, which is such a horrific epidemic across the world. I lean my head against the wall and continue watching.

After a few minutes I feel his hand on my knee in what I think is a gesture of comfort. My heart flutters timidly.

Despite appreciating his action, I shiver and flinch away slightly. My subtlety must've really been lacking though, because he looks at me with an apology in his eyes and tucks his hand back meekly into his lap.

*Why do people love physical touch so much?* I experienced this all through the rest of college as well and I still never learned to appreciate it, never trained myself to not act as though I'm repulsed each time. *I wasn't even repulsed!*

Old habits certainly die hard. "Sorry," I whisper even more quietly than before, in an attempt to show my reaction wasn't anything against him. I think he must understand because one side of his lips quirks up a bit and he just shakes his head gently as though it wasn't that big of a deal.

I try to forget about it, and through the rest of the movie I lean over a few times to ask about translation or cultural meanings and he graciously explains to me each time.

When the movie ends, I'm fairly tired. I think it's in part because of all of the people and socializing earlier, but it's also because of the weight of the movie. Despite the sorrow, there was an underlying love, and in the end the girl is able to leave, so while I wouldn't say I loved it, I also didn't hate the movie.

As everyone files out, I begin to pick up some of the cups left around me. Dash briefly looks at me with curiosity before taking the ones I've gathered to where I assume the kitchen must be. He returns and grabs a few more from me before I gather the rest and head in the direction I'd seen him go.

In the kitchen only Violetta and Luc are left. "Kit I can't tell you how glad I am that you decided to come! I hope I'll get to see you again soon. We're at my house a lot, so feel free to get comfortable," she curtesies gracefully and then giggles to herself, "Sometimes we do stuff elsewhere, so I'm sure Dash can let you know all the details. Can I actually have your WhatsApp though? I'd love to hang out with you!" She's so inviting it almost gives me a renewed energy.

"She doesn't give people her number, Muñeca," Luc says and then smiles jokingly at Dash.

"Nope. Already tried that one," he responds.

"Sure, just pass me your phone." I say while smirking at Dash.

"Dios mío. Must've just been you, Dash," Luc taunts again. "Can I get it too?"

"Sorry, I don't just give my number away willy nilly Luc.

You've gotta earn it," I chide.

"What? How did Violetta get it then?"

"She's endearing and sweet. It's cute." Violetta winks at me in acknowledgment of my response.

"I'm not endearing or sweet?"

Dash chimes in beside me. "The problem is that you're not cute Luc."

"I think you're cute," Violetta replies, sneaking up to kiss his cheek.

"You're biased," Luc remarks—discrediting her—while simultaneously pulling her closer into his side.

"Luckily for you," she says, elbowing him gently in the ribs. I laugh quietly. Yep, she's earned it.

"Well one day I'll get it for myself. If he can get it," he says nodding his head to Dash, "I should have no problem." I blush at that statement. Of course Luc would know that I eventually gave in. How else would I be here tonight?

"Right." Dash rolls his eyes. "Well we'd better head out. Thanks for hosting, Violetta. We'll see you soon." *Why is he assuming I'll be joining him again?*

"Yes, thank you, I enjoyed it," I say as I'm ushered out the door. *Oh right. I forgot. His motorcycle. Gosh dang it.*

He passes the helmet to me and I hop on behind him again. Even though it's only been a few hours, the air has more of a bite than before and I shiver a bit. For the remainder of the drive home I don't mind wrapping my arms around his waist a little tighter. I try to tell myself that this is simply because of the chill in the air, but I'm not quite convinced.

We approach the house but stop nearly a block away so that the sound of the bike doesn't wake anyone. Luciana and Elena may be awake still, but Isabel and the boys have definitely gone to bed even though it's only approaching midnight.

Hah, home at midnight, like I'm Cinderella again, except not quite. *I can't say I wouldn't mind being Dash's Cinderella though.* Freak, that's not relevant right now, I'm trying to start as friends, and stay as friends. *But he's so cute. But also, maybe not a Christian.* Plus, Cinderella is so basic, I'm much more like Kida from Atlantis, or Mulan: strong, fierce, sacrificial, the ultimate female warrior. At least I hope to be.

Anyway, we stop about a block from the house and I assume he'll just say goodbye there, but he walks me through the gate. Silence clings to the air for the few steps until we reach the door and I hear him inhale a deep breath—one of the ones that indicate someone has a lot on their mind.

"I, I hope you're alright." He states it simply, as though he doesn't want to overstep some unwritten boundaries.

I'm not sure how to reply so I shrug off his concern. "Umm, yeah, no worries."

"Adelina," he sighs in exasperation and corrects himself, "Kit, you don't have to be tough all the time, you know?" He looks earnest, but also cautious, as though I may hit him for his comment.

I stare at him blankly, trying to find an adequate response. "Yeah, I know," I reply simply.

"Do you?" He asks with genuine interest. Despite his concern and sincerity, I become annoyed.

I look up and I'm sure my furrowed eyebrows display my clear frustration. "You don't know me Dash, and I don't have to explain myself to you. I know I don't have to be tough all the time but thanks for the wonderful reminder." I roll my eyes and step toward the door.

He delicately touches my arm and turns me back around to face him. "I'm sorry. It's just, from the few times I've been around you it seems like you always have this guard up. You act like nothing bothers you, and I'd imagine that even if you were hurting—though you say you're not—you'd try to get through it on your own."

"So what if I try to get through it on my own? I'm in a different country, with a different language and culture, and people I don't know; it's not like I have many options," I huff back, trying to redirect the anger and sadness building in my chest. Why is he saying this stuff?

I hadn't realized, but his hand is still on my arm and he pulls me gently closer to him. "You have me. And Luc and Violetta now, too. Plus that girl you mentioned earlier at one point this evening, Jo. You're not alone and you don't have to live life as though you are."

The rare emotions I have are already in gear from earlier tonight and tears are threatening my eyes. Though I'm fairly confident that they won't escape, I send up a prayer in hope that they don't betray me.

He needs to stop saying these things. But he's right, I do feel alone. Yet, I know I can't really trust him, or anyone else. God and I have it under control. "Thanks," I finally respond, hoping to just end the conversation so I can get inside.

He ignores my concise attempt at goodbye and seems to take it as an invitation, wrapping me delicately in a hug. He quickly lets go when he seems to remember my discomfort at touch and pushes me back a bit, releasing me. "Anyway, I'm glad you decided to come. It was fun to see you interacting with Violetta!" He laughs a bit at this comment, trying to remove the tension buzzing through the molecules around us. "Maybe you two could hang out more. Or the four of us could hang out?"

I try to move past everything that just happened, too. "Maybe. She is really sweet. And Luc is fun. There's just one problem." *I don't know what your intentions are.*

"And that is?" He probes.

"Four is a crowd," I say while a smirk pulls at my lips.

"Well, Luc doesn't have to come."

"Luc is entertaining, I don't mind hanging out with him."

"You don't want Violetta to come? You've enjoyed hanging out with Luc and I that much?"

"She's wonderful too, I couldn't ask them not to come together." A curious look grows across his face as I begin to smile bigger.

"I see…" he pauses dramatically. "You're scared of me," he jokes, trying to throw back what I'm handing him. The only problem is that he's not wrong, especially after what happened a few minutes ago. I laugh anyway, trying not to show my discomfort. "Well okay, if four is a crowd then how about the two of us?" he continues. "I'm free most of tomorrow. Are you doing anything?"

My mind shuts down immediately and my laughter is drawn from the air. Ugh no, if he's not busy that means he won't be going to church. While I'm disappointed, I can't just ignore him. Friends it is, I suppose. "Tomorrow's Sunday so I'll be going to church in the morning. Then Jo and I usually go eat afterwards," I reply, trying to politely indicate that I'm busy while also letting him know that me going to church isn't negotiable.

His eyes flash and I'm curious as a smile grows across his face again. "I could join you," he says a bit too enthusiastically.

"Well I mean usually it's just Jo and me at lunch, but I could see if she wouldn't mind you joining us."

"Oh, well sure, that too if she wouldn't mind. But I meant that I would love to join you at church," he replies enthusiastically. I'm sure my face drops in astonishment at this remark. *No way. He wants to come with us?*

# 9

I wake up extra early, eyes wide and mind jittery. I get ready like normal, deciding not to wear anything extra fancy even though I want to dress up a bit more. To fill my time I try reading. On any other day I could fall into my book and get lost; this morning I'm too distracted.

Of course I immediately messaged Jo to freak out last night after Dash left. This was probably one of those call-without-hesitation moments, but she knows that phone calls make me anxious so her response flew back immediately in all caps. She was just as excited as I am because, even though we don't know where he stands in his faith, the fact that he is coming with us or that he shows interest at all is definitely a victory.

Except maybe I shouldn't get so excited. If he is religious or open to faith, I may end up liking him more and I'm not ready for that, plus that's not the same as genuinely loving Jesus. I've been here a little over a month, which means the ending to this experience is closer now than when I first arrived, obviously. I can't start to like him. Well, I can't start to like him even more. My heart pounds at the small truth I've just admitted to myself.

The past few Sundays Jo and I have been meeting up right before service, but we agreed to walk together today instead. Dash is meeting us at the church so I didn't want to risk running into him before I'd found Jo.

As soon as I open the door Jo starts rambling on in excitement. By the time I've tuned in she's already trying to reassure me. "I know you're freaking out, but it'll be okay. I can see in your eyes that the bricks are starting to stack up one by one to keep yourself away from him and the possibilities. Knock it off, stay open, and only build the wall if he proves to be rude, or lame. You don't have to start ahead of time."

I know, I know, I heard this all through the rest of college: be vulnerable, don't be so closed off, trust people. Sounds great in theory, sure, but it doesn't always play out so well. Sometimes it just means you get hurt more in the end.

"Suffering produces hope, Adelina." Daisy reminded me of this often, every time I made excuses to close myself off from people. Of course she's wise enough to speak Scripture—I can't deny it.

Endurance, character, and hope, the promised gifts we receive in suffering. It's pretty much the equivalent to 'whatever doesn't kill you makes you stronger,' except more sophisticated and more inspiring. Nonetheless, it's much easier to understand as a concept than to actually embrace and live through.

"Thanks, Jo. I love it when my first interaction with someone in the day is a lecture," I reply when she finally finishes. She just laughs and ushers me out the door. As we walk, she tries to avoid the subject of Dash as much as possible, though she can't help but smirk at me every so often. As we near the church she finally breaks. "I hope he isn't late. Last week they said this message was going to be interesting and I'd like to sit—."

"He's early," I interrupt with a low gasp when I catch sight of Dash standing out of the way near the street. He's not in overly formal attire but he certainly cleans up nicely.

94

"He definitely doesn't look like the punk surfer you've described," she says, reading my mind. She waves at him and he looks surprised. *What in the world Jo, now he knows that I've been talking about him!* I glare at her so that she gets the hint.

He steps toward us and extends his hand. "You must be Jo, I'm Xander, but everyone calls me Dash. Thanks for allowing me to intrude on your morning with Adelina." He smiles invitingly at her and continues. "While I'm glad to have the opportunity to join you for service, I may skip out early and allow you to go to lunch on your own." Jo and I both look at him silently for a moment.

"Oh my goodness, no. You have to stay for lunch as well," she protests. She should stop now; I wasn't totally against him bailing.

He smiles at her again, revealing his dimple and scrunching the birthmarks around the corner of his eye this time. "I guess we'll see," he responds. "Are you guys ready to head in?" I nod and he leads the way as though he's been here a hundred times. He walks toward the front and then steps aside so the two of us can step into the row in front of him. Jo and I exchange a look of surprise and confusion. Jo of course speeds up a bit to make sure she's in before me so I have to sit beside him.

He smiles dashingly as he turns in to sit down. Wow, that word will forever have a new meaning. Hopefully his name will uphold the respectability and allure of the word. One definition of the word dashing is to be energetic and spirited or lively. The other, which is what his smile demonstrates, refers to that which is elegant and gallant in appearance and manner. Gallant, what a word! He really ought to match up to his name. *Or maybe not, that'd be easier.*

We've only been sitting a moment before a few people step to the front of the church. I've experienced a few different styles of church and worship, including psalms sung directly from Scripture or not singing at all, a super conservative church that sang only hymnals, as well as churches which sang a mix to appease older and younger generations.

The worship here has been one of the most enjoyable styles by far. One, hearing people praise our God with a different language is a pure testament to his power and majesty, and it awes me ceaselessly. Secondly, everyone sings with so much passion and energy.

I'd seen videos of people worshiping in Africa, dancing and chanting and clapping in the aisles, and thought it looked both incredible and distracting. The style of worship here is so similar to that, and it isn't as distracting as I'd imagined it would be. It somehow connects me more with the people and helps me find greater joy in God, rather than merely reciting words. It even helps me focus on the messages and keeps my mind from wandering too far.

While those of us in the audience don't dance too much, there is a group in the front that dances beautifully, and it definitely brings recognition to all of those verses that say there is a time for dancing and that we should worship with music and dance. Often people would dance for joy after suffering or mourning, and in this setting it is as though we are dancing to rejoice in the fact that we have all come to new life. I love it.

Looking to my left, I see Jo's eyes are closed and her arms are lifted in surrender. I can't help but feel such gratitude that God has blessed me with someone like her to experience this journey with. As I peer right, I can see Dash's mouth moving to match the words being displayed in front of us and I'm again caught by surprise. Listening now I can hear his voice. I hadn't noticed it before because it's a bit deeper than when he is speaking normally. While it isn't the smoothest voice, the low sound gives it a richness that compensates.

I watch him for a moment longer. His face is radiant and consumed by worship and adoration. Then as his arms reach out near his sides I can see a full line of inked tattoo stretched across the forearm nearest to me. While I'm not at the most pivotal angle, I can still read the slightly swirling upside-down letters: *Cuando soy débil, entonces soy fuerte.* It's the same Scripture he has written on his WhatsApp account so it must really have some meaning.

From what I've realized, he only has these two tattoos. The one on his neck, which is bold and beautiful, but also intimidating, is a clear contrast to this one, which is delicate and peaceful. It's intriguing and I'd love to know more about them and why he got them. Finding myself distracted by the tattoos and the ways he worships, I remind myself that now is certainly not the time for wandering thoughts.

This is not good. I redirect my attention to the group in front again. He must sense that I've been looking at him because he peers over at me and smiles while he continues to sing. I think he also catches a hint of my surprise because he bows his head a bit before pointing it to redirect me toward the screen and lyrics. Right.

Paul said that sometimes it was better to be single because then a person is only anxious about the Lord. I'm beginning to understand that even better. I cannot get distracted.

I'm quiet as service gets out and I listen as Dash seeks to make conversation with Jo. She tries to engage with him as much as possible, but she's also trying to talk to me subtly through her glances. I'm fine, but the service just happened to be about Ruth, who's probably my favorite woman in the Bible, and I'm busy processing through the message right now.

Dash seems to notice I'm being quiet but doesn't bring it up. I'm not really sure what's going through his head, but he finally announces that he's going to leave us for our lunch and head home. Jo immediately snaps back and apologizes before again telling him to join us. After a little prodding, he reluctantly looks at me as though for approval. When I nod, he agrees gleefully.

I ultimately speak up when we're trying to decide where to go. Jo definitely won't let us go where she works, but admittedly it's one of the best places. Finally Dash interrupts and suggests a new place I've never been to before. "I completely forgot about that place. Yes, I've never taken her there. So glad we invited you." Jo is beaming at Dash and he can't help but smile back. They each peer over at me for confirmation, and I only shrug because I really can't give input.

He leads us to a casual restaurant on the beach and the smell as I approach is incredible. Dash smiles over at me expectantly and I can't help but smile back in approval. "Kit, you're going to love this place. Can I order for you? My favorite meal is to die for!" Jo interrupts us.

"Shouldn't I get to pick her first meal since the restaurant was my suggestion?" Dash jokes. Jo hesitates and Dash takes the opportunity to scurry to the front and order for all of us. I immediately look over at Jo, who stands staring agape.

I can see she's a little frustrated but pleased at the same time, so she moves on to find us a table, sitting contentedly and then pulling me in beside her. Dash comes and sits down across from us, eyes glittering as though he hasn't done anything wrong. I mean, technically he hasn't, but him ordering for us certainly isn't normal.

We watch him for a moment and he doesn't react at all, perfectly comfortable in the silence. We're all quiet until the food comes out and each of us has a different meal. Finally Dash speaks up to tell us what we each have. When he describes mine as Sopa Negra or a black bean soup, I'm a bit disappointed, but as soon as I try it my taste buds melt. I look over and I can see that Jo is loving her meal as well. We're each transported back to the table and reality when he speaks up again.

"Adelina, what did you think of the service?" I see Jo look over at me, confused as to why he's just used my first name. I don't get it either, so I just shrug back silently. Or maybe she's as thrown off as I am by the fact that he's asking about the service.

I look back at him and he's patiently waiting for a response.

I don't know what to say yet and I don't know why he'd be

interested, so I brush the question away with my own. "Well, Ruth is one of my favorite books, so I've read it quite a few times, but this morning brought up a few new thoughts. What about you, what did you think about everything?"

He hesitates for a moment before responding and it's almost as though he's discontent with my response. "I enjoyed it. I generally like the guy who spoke today. I've been there a few times before on my own, but Violetta started dragging Luc to another church farther inland a few years ago and I've been going with him to that one ever since. It's a little more out of the way but the theology is solid and the worship is connective."

He pauses for a brief moment when he sees Jo and I exchange a look of astonishment and confusion. The look in her eyes is slowly shifting into excitement, but I'm sure that fear and anxiety are probably flooding my expression. I mean holy cow, he just said "the theology is solid." *Don't flip.* Jo looks at me and I see that she's also trying to tell me not to freak out.

Dash ignores our silent conversation and speaks up again. "What did you mean when you said the sermon brought up new thoughts? I take it you know it fairly well if it's your favorite." He addresses me again and I'm not sure how to respond. Too many thoughts are still swirling in my mind, and some of them I'd probably prefer not to share. I mean, I guess I'd prefer not to share any of it. He needs to stop asking me questions.

He sits attentively. Jo turns as well, looking at me patiently. I'm starting to get anxious, but I don't think I'll get away with saying nothing.

My lips purse as I try to compose my thoughts. "In the service this morning, as in many others, we discussed Ruth's faithfulness to Naomi and her willingness to leave her family to marry another man as Naomi suggests, and most importantly to serve Naomi's God as her own. Her loyalty is astounding, without a doubt, but there is more to this.

"There's one part of text where people tend to freak out or joke about Ruth being really forward and how her actions are sketchy right, as though she's pretty much just begging for Boaz to sleep with her, some even suggest that she did." They stare at me as I ramble. "Anyway, for her to approach as she did is normal culturally. Many people don't understand but to lay at his feet as she did is what servants do to their masters as a sign of respect. When Boaz wakes, she asks for him to spread the corner of his garment over her. This, in their day, would mean that she is stating she is a widow and he should take her as his wife. She's asking for his protection in both of these actions."

I'm on a roll now and the teacher side of my spiritual gifts is definitely coming out. Plus, this is a topic I'm intrigued by, so I continue despite not wanting to talk to begin with.

"Additionally, in Israeli culture during this time, a woman was legally entitled to a kinsman-redeemer, or someone who could maintain her husband's family name. The relatives of a widow are bound by law to marry her if she does not yet have an heir, in order to carry on the name of her first husband. The relative may refuse, but this is very disrespectful and those who refuse are often shunned to an extent. Also, if the man doesn't take action to accept or refuse, or if he is unaware of his role as the kinsman-redeemer, the widow may seek out the man. In a way, this is what we see in the case of Tamar as well in Genesis.

"Anyway, Ruth seeks to present herself to Boaz in acknowledgment of the law and she does so in a way that is modest and submissive, not sexually as some suggest. Of course, unbeknownst to her, and Naomi as well, I'm sure, there is someone else who is closer in the family tree. So, Boaz assures her that he'll converse with the man to see if he'll fulfill his duty. Shortly after this he suggests she remain the rest of the night. Again people assume negatively of this scene, but more likely this was suggested to protect her.

"It wasn't that he wanted to keep others from assuming that she was coming to him as a prostitute, but to make it so that the closer heir wouldn't assume her to be trying to work around him in search of someone else as her husband. This would have been incredibly dishonoring. Moving on in the story, the closer relative refuses and Boaz takes Ruth as his wife and in the end the faithfulness of each of them causes them to step into the lineage of Christ."

I pause because I don't think I want to continue. This is all part of the story I've known for a while, but it isn't the part that connected with me this morning. That part is more horrifying than fascinating and I'm thinking I may be fairly frustrated at my epiphany. It's her willingness to try again, and even to try at all—to try at love and vulnerability. I don't understand it and it scares me.

They're both looking at me somewhat stunned that I've just rattled off so much information, but I think Dash knows I'm still holding back some of it. After a moment he asks, "So what have you been thinking about this morning that was new or different? What is your grand takeaway or your moment of conviction?" Geesh, he's really prodding, isn't he, and with words like 'conviction' nonetheless.

Each moment makes me want to share less and less, but his eyes are so kind and inviting that I also feel a deep desire to share with him. I take a deep breath so I can explain my new thoughts, hoping it'll make some sense.

"Ruth had already risked love. She left her home and her family for a man who was not even someone of her own nation. She gave up all comfort for this man, and what happened? He died. It was all seemingly purposeless. Yet she persisted nonetheless. She didn't run back to what was comfortable or easy, she stayed faithful to the Lord and when he asked her to try again, she did so obediently."

I think briefly of the girls I'll be working with at Hogar de la Esperanza who have also lost so much and will have to learn to trust again.

"She chose to approach love again despite the risks, and in the end, she receives many blessings as a part of the genealogy of Christ. The whole thing was aligned so perfectly, and despite the hardship, she fought for the relationships around her and she obeyed God in them—putting him and others before herself. She faced suffering, but she came back in obedience to find joy in embracing relationships again through vulnerability."

Dash looks somewhat confused about my response, like what I said is clearly obvious and makes so much sense. He obviously doesn't understand why it's caused me so much vexation. On the other hand, Jo is beaming at me because she knows this is another tally on her side of the scoreboard. She knows my three deepest fears: vulnerability, intimacy, and commitment; and this 'moment of conviction' as Dash so aptly put it, targets each of those. She's stoked, and she's gloating in her victory.

What she doesn't know and understand is that just because I'm convicted to be more vulnerable or to seek relationships, it doesn't mean I'll follow through. The fear of it is my Achilles' heel, the chink in my armor, my kryptonite. It's my thorn, and it doesn't seem to be going away any time soon.

# 10

While Dash tried to ask more questions to understand, I brushed them away and our attention shifted back to our food. We left after more light chatter—him heading back to his house and me joining Jo at hers, with him promising to see and talk to us again soon.

The rest of the afternoon we've stayed inside watching Harry Potter and some other movies. Her brothers got home a bit ago from the city, each tromping in carrying bags. The two eldest brothers even brought back little candies for the two of us.

While they make fun of Jo and claim she'll always be the baby of the family, even though she's technically in the middle with two older and two younger brothers, she laughs and rolls her eyes, happy this is one of the times when they're all getting along rather than fighting. Eventually they each retreat to the rooms they share, the two eldest together and the two youngest together, and we're left to continue our movie bingeing.

While I jump up to sort through our options for the next movie, Jo speaks up and startles me. "You know we're going to talk about what happened at lunch today right?" Ugh, no I didn't know that; I don't know why it's necessary.

"Mmhmm, just not right now okay?" I ask, in hope that eventually she'll forget about it or just choose to move on.

"Adelina." She never uses my first name and she sounds way too intense right now as it comes off her lips. "You are literally ignoring what you heard this morning. You're already trying to run from it. Why do you keep doing that? I'm not going to move on and I'm certainly not forgetting. We're talking about this tonight." She sounds serious.

My face falls. Beyond the fact that I don't want to discuss it, I'm exhausted. I've been with people all weekend and I'm beyond drained. It'd probably be best in every way if I just left early.

I stop shuffling through the movies and look back at her. "Jo, I can't today. I'm tired and really just need to head home I think, go to bed early and get some good rest. I'm sorry, but later," I tell her as I move to the couch and gather my bag to leave.

She looks at me and her eyes reflect hurt and disappointment, but I can't please her right now.

Dash and Jo have each been trying to message me for the past two days wanting to chat or hang out. I'm kind of ignoring them. I've been steering clear of the house and other places with Wi-Fi so that I have a bit of an excuse to not respond, but I still know that I'm avoiding them, and I feel a little guilty about it.

Dash stopped sending messages some time late last night and I don't know if it's because he's given up or because he's busy. Jo has only increased her messages, however, and she's just threatened to come to my house.

If she genuinely follows through then she'll realize that I have absolutely no legitimate reason for not responding to her. If I've learned anything over the past little while being here, though, it's that she has a strong will. I don't want to take any chances, so I message her back and promise her we can hang out soon. As I turn back to my book, I hear the gate rattling from the front of the house. My heart jumps. "Un minuto," I yell out quickly in annoyance.

Clearly my message must not have sent through quickly enough. She sent hers about twenty minutes ago and, because I was so wrapped up in the book, I only saw it a moment ago. Maybe she did come over already.

That's annoying, maybe we won't be hanging out later after all. I mean, if she's going to barge in on me now then she definitely doesn't need to see me later. I yell out again as I go to let her in, "You seriously couldn't just patiently wait for me to respond? I was going to talk to you eventually and you knew I wanted time to think about—"

Dash is leaning outside, arms resting through the rungs of the gate with a look of astonishment on his face. I'm sure my expression matches his because I certainly wasn't expecting to see him at my door. The corner of his mouth tips up slightly. "Think about what?" he asks gently after a brief moment.

About him, and the sermon—about my feelings. "Oh, um, I thought you were Jo." I pause a second because I don't know how to pull my foot out of my mouth.

He laughs, "Really? Well, I'm glad that was for her and you're not upset at me."

"What makes you assume I'm not?" I say, impressed by my ability to contain all of my smile except for a small quirk that tugs up the right side of my lips.

He hums lightly, "Right. Well, I suppose I'd better be going, then. You said you've got some thinking to do and I must be interrupting. The sooner I head out the quicker I'll hear back from you."

I think he's egging me on, trying to get me to ask him to stay. "You can't just assume I'll be talking to you any time soon after showing up on my front porch without warning."

"Unless I've learned poor English, I don't think you have a front porch." He says this haughtily as though he's somehow earned himself the right to speak. "So, will you let me say what I came here for?" I lean dramatically on my hip while I wait for him to continue. He gets the cue. "I thought I'd show you one of the typical tourist attractions of our city. A todas las gringas les gusta." *All the white girls like it? How many has he taken there to know that?*

"You take all the beautiful gringas to this place then? No thanks. I'm content with my book." I'm not a typical tourist and he can't just win me over like any of those other girls. In my now genuine frustration I start to shut the door.

He tries to step forward but is met again with the gate that I didn't get around to opening. I see a flash of embarrassment cross his face, and it catches me off guard. "I didn't mean it like that, I just know it's a place people like to go. I also wouldn't mind staying in to read though, if you'd let me join you." There's the Dash I'm more familiar with. *He's so confident.* He acts as though I'm dying to spend any time with him I can.

While his words are somewhat cocky, the look on his face is sincere. I remind myself I'm merely trying to be friends with him, so hanging out isn't a bad thing. And I guess I'm a little more than *slightly* intrigued by his offer.

I pull the door back open, "My book is pretty good, you're telling me you think this would be better?"

His concern fades and the smile flies back onto his face. "I certainly hope so."

I nod my head and toss him the key to the gate before signaling for him to follow me. When I get to the kitchen, I grab some money from my bag, put away my book, and write a note in case Isabel gets back before I do.

She and the kids all went into the city for the day, and I told them I'd be hanging out at home.

Dash is standing just inside the door when I come back. I'm not a great host, as I kind of forgot to invite him to sit or get a drink or anything, but instead I just rush us back out the door, hoping it didn't matter too much. I look around for the bike and stop short. "I didn't bring it today, I thought it'd be nice to walk," he says, reading my mind.

Oh shoot, I'm not sure which I'd prefer, the uncomfortably close ride or having to talk the whole way walking. "Sounds good," I say, though I think my voice may lack some conviction.

He starts directing us toward the beach and my heart sinks a bit. I love the beach, but I don't know why he would've made such a big deal about it.

As we walk, the air around us is quiet for the first little bit and it feels slightly awkward. We get into step with one another after a few more minutes and he finally speaks up. He asks questions about who I am and life back home. I don't mind as much today because he tries to keep it pretty light. I stray away from talking about myself, what I love, and who I really am, by highlighting activities or other people. I don't have too many friends so it's easy to get through the basics of all of them. Then I highlight just a bit more of why I'm here with Hogar de la Esperanza. He becomes quieter after that, probably just because I'm mentioning prostitution again like during the movie.

This whole scenario feels a bit weird but I'm trying not to have a mini meltdown. When he pauses for a moment, I jump in to ask questions, taking the spotlight off myself for a little while. He doesn't seem to notice that I'm redirecting the conversation, or if he does, he doesn't comment on it.

As we get nearer to the beach he doesn't stop, he just kind of steers us to the left and continues walking. I don't ask any questions because I'm busy trying to figure out what he's doing and where we're headed. I think he can tell I'm confused because I hear him laugh quietly to himself.

After about ten more minutes he points to the left. "This is us," he says plainly, and his usually simple smile isn't subtle at all.

He's brought me to the marine park! The pit in my stomach goes away and is replaced by excitement. From what I've seen, parts of the place look like it's really only for children, but animals are animals, and I couldn't care less how old we're supposed to be.

Walking in, it doesn't seem like the clerk selling us our tickets recognizes Dash, so that's a good sign that he really doesn't bring all of the girls here. *Adelina, why do you care if he does, you're not together.* The older attendant looks at me questioningly, but after a little while Dash is able to convince her that I'm a resident, even if only temporarily, so I get the cheaper price. I reach into my pocket to grab my colones and am stopped short. He comfortingly clasps my shoulder lightly and my frustration evaporates quickly into appreciation as he extends enough money for the both of us to the lady.

I thank him and then go quiet again, trying to debate his intentions. After a few minutes he stirs me out of my thoughts when he speaks. "Do you care where we go first?"

Of course not, I don't know what's here or what's best to see. "I'm at the hands of your service, sir. You can be my tour guide," I say while directing him forward with my hands and a low curtsy. He chuckles and bows before leading us away from the building and off to the right.

"I used to bring my brother here a lot when we were younger. Matías is twenty-two now and isn't around, so we don't really visit often anymore. I haven't been here in many years."

I'm confused when he says this and my eyebrows frown in thought. If Matías is twenty-two, that means he's older than I am, which puts Dash even older than I'd thought he was. My heart pounds at the thought.

I hesitate and don't say anything yet as he continues. "His favorites were always the crocodiles, I'll admit they're pretty cool, so we'll go there first. That way we can start well and end just as well, if not better."

I listen intently as he tells me more about his brother and their relationship. He stops talking for a second as we approach the outdoor enclosure and I take the chance to speak up, "This may be an odd question, but you said your brother is twenty-two, so, umm, how old are you then?" He smiles crookedly at me and I don't know what that means.

"How old do you think?"

I assumed he was about twenty-two, max. I thought he'd be close to my own age but maybe only a bit older and I tell him exactly this.

He's quiet before throwing my own question back at me and asking how old I am. He's dragging this out more than necessary so I decide to answer, "Almost twenty-one."

He thinks for a moment at my response before answering for himself. "I just turned twenty-four a few months ago." Oh shoot, what? That's a little more than a three-year age gap, I'm shocked; he looks younger, still very mature, but not twenty-four.

I remind myself that his age is irrelevant. One, we're just friends, and two, age is a social construct.

"What does almost twenty-one mean, is your birthday soon?" he asks, pulling me back from my contemplation.

Dang it, I knew I shouldn't have said it like that. I hate telling people when my birthday is and it's really awkward trying to avoid the conversation. It's not that I don't appreciate when people celebrate my birthday, I just think it's dumb to celebrate someone extra on a specific day when we should show love all year.

I decide that while it's awkward, I may have a decent chance at avoiding the topic so I look into the first pond at the crocodiles, ignoring Dash beside me. There are two in this enclosure and they're equally fat and squatty. One is trying to waddle toward the water and the other is lying on its stomach near the edge of the habitat.

Dash turns his attention from me and toward the crocodiles as well. He informs me that one is female and the other is male and, while generally they wouldn't put one of each gender together to minimize the babies, these two were found together in the wild.

"The female was injured and the male stayed with her, bringing her food and caring for her. When they tried to bring her in, the macho man here charged the rehabilitators. Then they decided it'd probably be best to bring them together. They've been together now for about thirty years in captivity, and it's estimated that they were about twenty years old when they were found. Fifty years together seems like such a long time." *Yeah, too long.*

"It's really incredible actually. Unlike a fair number of animals, crocodiles are monogamous creatures, you know." He states this simply as though I should know that. "I guess in quite a few ways they're a bit like people. I don't think that's why my brother always loved them, but it's what I find most fascinating—the way their love and commitment to one another endures for so long. These two are my favorite, but there's another over here. She's by herself, which is kind of sad, in my opinion. Alone for all of her life, no one to love her and no one for her to love." *Umm, hinting much God?*

He directs us to the second pond, and there's a different species of crocodile in here. She's under a tree and it looks like she's younger. The smile stretching across her face is more inviting than frightening, and I'm surprised when Dash tells me she's only been here about five years. When they first brought her she was a little older than a hatchling, and they let people in the city hold her. That was the last time he and his brother came, just to see the new spectacle.

His voice is soft and gentle as he speaks about the animals and his brother. For some reason it makes me feel some reassurance, as though I can talk to him, even if it's so insignificant. "My birthday is this next month. It'll be the third birthday in a row away from my family. Not a big deal, though."

His eyes are curious but his smile is just as gentle as his words were before. "You're not going to tell me the date, are you?" he asks.

"I guess we'll see how good of a guide you are," I tease. "Plus, maybe I won't be talking to you by next month anyway, so the date may not even matter." The first part, while a joke, is my attempt to evade the topic. I'm hoping he'll forget about it by the end of the afternoon. This second part is less of a joke, but I keep my tone light so he doesn't think I'm serious.

Jo would be annoyed at me; she'd know this was a layer of bricks I was laying. How could I not, especially now with his 'crocodiles are monogamous, like people, and it's fascinating' speech?

# 11

While part of me is now ready to leave, Dash confidently directs us to a small pool on the farther end of the park. When I look into it I'm amazed by the large sharks swimming around. They don't look dangerous at all, probably because they're all circling near the base of the pool and their mouths curve around the front of their bulky heads to resemble pleasant smiles.

Dash informs me that they're nurse sharks and mostly harmless. I lean over and put my hand into the water. "Mostly harmless," he cautions as he leans in beside me. "While they're bottom dwellers, they will bite if upset or bothered." We stay like this a little while, brushing our fingers across their sandpaper-textured backs.

One large gray shark rests beneath us, allowing us to pet its back for a period of time. While dragging my fingers down its side, I flinch and pull back as my hand connects with Dash's instead of the shark's skin. *Seriously, you're petting sharks and yet you flinch away from him?* I chide myself.

He doesn't make any sign that he's offended, but we move on shortly thereafter, me placing my hands deeply in my back pockets and him clasping his together in front of him precautiously.

I know we missed a lot in the center, but he must be saving those because we shuffle into the next building and are instantly shrouded in a dim, glowing darkness. The light brightens as we approach a large aquarium. It is bustling with color as the various species of fish and other aquatic creatures shuffle around the tank. They are all so vibrant and exotic, and I'm enthralled by the differentiation. I've seen many aquariums before and I've been snorkeling a few times, so much of what I'm seeing isn't new to me, but it's all incredible nonetheless.

Dash begins telling me another story about him and his brother and how they'd create lives and tales, intertwining the creatures in the tank. The tone he uses each time when speaking about his brother is almost sorrowful but the joy of the memory bleeds through in it as well. I'm curious but remain silent. Within moments he's diving into a story of adventure, romance, and danger, tying the lives of various animals together.

It's hilarious and witty, but at one point I find myself distracted by the aqua hue that is shining on his face. The ripples of the water and the reflections from the glass cast deep shadows and alternating flecks of light across his eyes or lips and down along the side of his jaw. *Dang, he really is attractive.*

His eyes flit toward me to make sure I'm still engaged in the story and I catch them briefly before I hurriedly look back into the water. He smiles and grows quiet as he reaches the 'happily ever after' moment in the tale and I look back at him once more quickly before moving on. *I need to stop.*

I walk to the center of the room where there is an interactive pool. We're able to pet a few of the different starfish that rest at the bottom, so I dip my hand in again but slide over as Dash comes beside me—not wanting a repeat from the shark tank.

We move on shortly and fall side by side as we walk down the hallway toward the exit. I feel a bit uncomfortable as we walk because I feel like this could easily be a date. To add to my wandering thoughts, his arm brushes near mine and I imagine how I could casually slip my hand into his. I feel my face flush at the thought. *This isn't a date. You aren't even friends yet.*

"What are you thinking?" Dash says, graciously interrupting my thoughts, though I am definitely not going to answer that question specifically. He interjects again, moving easily past his original question. "Actually, are you enjoying yourself?"

I don't have to avoid that question; the response is easy enough. "Yes, I love it!" I exclaim, somewhat at a loss for more words as we step up to the sea turtle tanks.

From the look of it, this is our last stop and I'm stoked. His voice reaches a hushed tone as he goes into storyteller mode again. "My mom always preferred the sea turtles to the other animals. She came with us a few times but normally had to work, so it was truly a special occasion if she made it. She'd say that the turtles were more than only beautiful and unique; she told us they were also strong."

He shifts his tone again, remembering a rendition of his mother's words. "For sea turtles, life starts rough. Their eggs are laid underground, and from there, the turtles must break out and dig their way through the sand. They emerge in darkness and must find their way to the ocean where they face pollution, poaching, habitat destruction, and many predators. They're at a disadvantage from the beginning, yet they endure and fight through the struggle to keep living. 'Somos tortugas marinas, mijos.' We are the sea turtles, she always used to say that. Not all of life is perfect and our environment may work against us, but we are strong."

The lull of his Spanish story quiets and ends. He shifts back to the present, "Four of the seven species of sea turtles in the world are now endangered and the others are on the brink of facing endangerment. I don't know why I made this our last stop, I guess I just felt as though you might appreciate the unity between beauty and strength. I mean, I realize I don't know you all that well, and I'm only beginning to see parts of who you are, but I believe these qualities seem to fit you well also." I feel the heat rise up my cheeks and stream down my neck at his bold but endearing statement.

I don't know what he sees or why he thinks that. "That's kind of you to say," I respond awkwardly.

My words are worthless, but I hope my eyes reflect my gratitude. At the same time, the way he's watching me and the words he spoke are making me feel exposed. To say that I'm trying to hide inside of myself would be an understatement.

"You ready to head back?" I ask, hoping to escape.

"Aren't you hungry?"

Is he kidding? My stomach has been eating itself for hours because I didn't have anything at all this morning.

"Umm, I don't really think so," I lie, not wanting to be a burden and wanting to get away faster.

"That's a bummer. I was thinking we could eat at the park here, I made quesadillas earlier. I'm sure they're cold but probably not too bad." Now I notice the backpack he has slung across his shoulders. I think through my impatience and then I nod my head maybe too vigorously at the new proposition. He laughs before leading us to sit at steps arranged like an upside-down triangle of bleachers.

We're staring out at the park area in front of us where there's a children's pool and some other tables. I eat quickly. "That was fast, you trying to get somewhere?" His remark puts me on guard. While I'm not trying to leave completely at the moment, I'd like to cut this encounter as short as I can to avoid any more intense staring or mind wandering.

While contemplating a response to his question, one of the elements before us catches my eye and I stand so I can go to it. Dash eyes me inquisitively and sets down his food as though that'll help him understand better. I merely smirk at him and turn around, taking off toward the jets of water that are streaming into the air.

I let out a short shriek as the water rushes at me. Crap it's cold! I hear Dash laugh, much closer than I'd expected. He's gotten up and now stands just outside of the zone of water splatter.

Despite his distance I try to cup my hand around the base of one of the jets at the precise angle to send it shooting his way. Bullseye. He yelps and comes running in after me. "You'll regret that." He laughs and I yell, splashing more water his direction. He's quick, though. I rush off into the grass but before I've gotten ten feet he comes up behind me quickly.

Before I can register what's happening, he's scooped me up and taken me back to the concrete. He sets me down right in front of one of the spouts and wraps his arms around me so I'm helpless to go anywhere. I honestly don't mind it as I can feel the pulse of his heart against my back and the rush of his breath near my face. *Of course you mind it. What is happening?*

He's too close.

I start struggling against him, hoping he'll loosen his grip. My nerves overwhelm me as we wait for the water. "You know that if you stay here holding me then you're going to get drenched too, right?" I chide, hoping by some chance he'll let go.

My head and heart are battling as he laughs, "I think it'll be worth it."

What'll be worth it? Is he talking about the fact that he'll get to watch me get doused with water or is he talking about the fact that he gets to keep holding me like this? *Holy cow this spout is taking forever.* We wait what feels like decades as various other water jets fly into the air sending some of their spit at us.

Finally, the water streams right in front of my face and fans out in an umbrella, covering us both as it rains back to the ground. Dash releases me and we both shriek, running back to the cover of the trees and the bleachers.

Why did I start that? That was too much. Now my heart is beating erratically and even my brain is starting to lose its logic. I look back at Dash, sitting on the lowest bench with his legs outstretched and his face upturned to the sun as he chews the final bite of his quesadilla. He looks completely pleased with himself.

Okay good, he's done. That means we can leave now. The only issue is that he looks so at peace and the sun on his already golden skin is dazzling. When he opens his eyes I'm even more floored by the way the light reflects on the halo of gold around his pupil. He smiles at me and my heart melts. *I'm done for.* The curve around his eye has crinkled with his face and the dimple at the corner of his mouth is trying to show through. Seriously? How can he look like this?

The way he spoke all afternoon was so fun and entertaining… how he served and engaged with the people at Violetta's, so genuine… he spoke so caringly of his brother…his sarcasm was so feisty…his confidence…the kind words he said to me earlier…his persistence…the way he seeks to know me….

My mind is rattling off the various things I've seen in his character so far that I already appreciate. Not to even mention the fact that on Sunday he demonstrated his faith may not be just for show but that he could actually love and follow the Lord.

No, no, no. Less than five months, now. You don't do relationships. It couldn't work.

My mind is now battling itself: listing the things that make him so intriguing, making him a possibility, and listing the reasons why it would never work. I'm ignoring the voice that's trying to pry through my swirling thoughts. *Be still, Adelina.*

# 12

"I'm so nervous, Daisy," I say to the quiet face on the screen in front of me. "Things are so different when I'm with him; it's not like any friendship with a guy that I've ever had and we've been spending so much more time together since that day at the marine park. There have been days with just him and I, days with Luc and Violetta, and even days when Jo has joined us and we've become a little pentagon."

She continues staring and the intensity in her gaze almost makes me wonder if the connection is bad and I've lost her, but her slow, steady blinks assure me she is listening intently.

"Honestly, Daiz," I sigh, using her nickname, "If there isn't something on his side then I swear I'm delusional. But he still hasn't said anything and it's confusing. Especially because I know that our cultures are different and Latinos are generally more flirty in general. I want to ask what's going on but then maybe I'd have to acknowledge where I'm at and what I'm feeling, and I don't want to admit that to him. Or myself. I feel like our hearts are already linking and it scares me."

I look at the familiarity in her eyes and knows that she's also thinking of her favorite verse, Proverbs 4:23, which reminds us to guard our hearts. I can't help but think that I've already failed. But I'm trying so hard. I have to protect my heart from him and the pain he'd cause.

She sits quietly before speaking slowly. The intentionality seeps through each word. "Kit, first and foremost I want to remind you to look at who your God is always, and in this. He cares for you and knows you. Remember to look to him first. Fear is not from him. Then I want you to look at every piece of the situation. Look at why you're scared. Look at what could happen in either case, whether something does or doesn't happen between you two. Analyze what God could want for you in this time. Settle your heart and mind, and then approach it all in peace."

Her words are simple and she follows them with a few questions that make me really dig into my heart to understand what's happening on my end. I really am living in so much fear. I want to cut everything off now in order to prevent things from going further than they already have. While it would hurt, I know it wouldn't be as bad as saying goodbye months from now after we've grown so much closer, which I know without a shadow of a doubt is what would happen.

The speaker on my phone is filled again with her voice and my thoughts take a quick pause. "It's good to think of what it could mean for your friendship when you leave, but you also have to think about now. How do you pursue clarity more than intimacy in this time? But also, how can you be open enough to let down your walls? What if this is what God wants for you to pursue? You can't shut it down because you are terrified. I know he hasn't said he wants to pursue you, but his actions and words, from what you've shared, demonstrate that he's leaning that way. It's possible, and even though you'll leave, who's to say you'd never come back? You know as much as I do that God could use your heart for human trafficking victims to bring you back eventually. Nonetheless, be present now. Go step by step in whatever way God leads."

She says this with finality and I know that she doesn't have more to say on the matter. The words ring in my ears, I just don't know if they've made it to my heart or head yet. There is so much uncertainty and too much risk to step forward, and while God hasn't said to run, I also don't think he could be telling me to step forward. Right?

"We couldn't help but overhear you on the phone with your friend," Elena's gentle voice comes into my room as she and Luciana stand hesitantly in the door. I'm grateful for their company, which has been less frequent lately.

I nod to usher them in and they seat themselves cross legged on the floor. I scoot off my bed to join them and wait for them to speak first.

They both look slowly around the room at their brother's things that still remain on various shelves. Luciana is breathing heavily and Elena's cheeks are faintly pink. I inch forward and grab each of their hands in my own. I see the sorrow on their faces.

"Lo extrañamos muchísimo Adelina," Elena finally says, breaking the silence to announce how much they both miss their older brother. "We did everything together, and now he's gone."

I don't know how to respond well or how to comfort them so I sit, listening intently.

"We're sorry, Kit," Luciana says, catching me off guard. "We've talked since that day at the beach and we know you were right. I think," she pauses to gather her thoughts. Our minds flash back to that day when they were so withdrawn and resisted joining their brothers in the water. "I think we both just wanted to protect ourselves. See, when Gabriel died, we both broke down. The boys were almost too young to really understand what happened, I

120

think, and Gabriel had meant everything to us."

"He was our protector, our best friend, our hero," Elena jumps in. "I think without really knowing it, we retreated and left our family behind, too. As I was coming into my teen years, and Luci was becoming a pre-teen, we already had a lot of attitude so mom assumed it was just puberty."

"Pero no lo era," I say, trying to let them know I understand that wasn't the reason.

"No, it wasn't. We couldn't hang out with the boys anymore because they reminded us of him. Poor Manny. He is just like him, so we hid from him the most."

"You were wrong in one element," Luciana references back to the memory again. "That day at the beach, we weren't trying to just be beautiful or whatever. We had just forgotten how to interact with them. Like you said, we needed to be intentional with them."

"Todavía tenemos que serlo. Maybe even more now."

I nod my head in realization of it all. Of course they've ostracized themselves from their family. They want to protect themselves from getting hurt.

Luciana breathes deeply and speaks again. "Anyway, we want to thank you for challenging and encouraging us. You reminded us of what's important: to cherish the time we have with the people we love."

"We've been so worried about protecting ourselves that we've missed out on what we have now and who we're with. And, well, we couldn't help but think, when we overheard you speaking to your friend, that you're doing the same now." Elena's comment slaps me in the face.

Immediately I begin to stutter back a response but the look in her eyes quiets me. Luci lays a hand on my knee, "We understand where you're coming from, and we maybe get it even more since we know where he has come from in his past as well, but we still think you should go for it."

Of course they do; everyone but me thinks I should jump into it.

I nod at them, even though I'm not sure I'm agreeing yet. I need time to think about it and Jo said she has plans for us to spend quality time together. I can wait a little bit before processing everything.

# 13

My phone dings and I roll over unwillingly. I glance at my phone, checking the time. Six o'clock. Stupid. I groggily swipe the message to open it and my heart stops momentarily when I read it.

> *Hey gorgeous! Are we hanging out again today? I have an idea of something really fun we could do if you're not too busy with someone else. ;)*

What the heck? Is he serious? I sit staring at the message for another minute before I realize my idiocy. The message is from Jo, not Dash. Did I want it to be from him? *Of course not. Well, maybe.* I type back hurriedly.

> *Of course! Wouldn't want to tour CR with anyone else. But why are you waking me up so early?*

I feel kind of bad because part of me wonders if I was being totally honest in my second sentence. I love wandering with Jo, and while I've been happily avoiding Dash the past few days, I'm almost starting to kind of want to be around him.

I don't think she's realized what I'm doing yet, but if she knew I was adamantly avoiding him and using her as an excuse she'd kill me. "¡Estás huyendo!" She'd yell at me again as though I don't already know I'm running.

Anyway, I don't think Dash can tell anything weird is going on. I try to message enough to make it seem like we're still friendly acquaintances. And I've been talking to Violetta as well so maybe she can let him know things are fine.

*They are fine.* I reassure myself as Jo's new message comes in.

> *Jo: We've got an appointment to be somewhere at 8:30 and the drive is going to take about an hour and a half. You still down?*

> *Me: Yep. Do I need to bring anything?*

I don't really have any reason not to go, so my response is immediate and unreserved. Without delay her response pings through to light up my phone again.

> *Swimsuit. Sunscreen for your gringa skin. Just kidding, you're tan enough now that you may not need it. Snacks for the drive if you want? I'll be there at seven, so you'd better be ready okay.*

> *Oh, and don't bring nice shoes or clothes.*

Now I'm definitely intrigued. I scurry around the house so I can grab my suit. I slip it on quickly and then hurry to swipe a few snacks from the kitchen and toss them into a bag. Finally, I go back to the living room to let Isabel know I'll be out for a while. I'm sitting for only a second before I hear a horn outside and rush out the door.

I stop abruptly, still inside the gate, at the sight on the street just in front of the garage area. Luc's stupid Jeep. Are you kidding me? A million things are running through my head now. Annoyance, curiosity, excitement, frustration. Why are they here?

Violetta waves excitedly at me from the window and Jo smiles from the back seat. Luc continuously honks the horn obnoxiously;

124

he'll for sure wake up my neighbors. With the fact that Jo contacted both Violetta and Luc, I can only imagine that she wouldn't hesitate to message Dash as well, which means that he's probably on the other side of Jo in the back seat. So, not only is he coming—when I was trying to avoid him—but I'm also going to have to be next to him for the whole hour and a half.

Can I ignore him? Is that too rude?

I finally get my feet moving to unlock the gate, and I smile politely as Dash hops out on the other side to let me into the middle seat. He's still just as handsome as before so that's even more aggravating. I guess I deludedly thought I wouldn't care somehow.

Jo beams at me as I slide in beside her. "I hope you don't mind that I invited them. Dash messaged to ask what our plans were for the next few days, since you told him we were hanging out. He threw out some suggestions and I decided he should come right along with us. And why not invite Luc and Violetta as well?"

I can see in her eyes and can tell by her tone of voice that she knows I was avoiding him. I can also assume she probably knows she was my excuse, and she's not super happy about it. Her tone is light enough that no one else can probably tell, but I know, and I smile sheepishly at her.

"Yeah, sounds good," I say with as much enthusiasm as I can muster while squeezing her arm gently to express my apology. She gives a devilish grin, knowing their invitation is payback enough.

I'm just wondering why he messaged her in the first place. When did he even get her number?

Violetta is giddy and joyful as always, spinning around in the front seat to squeeze my knee in greeting. "I'm so glad you invited us, Jo! I've never done this before. Kit, I hope you like surprises because none of us are telling you what's going on. Sorry." Luckily for them, I don't mind. Though the surprising fact that they were all going to be joining us is probably one I could've done without. *Stop,* I berate myself. *It'll be good.*

Luc peers back at me in the mirror and smiles. "Estás atrapada, hermana. My homie Dash on one side and the punk on your right wouldn't let you out for anything; you're stuck."

"Lucas, you know that's not true. You act like we're kidnapping her." Dash smiles at me apologetically.

"Heck no, I'm with Luc. He could go to the moon and I wouldn't let her out. She's lucky she wasn't blindfolded." Lovely, Jo, thanks.

Dash thinks for a moment and shrugs. "What the heck, sorry Cariño, you're stuck with us I guess."

Excuse me, what?

I think Jo notices me freeze. Heat rushes up my neck. He seems like he's maybe embarrassed, too, but looks out the window as though he didn't just call me Darling. It's casual when Luc uses terms of endearment because I know now that he's joking or it's just him being friendly rather than flirting, and from the guy with the fish it was fine because he's older, but from Dash maybe it's more of a term of affection?

I'm frustrated that I don't know what he means by saying it and I'm more annoyed that one simple word has had such a huge effect on my thought process.

Thankfully, that direction of conversation dies quickly as Violetta begins telling us about the new party she is planning. I swear this girl is friends with more people than I've been friends with my whole life. And she doesn't just halfway care about them either, she genuinely loves each and every person she interacts with. It's fun to listen to her talk about it all, overwhelming a bit, but definitely enjoyable.

As Violetta winds her story down, I pull out the book I started yesterday. I'm surprised at how far I've gotten already and also by how good it is. A few of my roommates from college, Eleanah and Sisla, have been harping on me to read it for months now and I finally gave in. They told me it was a story of love and pursuit both from a man and God, so naturally, that

126

first part drove me away for a while.

My eyes trail page after page through much of the drive but after a while I have to stop because I'm feeling a little queasy. I close the book and hold it on my lap, looking out at the road as I try to breathe and wait out the head-spinning, stomach-swirling sensation I'm beginning to feel. I close my eyes, hoping that by removing the external stimuli I'll recover more quickly to get back to reading again.

My breathing slows as exhaustion rolls over me from having to wake up so early. While I have been fairly consistent in waking up early to go to the beach for my reading time with Jesus I've been going a little later than normal, and contrast between the couple hours of extra sleep compared to my early text alarm from Jo has thrown me off.

I startle some when the book slips from my lap and I try to grab at it. My fingers grasp nothing and I open my eyes to retrieve it from the floor where it must have fallen, only to find that it didn't slip, but rather was stolen.

Dash has it between his hands, back cover up as he analyzes its contents and plot line. *Well this is embarrassing.* It's a romance, like an epic romance. Not even a fantasy or dystopian novel with elements of love but a full-blown romance. Drama and adventure and enchantment, la, la, la. The only saving grace I suppose is that the story is based off Hosea and Gomer in the Bible.

"*Redeeming Love*, huh?" I can't tell if he's saying this mockingly or with intrigue. "How is it?"

I perk up more when I realize this second question sounds more curious and pensive rather than judgmental.

"It's not bad so far. Definitely interesting." I choose not to really expand. The truth is that it's more than kind of good. In fact, by the time I finish, it may be my new favorite book. With Dash beside me, I also realize it's pretty convicting.

"Care to elaborate on that at all?" he asks as I'm thinking about it more. My previous thoughts definitely don't encourage me to elaborate, but he just watches me, waiting. *Why does he always do that?*

"Well, the story is essentially about a man and woman and their attempt at romance." I keep my intonation dry, as though it's not really that significant. "The man desires a wife to settle down with. However, one day when he sees a beautiful prostitute, Angel, walking down the road in town he hears a voice, whom he knows to be God, telling him that this is her; this is the woman he's going to marry. Of course he's thrown off and confused but he knows that he must follow God's will. So, he goes to the brothel and fights for her. It continues to be a battle between them as he tries to love her and she tries to keep her guard up. As you can probably imagine, she'll relent, stop running, and fall in love with him, yada yada yada. Or at least that's what I imagine will happen."

I shrink back into myself, realizing that relating the synopsis to him only convicts me even more, and the look I can see on Jo's face from the corner of my eye is smug and knowing. Again.

Yes, I'm running away right now. I may not be a prostitute, but my heart is definitely like Angel's: hesitant, shut down, and surrounded by three million barriers.

The others listened intently as I spoke and now that I've finished it's quiet. Dash just stares at me for a moment. "But isn't it worse to continue pushing back? Doesn't she suffer more?" His questions rattle off, expressing his confusion at her choice of actions. It doesn't completely make sense, I know, but at the same time it does.

"Yes, yes, and yes, to all of the above." I respond shortly, unsure what else to say in response.

"Then why does she do it?" He asks genuinely, trying to understand.

"Because," I pause, trying to evaluate the best way to answer his question, "the idea of a lasting and unshakable love is too good to be true, a flawed concept, and the temporary pleasure isn't worth the inevitable pain."

When I fall silent and peek up at him his eyes meet mine with tenderness. I flit my gaze toward the ground in avoidance. I'm unable to look back, because his look said it all.

He's just realized, in the same way that I've always known, that these were her thoughts just as much as they are mine.

# 14

I don't know what it is about my answer, but Dash sits quietly watching me. He holds the book in his lap and runs his fingers over the cover, analyzing. Neither of us says anything for the rest of the drive and I can't help but feel self-conscious.

Finally, in the midst of the tropical trees and forest, we come to a farm area. We stop at a large building and what appears to be some type of stable. I look inquisitively at Jo and she smiles back before jumping out and running into what must be the office. Next thing I know, we're each being directed toward horses.

She smiles at me emphatically when she tells me about how she used to ride them all the time as a young girl. Before she lived in Puntarenas, she lived with her family farther north where they worked at a tourist horseback riding place similar to this one.

She was young, but they let her go on the rides often until she was old enough to lead the tours herself. As she swings her leg swiftly so she's sitting up on her horse, I can see the ease of it all coming right back to her. "Five years off a horse and I've still got it," she beams at me before backing her horse right up beside mine.

Luc looks like he's freaking out a little and Violetta is trying to reassure him. Dash, of course, looks perfectly comfortable as he directs his horse to my other side after helping Violetta calm Luc. "He's never ridden before and his fear is spooking the horse," Dash turns to tell me. "You, on the other hand, look like a natural. She seems to like you," he says, gesturing to my horse.

She's beautiful. The front of her body is a deep rich brown and her backside is all white with what looks like paint splattered brown near her stomach. A few large paint spills of brown mark her hind legs, and a white streak traces down her face.

I shrug, "I don't know, I just like animals." He smiles at me. "You look pretty comfortable yourself. You got a story like Jo?" I inquire.

He looks bothered for some reason by my question or whatever memories it stirs. "Umm no. Our stories are quite different. Before my mom passed and when my dad was around we had a decent amount of money, so we got to do a lot of the typical tourist things." He hesitates for a moment, "This was always one of my parents' favorites." I didn't realize he spoke of his mom in past tense because she'd passed away, I just assumed it was because they hadn't been together for a while. And he hasn't mentioned his dad before, yet he mentions him now with longing.

I turn when I hear Jo click toward her horse, directing it behind our guide who has appeared. Our conversation takes a lull for a little while as the guide gives us a history of the land and leads us into the lush forest. When the guide is quiet I look to Dash, who has come up beside me again.

"Where is your dad?" I ask after a moment, wrestling with myself and whether or not I should bring it up. He hums, either because he's confused by my question or he didn't hear me. I'm not the queen of subtlety so I just say it outright. "You said you used to come here when your father was around, that implies that he's no longer around, and I was wondering where he is, what's changed?" His face drops a little. I'm certainly not treading lightly.

131

"I'm sorry, forget I asked," I stammer, trying to soften the shot I already took.

"No, it's okay; it's my life. Dad was put in prison about ten years ago."

His quiet keeps me from prying further. I feel really bad for asking, even though he says it's not a problem. The regret must show on my face. "Cachorra, no te preocupes," he says sweetly, smile returning back to normal. I look at him quizzically. I understand the don't worry part. *But what is cachorra?*

He points ahead, redirecting my gaze to the spring beside us that quickly becomes a rushing waterfall. I feel even more stupid now. I've hardly been paying attention to what's passing because my focus was on Dash and his words. This was definitely easier when the guide was talking.

As our horses get nearer I see that Jo is already off her horse beside the falls. "¿Lista?" she asks me, though I'm unsure what I'm supposed to be ready for.

I swing down off the horse, directing my attention purposefully away from Dash again. "Umm, yeah, what are we doing?"

She begins to slip her shirt off, "We're having a spa day!" she exclaims. "But don't be expecting a massage or anything, I mean unless…" She looks slyly over at Dash who's circled back to Luc to help him down.

"Shut up, Jo!" I squeal in frustration.

"Sorry, but I saw you watching him, and it's not like he wasn't staring right back."

I shush her as the others tie their horses to where ours are resting and then walk to join us. Luc begins taking his shirt off immediately and yells, "Last one in eats smelly eggs," as he heads for the falls. I'm distracted and laugh at his mix-up. "The phrase is 'Last one in is a rotten egg,' Luc," I tell him when his head resurfaces after jumping in.

He laughs and shakes his head. "You can't be an egg; you can only eat them." I shake my head back at him and chuckle to myself. He must be doing a lot better now that he's off the horse.

Everyone else laughs at the exchange, too, but they aren't as distracted as I am, so of course they're all in the water before I've even kicked my shoes off.

They're all looking at me now and waiting for me to get in. I dive quickly, trying to avoid the awkward moment of insecurity while I stand in my suit before everyone. When I come up, they've all turned to create a type of star, standing with the water at varying levels. The water is sitting toward the middle of Luc's stomach and lies right above Dash's waistline, exposing his entire chest.

He's definitely on the tall side compared to most of the guys here, then there's the broad shoulders, rich dark tan, and tattoo on his neck that is exposed again. I'd forgotten it was there, though at the moment it's on the opposite side of me and I still can't tell what it is.

Ugh, what am I doing? Stop. Move on. He's really not even that attractive.

Who am I kidding? That's such a lie.

I'm caught off guard when a burst of water catches me in the face. I sputter and spit the water out of my mouth before noticing Luc and Violetta, who are on either side of me, doing the same, as Jo has just sent a rush of water our way. She smirks at us as though she's trying to start a war, but when she catches my eye I realize that she was pulling me out of my momentary lapse of cognition. I smile gratefully toward her as Violetta thrusts water at Dash and Jo. The battle has begun.

Water goes flying in every direction, ricocheting off the visible skin. The guys are an easier target because they're farther out of the water, but they're quicker than we are. I swirl around Luc, trying to use him as a shield but then Violetta comes around so I give up my spot to her. He is her boyfriend, after all.

As I step out of the way I'm hit on the shoulder by something thicker than water. I look down and see a clump of dark, green-brown mud splotched against my tanned skin. "Sorry Kit, but I told you we were getting a spa treatment." Jo is overjoyed with the new level this game has taken.

I join eagerly and before long she and I are smattered in muddy gunk. From the corner of my eye I can see that Violetta and the guys are a little taken aback by what's happening between the two of us but I don't care.

Thankfully, they don't join in, and Jo and I just go back and forth. We're rolling with laughter and the battle has now become an art competition as we try to create the best designs down each other's arms and backs.

After a little while of our own personal spa day, we cease and return to the group, not bothering to wash ourselves clean, but leaving our war marks. I'm next to Dash now and he simply smiles at us both with curiosity.

Then, before I know it, his left arm reaches out to gently grab my shoulder while his right hand comes up near my face. He hesitates.

I'm stunned to paralysis again by his touch and can't move when his hand cups my cheek. His thumb slides gently just under my eye as though he were wiping away my tears. Only when he speaks, sheepishly telling me I almost got mud in my eye, do I come out of my immobile trance.

I nod my head bashfully and step back quickly. The resistance of the water I'd forgotten was there throws me off some and I trip disgracefully. His hand reaches out and catches me again, steadying me and making me more off-balance all at the same time. "Sorry," I tell him while trying to smile so it appears as though I really wasn't as fazed by his touch as I seemed to have been. He only nods politely and releases his grasp on my arm.

I can see the hope in Jo's eyes—the anticipation and expectation of what could happen flit behind her eyelids. I frown at her and the look immediately disappears. It doesn't matter, it was just a kind gesture.

When I look up again I realize that Luc and Violetta are laughing and messing around as they outline each other's faces precisely with the mud—like a normal face mask and not an abrupt attack as Jo had done. Supposedly, the mud here is really used for cosmetic purposes and this is one of the most popular tours given.

Jo sloshes through the water to Dash with a glob in her hand. He raises his arm defensively, as though she may throw it at him, but she giggles airily before shaking her head to let him know that's not her intention. He squats lower and she smears it all over his face, avoiding near his eyes. He gathers some more, running it down his neck and over his shoulders. Is it weird that he doesn't even look that bad?

I notice now that he's avoided the spot on the ride side of his neck where his tattoo lies and it's clearly displayed. Covering about half of his neck in the center there is the back of a bird in flight. The tattoo isn't extremely large, but the detail is immaculate. The tips of the wings are black, transitioning to blend with an Egyptian blue. This light-dark mixture splays up its back as well and then lightens into a more predominantly pure blue shade at the bird's head and into two short black plumes that come from the forehead. The bird's head is turned slightly as well, displaying a brighter white in contrast with the black necklace that separates it from the blue back. The long, pointed tail feathers are also an iridescent blue, though the color here is deeper and darker. The whole thing is fascinating.

I hear a light splash behind me and realize I've been staring again. I quickly turn away. I'm surprised when I see our guide looking in at us all expectantly. He tells us to get together and we line up, mud caked and all, to smile for a picture.

In trying to maintain our balance in the water together, Dash slips his arm around my waist. Immediately, my stomach and heart stir with buzzing again. Only when I hear the camera shutter close do I realize that I definitely had forgotten to focus on smiling.

"Ayúdame Jo! Come on, you heard him yesterday. He wants to know if I'm busy tonight. I need an excuse." I'm definitely pleading.

"No way Chica. You already used me to avoid him enough. Just go, you know you have nothing better to do." I roll my eyes at her stubbornness.

"That's not the problem. The fact that I'm not busy doesn't automatically make me want to go."

"Pero sí quieres ir, y lo sabes. There's no way you could convince me you don't want to go. I saw the picture after we got back from the falls. Smile or not, you certainly didn't look too upset about him tucking his arm around you." I groan, regretting telling her why the picture shows my face depicting pleasant surprise.

I regather my composure and pull my leg up beneath myself as I turn on the bed and raise my eyes to meet hers. "You know I can't hang out with him, Jo. Yes, he is beyond attractive; yes, he is fun and adventurous; he's smart and servant hearted; yes, he loves the Lord. I mean, there's more, but—" I get quiet, trying to think of the right words. "I know this sounds beyond dramatic and I haven't known him too long, but I guess if I could choose what I wanted my husband to be like, Xander would be it. Or pretty dang close at least. I mean, I guess, I think he'd be a good option anyway." Saying just these few factors out loud causes my heart to constrict before I finish my train of thought.

"But none of that matters right now with where I am in life. Even if I could stay here or come back, I'm not selfless enough to put him first. I'm too closed off to let him into my life at any real and significant level. Plus, remember in 1 Corinthians when Paul is telling the people that it's good to remain single? He says if you're single don't seek to be married because even while it isn't a sin, it will bring more worldly troubles and it will draw your attention from God. Yes, it is also good to be married, but maybe that's just not for me. I don't trust enough and I don't have enough hope."

I finish speaking and her face radiates pity. "It's like this," I start, attempting to give another picture. "You're standing on the edge of a jungle. Many people have been here before you and they say on the other side of the jungle is the most beautiful landscape you will have ever been to, with many awaiting adventures and joys. However, while stunning and exciting, the jungle is filled with vines, predators, and other obstacles.

"So, in search of this paradise, many try to avoid entering the jungle. Some try to find tunnels underneath it; some try to fly over, many seek ways around, but inevitably the only solution is to go through, and in the end almost everyone decides to risk it.

"Well, that's not me. Sure, the idea of paradise is alluring, but the risk isn't worth it. You see, most people are discontent where they are or they long for the paradise—but I'm not discontent. So in a sense, why fix something if it isn't broken? Why tromp through the jungle to find paradise if I already have my own little haven?" I grow quiet again, finally done trying to explain myself.

Jo's been sitting silently, watching me, but now she's gotten up and is shifting things here and there, tidying up her room. I think she's trying to discover a way to respond, to find some way to tell me I'm wrong. "Aye hermana," she says delicately. Her shuffling stills and she turns back to face me.

"Maybe Dash does have all of these wonderful qualities, but that doesn't make him perfect. And aren't you flawless either. You'll never be selfless enough or open-hearted enough to love anyone perfectly. That's why God must fulfill us, not another person—even a boyfriend, girlfriend, or spouse. Secondly, the purpose for you may not be to reach paradise or whatever you'd like to call it. Maybe God is merely asking you to trust him as he takes you swinging through the vines, following him through the jungle, no matter the final destination."

She pauses, watching me intently as I fumble with the comforter. "Also, you keep trying to say you don't care, but there's one key thing you said that tells me otherwise." I stop my twitching. She's waiting for me to ask what she means but I'm not going to. She sighs, exasperated, but then her smile grows wide. "You called him 'Xander.'"

I'm confused. "What? Called who 'Xander'?"

She just blinks at me. "Seriously, Kit! Dash of course. No one calls him that. I pretty much forgot that was even his name." I somehow grow more silent. *Did I do that?* "It was right before you claimed that he is pretty much your *ideal guy.*" She bats her eyelashes at me dramatically as she says this and my eyes grow wide. I think she's right. I did say both of those things, didn't I?

Man, I'm delusional.

"So you see that this is serious, right? I can't hang out with him. Especially not just the two of us." She comes to join me on the bed again. "What about, 'guard your heart above all things,' Jo?"

"True. This is difficult." Finally, she gets it. Now maybe she'll cover for me.

"But, maybe you can hang out with him tonight and then tell him in person that you need to stop hanging out one-on-one. He's practically taking you on dates but without the commitment, and that's just the easy way out." Well she's a little closer to the mark now, but that's not quite helpful.

"Yeah, Jo, and how do I say, 'Hey, so I'm starting to like you but I know I shouldn't and need to protect my heart, so we can't hang out just the two of us anymore,' and make that not awkward and weird and embarrassing?"

"Well, if you think about it, to start, you can get to know as much as you really need to know about someone while in a group setting. So technically, it's not even him, it'd be any guy. Which means that you don't need to hang out with any guy one-on-one unless he's pursuing you."

"That's it, that's how I'll say it."

"That could work. And then, it could also work as a way of telling him to step up and pursue you if he wants to hang out in more intimate and personal settings." Her anticipation rings through her voice.

Hold up, what?

"Backtrack, no, didn't you just hear me say I can't do that?" I protest.

"Mmhmm, yes, and I also heard the hope in your voice. Kit, I know we haven't known each other long, but I know you. You're not allowing yourself to realize it, but you're secretly dying to know him more and you really wish he'd ask you out already. Maybe he just needs a little push."

Maybe she's right. No. I don't want him to get a push. That's too risky.

The ever-so-quiet but obvious voice comes to my mind again. *Trust in the journey through the jungle.*

# 15

Despite my many protests, when Dash reached out again, I couldn't deny his invitation to join him for the evening. He refused to give me any details other than the fact that it would be 'chill' and enjoyable.

I clamber off the back of the bike as soon as we stop, removing my helmet and finger combing my hair. Multiple kids, probably aged anywhere between twelve and nineteen, are all outside and have turned to stare at us. I feel the heat rising up into my cheeks.

Just like all the homes and many other buildings here, this one is enclosed by a gate. Unlike most of the other spaces, this one also has a sizeable open area outside, which is where all the students are now standing. There are two hoops on opposite sides of one another, creating what appears to be a type of basketball court, though some students are using it as a soccer field. I look toward my right to continue taking in the setting and to my surprise I see a small half pipe on the other side of the outdoor patio. While I imagine it's used for skateboarding, duh, no one is using it at the moment.

"¡Pura vida mae!" one of the teens yells out in greeting as Dash pulls open the gate. The older boy gives him a smirk and whispers something which causes all the other guys to begin laughing quietly while shoving one another.

I've seen this enough that I know they've probably just made a comment about me. Dash and I both try to ignore it and he walks over to the group of rowdy guys, greeting them elatedly. I trail behind hesitantly, not sure of what exactly I'm supposed to do or what's going on.

As I step up beside Dash the guys all quit their clamoring but still bump one another subtly. He looks over at me and smiles brightly. The crescent ring around his eye collapses slightly. "Chicos, ella es Adelina."

"Hola," I say finally, trying to ignore how my name always sounds with his accent. They all respond with overzealous greetings and I have to try not to roll my eyes. I don't know what they're thinking, if it's about me—or Xander and I—or something else altogether, but they're certainly entertained.

Dash talks with them for a few more moments and then nudges me to indicate he's moving on. I look at him curiously, supposing that he's signaling for me to join him. "This is the church I go to, tonight is, what do you call it, youth night, with all the kids. I wanted you to see it, where I work."

He works here?

"What do you do exactly?" I ask, trying to hide my apparent surprise.

"I'm one of the leaders for the students, not a pastor though. On Tuesday nights, like tonight, I usually lead one of the small groups for the guys in secondary school. The rest of the week I try to organize outreach events and activities to keep the students occupied and off the streets."

Still stunned, I ask, "What made you want to do this?"

He shrugs meekly at my question before answering simply, "I was searching for something when I was younger and got into some bad stuff, like a lot of the kids around here. A few years ago I realized that only Christ can be the thing that—" He pauses, trying to decipher the best words, "Well, I guess I realized that following God is the only thing in life that brings everything I wanted: adventure, risk, challenge, love, purpose."

He's smiling as he says this, and I feel my heart speed up and constrict all at the same time. That smile and the words that preceded it have me utterly captivated. "I want to show these guys that they don't have to fall victim to the things the world says bring joy, I don't want all of them to make the same mistakes as the rest of us. Maybe something I say will resonate with a few of them. At least that's the hope—that they'll hear the spirit."

He says this with both joy and sorrow and I'm unsure how to respond. I mean, how do I say that I think what he's doing is beyond phenomenal and that I may have just fallen for him even more? *Oh man, I'm done for.*

I smile at him to acknowledge I was listening and to show my approval. I want to know more, but as kids start to shuffle inside I realize I don't have time to ask.

"While I'm sure the guys would love for you to join us, we wouldn't get through anything. We'd be too distracted," Dash informs me as he nods toward a group of girls I can join.

I blush, as I'm pretty sure that's supposed to be a compliment, and I don't know if he meant to but he definitely did just admit he'd be distracted too.

"Well, I think your guys may be distracted already," I say, nodding over in their direction. They're all watching us intently still. "Go entertain them or something."

We've gathered in groups, and I sit with the girls through the message. The frustration amongst my group is growing as the lesson is taught. We've just covered Ephesians 5, the chapter that depicts an idea of the roles for husband and wife. The chapter that states women must be submissive. Of course they're annoyed.

I think back to the beginning of my time in college when my understanding of the chapter shifted and I began to find peace in what it said.

The woman leading, Melissa, is trying to get the girls to understand the beauty in the passage but they're not necessarily buying it. I get it, but also, I now know there's such depth to those words that the girls aren't seeing. I'm trying to think of a way to address it when I remember what I overheard the girls discussing earlier: the idea of needing to be beautiful, the idea of being sexualized by men, and also the fact that they enjoy and appreciate the attention so they allow themselves to be used. It's only slightly different from the way they've interpreted the idea of being submissive, yet they prefer their idea and reject this one.

The ladies go quiet as I speak up and Melissa looks at me a little skeptically.

Like I used to, they all ignored the beauty in the passage. The depth that, beyond this being a portrayal of men and women in marriage, depicts Christ and his relationship with the church. They stopped listening as soon as the verse said "submit in everything," which means they didn't hear the valuable command given to men as well.

The word submit doesn't mean they are insignificant or worthless and only the husband has importance. Just as the church is not purposeless or without worth.

A husband is meant to love his wife even above himself, as Christ loved the church above his own life. The husband sacrifices and gives all he has for his wife. If she is cared for and flourishing, then he will be, too. Christ gave his life up for the church, and in the same way the husband should give himself up for his wife.

Headship is not domination. Husbands are not meant to control and command; they are meant to guide and build up all those in their care. In the same way, submission is not blind, forced servanthood. Women are called to affirm and nurture others while also receiving and honoring those in their lives.

The girls have also missed the verse that says we must be mutually submissive to one another, meaning men must be submissive to their wives as well, which removes the idea that only women are subjected to this command. Men and women may be called to different functions, but they are equally valuable and worthy, both in subjection to one another.

I try to depict this to the girls while they listen intently. They begin to ask questions, and in the brief pauses I can hear a whisper of Dash explaining the role of husbands to his guys. He's depicting the males' end of the Scripture, highlighting the fact that men must serve women and love them, not control them and make them follow their every command. I'm reveling a bit in this moment, seeing him and I trying to serve and lead the teens on our own yet with the same purpose.

Melissa has stopped looking at me with uncertainty and is now busy answering questions. The intensity and frustration has finally simmered down, so she prays to close and then notifies the girls that they are free to head out.

We all meander outside and surprisingly, many of the kids are still hanging around. The girls and I sit on the ground and watch as the guys gather around the half pipe in the courtyard.

The girls look at me curiously as Dash joins the others. It's as though they're observing my reaction, and I try my hardest not to have one. When I look back over at the pipe, Dash has a board in his hand and the other guys are watching intently. He laughs with them and glances at me quickly with a daring smile before dropping in. My stomach stirs from the look in his eyes.

He stops the board with only the tip resting on the edge before swooping back toward where he came from. I'm not too impressed yet, but the others keep watching in anticipation of what's coming next. He pauses only briefly before descending again and spinning the board to complete the 360 as he heads the other direction.

There are a few cheers at this one but then immediate silence. Apparently he's not done. On the other end of the pipe he kicks the board so it flips high above him in the air. He lands with his feet on the platform and catches his board on the edge across from the guys.

I think he's finished, but everyone still watches intently. He waits another moment. I turn to the girls on either side of me, and one simply points. "Mira," the other says, commanding me to watch. I look back and there's a kid bending down across the ramp from Dash, holding a second skateboard. I peer over at Dash again—he takes a deep breath to compose himself and lets it out slowly. I take a deep breath also but hold it in anxious anticipation.

He inhales again and drops in. This simple movement sends a gasp through everyone. He and the board appear to move in slow motion and when his board reaches the other side he jumps. Before I know what's happened, he completes a backflip. I think he'll crash as he's gone slightly crooked, but this new angle causes him to come smoothly back down, now on the other board being held out for him. Everyone erupts with a chorus of cheers and applause as he slides back down the other side simply and stops himself in the center.

I'm baffled. The girls sit in awe as well and the guys all jump down and crowd him. It's as though they've never seen this before.

The girl to my right informs me that he's been working on it for weeks, but this is the first time he's ever completed it all flawlessly. She then giggles, and whispers to me, telling me to stop staring before everyone notices that I like him. Like any wise teenager, she tells me I'm supposed to play it smooth and hide my attraction more.

My mouth drops. I mean, I guess me riding here on the back of his bike may lead them to have some ideas about our relationship, but I didn't realize I was so transparent about what I was hoping for. *Freak, Jo's right. I am hoping for something.* I smile at her innocently and try to make my face convey admiration while also being more neutral.

Dash has broken free from the mob of guys and is now coming over to talk to me, board back with the kid who I assume must be its owner. He asks me what I thought but I'm still stunned to silence so one of the girls speaks up, telling him it was awesome. He smiles and graciously thanks her. I shake my head in agreement and he smiles proudly at me as well.

I look around and realize many of the kids are now trickling out of the gates, as though this was all they were waiting for. Dash tips his head toward the gate in a way that lets me know he's asking if I'm ready to head out. I nod and hop up from the ground where I've been sitting. I say a brief goodbye to the few girls who are left before following him back to where the bike is still resting.

"That bad, huh?" He asks me jokingly.

"I'm literally so impressed I'm at a loss for words right now. That was incredible. Well, honestly the whole night was incredible. Just, wow, thank you. Maybe you could come when I go to get settled in at my internship, to see what I do as well?"

His smile deepens, falters slightly, and then returns easily. I think I notice a bit of pink hiding in his cheeks. His reaction, so genuine and appreciative, surprises me and I can't help but feel a flutter in my heart.

Just like all the times before, he walks me up to the gate. Tonight however, he hesitates longer and he's quiet as though he wants to say something. After another moment, to alleviate my feeling of awkwardness, I boldly, yet cautiously, ask if he wants to come in. He nods his head meekly, following me through the gate and in the door.

I don't really know what to do now so I just take a seat on the couch. He follows me and sits down on the other end. I'm feeling restless and uncomfortable so I abruptly ask, "Can I get you anything: water, coke, ice cream?"

"No, I," he pauses, "I just wanted to thank you for coming. It was really cool to see you interacting with those girls. I think it was probably really cool for them to hang out with someone who's closer to their own age."

I nod my head and smile meekly. "I enjoyed it. They had a lot of questions and were really willing to listen, which made it easier for sure."

"I also heard some of what you were saying here and there. You're very good at explaining things in a pretty simple manner. Like when you were talking to Jo and me about Ruth." *He remembers that?* "I admire how much you seem to know and the joy you express when sharing it." I appreciate what he's saying but I'm getting uncomfortable from all the compliments so I merely thank him quietly.

He acknowledges my thanks with a head nod but then looks at me quizzically. "However," he pauses, and I feel myself growing anxious as he formulates his thoughts. "I wonder if you're actually honest with people."

It doesn't seem like he knows how to pose the question he wants to ask, but I know what he means nonetheless. He's wondering why I'm so closed off to others and why I share about myself so infrequently. "It's not necessarily that I'm dishonest, but that I choose to stay quiet and to omit a lot of who I am when talking to people," I admit, being more vulnerable than I'd anticipated.

He looks at me expectantly, waiting for me to give some sort of additional response. "Care to elaborate?" He asks when he realizes I've said all I'm going to.

I hop up from the couch—feeling the heat of his eyes and the intensity of his question—and turn to walk into the kitchen. I project my response over my shoulder, "Not really."

I hear him come in behind me and when I turn around I catch my breath as he snags the carton of mocha ice cream out of my hand. "You're avoiding." He backs up a bit, allowing me to breathe again.

"I've just realized that there's little point in sharing when people only half care to listen."

"What do you mean?" He asks while digging through drawers.

"I mean that it's rare for people to actually care about what others have to say. They're eager to jump in with their own stories and thoughts. They ask questions out of courtesy, not curiosity," I reply, coming around him to grab two bowls and spoons, which I promptly set on the counter in front of him. When I reach for the ice cream he stretches it behind him and away from me.

He continues, stopping my wandering thoughts. "You're wrong, Cachorra. We do want to know. Or at least I do."

There's that word again. *Cachorra. It sounds endearing, maybe?* I stop my own train of thought and respond with a hint of challenge in my voice. "If they want to know they'd ask and then listen. They would genuinely care." I grab for the ice cream again since he's set it down on the counter, but he's quicker than I am and snatches it up again. I'm entertained by the taunting but am starting to get frustrated with that on top of the conversation.

"Isn't that what I'm trying to do?" he asks gently.

His comment makes me stop, because in some ways he's right. I just don't know why he's interested and there's no security in not knowing.

I stay silent while he picks up a spoon and pops the top off the carton, dropping it onto the counter. Smoothly he leans back against the island and scoops out a chunk of chocolate. Confidence radiates through every bit of his stance.

"Still nothing to say?" He questions, talking around the bite of ice cream he grabbed—straight from the carton, ignoring the bowl.

"I don't know what you want me to say, Xander," I respond in exasperation. "Now please get a bowl and pass me the carton, that's disgusting," I tell him as he goes to dip his spoon in again.

Really it's not that bad, but I'm a bit of a germ freak and right now it bothers me. Plus, I've read enough books that talk about the

148

microbiomes in our bodies—all of the tiny microorganisms that live on or within us, including bacteria, fungi and viruses. While the books were novels and not scientific, they got me thinking more and now it's a common thought I have. The microorganisms are all over and there are many in our mouths. Cute right?

Children always say that when you share food or drinks with someone it's basically like kissing them. This usually causes adults to laugh, but the kids aren't wrong. In sharing food, you share these microbiomes just like when you kiss—only many more are exchanged when you kiss. That's just one more reason to postpone it as long as possible.

However, looking at Dash makes me tempted to give it a shot anyway. He's smirking at me expectantly and his gloriously beautiful eyes focus on mine as though he knows exactly what ludicrous train of thought I just jumped on.

I guess I have been quiet for a while. Then again, I already spoke, it was his turn. As if on cue he speaks up, "It's not about what I want you to say. Say anything, just share whatever. You can't sit silently for that long and have nothing to talk about. I've noticed, your wheels are always turning. So, what is it? What do you think about?"

He continues without a moment's pause. "Who are you? What makes you tick?" He asks each question boldly while wagging a spoonful of ice cream toward me with each point. It's not an invitation to take it but I reach for the spoon anyway. To my further dismay he turns it back to himself and licks it clean.

"Ugh, you tease," I accuse. He flinches back slightly, pretending to be offended by my name calling. Well, if he wants to know, I guess I'll tell him, "For your information, I was thinking about your microbiomes and bacteria and how gross it is that you keep putting the spoon back in the carton."

I say this not as much because I'm disgusted, but more in a backward attempt to get some of the ice cream from him. It doesn't work, though my statement does cause his eyebrows to peak up. I smirk back at him, hoping this will weird him out enough that he'll stop interrogating me.

No luck. "That's it? Are you sure?" I nod hesitantly, not wanting to reveal the direction my thoughts really went.

"Well, as fascinating as that is, you still told me nothing about yourself. I mean of course I can infer from this that you're a bit of a germaphobe maybe. On the other hand, I'm thinking that you also have these microhomes or whatever, and I wonder if you're as grossed out by your own as you are by mine." He says this casually as though it isn't a possibly intimate question, which in my mind it definitely is.

He's waiting for a response. I could say anything, so long as I talk about myself. I look at the clock and it's way too late to be having this conversation. People always speak more boldly and openly at night because their frontal lobes shut down, allowing the rest of the brain that still has energy to run freely. I answer anyway. "I mean, I'm not grossed out, but I'm aware of it; so for your sake, I would've grabbed a bowl."

His eyebrows go up in amusement. "I bet. However, I'm pretty much done here," he says, tipping the mostly empty carton so I can see it, "and it's getting late." *Ugh, he's so frustrating. But so adorable.* He scrapes out the bottom of the carton and holds it on his spoon. "I'll give you a break tonight, but next time, you'll have to share."

I sigh with gratitude that the interrogation is over. I'm suddenly aware that he must have heard it because he smirks at me again. "Would you like some ice cream?" he asks as he finally offers the spoon to me. I take it without hesitation knowing it's the last we have.

The moment I put the spoon in my mouth, he chuckles and his dimple shows deeply, smile stretching across his face. He nods to the empty spoon, which I've now licked clean, "I guess my microhomes must not bother you that much," he proclaims as he heads for the door.

"Chau Adelina," he says as the door closes, leaving me no time to respond—though I'm not even sure I would've been able to if I'd been given the chance.

# 16

The chatter of downtown San Jose flutters around us. There are shops strewn in various buildings, and the majority of faces that flash by display determined anticipation. Jo and Violetta are no different as they each hope to find new outfits. I, on the other hand, am one of the rare few entertained only by my company and enduring only for the joy of the relationships.

I talked to Jo again about Xander, and she called Violetta for suggestions. This was it, her key idea: a girls' day in the city. While I think another trip to the pseudo spa would've been preferable, I'm trying to be open to new activities and opportunities.

For the majority of the conversation I'm tuned out, but my ears perk up as Violetta hits a roll in her story.

"I started hanging out with both Luc and Dash a little less than four years ago. He and Luc were wrapped up in some pretty bad stuff together for a while. It's not really my story to tell, but anyway, I first met Luc about seven years ago. His younger sister Katerina and I are pretty close friends and I'd always see him around her house. Man I thought he was so attractive, and he was always kind to me. I told her what I thought, but each time she'd just tell me, 'No hermana, no te debe gustar.' She told me not to like him.

"She'd tell me he was not in a good spot and that he was always acting sketchy and being weird around the family. Little by little though, when I'd see him, I would start small conversations, and eventually after a few years of trying to avoid embarrassment and insecurity, I asked if he'd come to my youth group with me. I didn't do a lot outside of that, so it was the best option even though I knew he wasn't the most religious. He eventually agreed, and a few months later he fell in love with the Lord. He left the situation he was trapped in and God completely redeemed him.

"Dash was always his closest friend but he wasn't buying into the whole Jesus thing. With what happened to his dad, he said a God couldn't exist. Luc kept inviting him though, and after about seven months he finally started going to church on his own.

"Luc and I were still just friends at this time but we hung out a lot and despite them being best friends, I'd still never met Dash. He was really elusive. Luc had told me it was because he was just weird around women sometimes and he didn't want to intrude on our time together. It took him about another year from that point to go all in. He really started to change and grow, and he started coming to church with Luc and me.

"Anyway, a few months later Luc officially asked me if I would be his girlfriend. I thought, 'Finally dude, what took so long?' Almost four and a half years later! Well really only like two years from the time when he actually became a Christian. He was really hesitant, and I appreciated it, but I told him to get past his fears and dive in. If we're going to trust God we have to trust him in relationships, too. We can't just wait for circumstances to change so we don't have to deal with our problems.

"He's honestly lucky I didn't drop him after a year of trying to just be friends; I was so impatient. I knew I couldn't have stopped hanging out with him, though, he's the only guy I could imagine myself with. Hopefully now he'll just get his act together to propose. I've been ready for that for at least a year also but nope, he's sure taking his sweet time. I think maybe he's felt weird with his past and also hasn't wanted Dash to feel excluded or abandoned, but I don't think he really has to worry about that as much anymore. So, yeah, we've dated about four years now and I'm head over heels in love still. Enough about me though, we have other matters to deal with."

I don't know how she's still alive because I haven't seen her take one breath since she started talking. It was all I could manage just to keep up with her story, and my mind is now jumping around with multiple questions.

What's their story? She mentioned Xander's dad, was it about when he went to prison? Why did Violetta have to include the part about not avoiding our relationship problems?

Jo is looking fairly perplexed as well but she has an amused smile on her face. She runs through her questions as we weave through a Vans store. She wants to know about their first date, their first kiss, when Vi knew she was in love, etc. I don't know how thoroughly she's paying attention to the answers, however, because the clothes recapture her attention every few moments. She touches everything of course, and Violetta looks intrigued and nervous in this atmosphere, but we hurry out and get to something more her style.

"Guys, I know what we should do!" Violetta exclaims after a few minutes of exploring. "We'll each pick out different outfits for each other and whoever makes the worst outfit look the best wins." I quirk my eyebrow at her. This does not sound like a good idea.

Jo ponders the idea for a moment before shrugging her shoulder, "As long as we don't actually have to buy the hideous outfit, I'm down." Oh no. They each turn to me and I remind myself why I'm here.

Once Violetta lays out the instructions and yells "¡Ahora!" we each take off in different directions and go back and forth through the store, circling around one another while trying to hide what we've already grabbed. When we meet together again we each have a bundle of clothes tucked in our arms. Our faces are plastered with overly eager and anxious smiles.

Violetta unloads her bundle first and shoves it toward Jo. After a few minutes she comes out in a bright purple paisley shirt and a pair of lime green corduroy capris. She looks like the complete opposite of her true self and it's hilarious. "I wanted to make you a flower!" Violetta is almost crying with laughter at this juxtaposition she's observing.

I snap a quick picture with my phone before letting Jo know she's free to go put on her regular attire. As she's changing back, I push my stack of clothes toward Violetta.

Jo joins me again and a moment later Violetta saunters out. Her legs are covered in a teal blue pair of tights that have neon pink diamonds running down the front. The main piece of the outfit is a royal blue romper with a ruffled layer over the shorts and cotton ball fluffs on the shoulders. She's also wearing the metallic blue fedora I snagged off a mannequin at the last minute. Wow, it's bad, but she's rocking it as she sashays down the aisle with all of the changing rooms on either side of her. She's about to head into the main store to strut her stuff but Jo and I rush to pull her back. She giggles to herself. "Okay, okay, Jo, whatcha got for Kit?"

My smile fades a brief moment in anticipation of what I'm going to have to put on. I shuffle away from their giggling behind me and lock myself behind the thin metal door. I slip everything on quickly and step out in a pair of high waisted button-up shorts that are covered with sequins like those weird pillows. They're a deep navy blue, but when I swipe my hand up my leg they shift to a mermaid tail green. On top I'm wearing a long sleeve, billowing yellow blouse. Together it looks pretty bad but I'm surprised by how much I actually like the shorts, especially because I usually hate all things extra and girly.

Jo speaks up and matches my thoughts, "Well the shirt looks like vomit, but you are killing those shorts!"

Violetta's eyes flash wide, "¡Esperen!" she tells us to wait as she runs out into the main store. Jo and I flash a look between us in confusion but immediately Vi runs back in with a shimmering gold flowy tank top. "Put this on instead," she commands.

Though timid, I do as she's instructed and realize that she wasn't trying to make the outfit worse, but she's trying to make it better. This mashup is really cute. The holographic gold mixed with the deep navy remind me of the stars in a deep blue backdrop sky.

"You have to get that outfit!" Violetta exclaims beside me.

"Yeah," Jo winks at her, "she may need it while she's here." I look at her with a twinge of fear burning behind my eyes.

I sigh in defeat and hesitantly pay for the cute new outfit.

We wander through more of the city, and they lead me to a hidden takeout place. Once we get our meals we go back to the main courtyard where we can watch the street performers.

It doesn't take long before Jo jumps back into asking questions. While I was hoping some of her questions were along the same lines as my own, they aren't. My questions were about Xander, who's just a background character in the story, whereas hers focus on Vi and Luc—the main topic. Duh.

"Guys, I'm confused," I say, interjecting on the pause that's broken in the conversation. They both look at me as though they've been waiting for this moment all afternoon. "I don't know what God's trying to do in my life but it's frustrating. I know I'm supposed to trust him, but I don't understand. I think I like Xander, clearly. I mean ya, I do. Ugh, I don't even like saying that. But I'm leaving soon. Leaving the city, the country, leaving these relationships. I just wish God would take my feelings away; it'd be so much easier. Right? What do I do?"

I stop to breathe and allow them to think through my minor explosion while I shuffle food into my mouth. They stare at me calmly and then Jo looks at Violetta as if encouraging her to speak first. She nods and looks at me. "Kit, what would you say is the purpose of any relationship?"

I furrow my eyebrow in anticipation, trying to identify what angle she's getting at. "At the most basic level it is meant to glorify God. Within that, it should portray who he is to the world and it is meant to bring each person in the relationship closer to him and to help strengthen their faith."

She smiles at my answer.

"In the past few months, do you think your friendship with Dash has brought you closer to God?"

This question is more complex. "Yes, I think I've seen traits in him I don't have myself and he's challenging me in my actions. But at the same time, I think I'm getting distracted and anxious, like Paul talks about, and it is frustrating. I feel like, in that way, my relationship with God is being inhibited."

Violetta sighs gently and gives me a tight-lipped smile, "Kit, beautiful, Jo and I have talked a lot, and I think we've both seen that you're able to open up more around Dash. You complement each other, but you're also very closed off and fearful. You want to look to God but you're afraid of what could happen if you trust him." She pauses and looks at Jo, who nods her head.

Jo looks at me and speaks up, replacing Violetta's gentleness with a serious intensity. "You and I have talked about how much you're hiding to protect yourself. Sometimes obedience has to come first even if you don't want it to. You have to jump and trust that God will help you land, even if you end up with some cuts and bruises. You aren't even jumping." She stops and lets me think through what they've said for a minute.

"Okay, yes, you're both right. Beyond just being attracted to him, I want the opportunity to see my faith grow. Heck yes I'd be horrified, but I'm also beginning to see some of the positive aspects. But if God is working in the relationship then I'd have to trust that whether it ends or not, it's still for the good of both of us and still for God's glory."

I stop talking and look down, overwhelmed by the conversation. My leg bounces rapidly and displays the nervous jumble within my mind. I regather my composure and look up, still fiddling with my hands.

Smiles grow across each of their faces. "So, you think maybe you'd date him if he liked you and tried to initiate something?" Violetta chimes in eagerly and it almost makes me take back everything I've just said. Instead I purse my lips and tip my head slightly in agreement.

Jo squeals again in excitement. "Good! Vi, show her!"

As soon as she says this my hands stop mid fidget and my leg freezes. My eyes grow wide as Violetta gently pulls a card out of her purse. The moment I recognize the postcard style format and a familiarly drawn fox in the bottom right corner, I inhale fear and exhale any semblance of courage I'd had three seconds ago.

# 17

My mind flashes to the card Violetta handed me before the weekend. I feel horrible, but I still haven't responded. I've just been a little preoccupied contacting internship advisors and the facilitators at Hogar de la Esperanza now that I've settled, and things are actually supposed to start.

At least that's what I keep telling myself.

We all hung out over the weekend so I did see him, but I couldn't bring myself to mention it. I guess he just must assume I haven't gotten it yet or I'm waiting. He should understand that, right? He didn't act weird or anything, so at least that's a plus.

I flip the card over in my hands, back and forth, as I sit on the bus. The heat radiating through the windows causes my brow to perspire, and my shirt is beginning to cling to my back. Maybe the sweating is also partially from Dash's message. Do I nervous sweat?

I tuck the postcard back into the bottom of my bag, careful to not smash it but laying it between two books. I have to pay attention today.

For the first time, I'm finally heading to San Jose to meet with the founder of Hogar de la Esperanza in order to hear more about their programs and their anti-trafficking efforts.

As the bus stops, I cautiously pull out my phone to bring up the map I screenshotted and begin walking toward the women's home. I know Isabel and the kids showed me the way, but I don't want to risk getting lost down here.

I walk quickly but the heat continues to beat down above me. When I arrive, a stunning woman welcomes me into the cool, air-conditioned building. Her wavy brown hair falls down to her shoulders and her eyes twinkle at me warmly.

She introduces herself to me as Mirari, the facility director. She guides me into the office briefly while she asks me questions about myself and why I was interested in being an intern with them. I'm hesitant to speak because the words in Spanish aren't familiar on my tongue. How can I express the sorrow I've experienced in watching friends deal with the trauma of abuse? How do I tell her of the many years of research I've done on the subject that have led me to knowing how many people are sold every year, of how many are trafficked under the pretense of receiving a better future?

I speak and then go quiet; my throat is closing and pressure builds behind my eyelids. Slowly I take a deep breath and see that the look in her eyes is one of recognition. I don't have to explain anything—she understands completely.

For the next half hour she shares her story with me. Like many other women in Central and South America, she was promised a life as a model in Spain. She'd met Severo, a handsome young man, when she was fifteen and he told her he could give her the world. He took her on dates and cared for her like few others had, before he introduced her to some friends in the business.

She went to Spain willingly with him, but once she got there she found that she wasn't going to be modeling after all. They put her in a small home with twelve other young women, none over the age of seventeen, and day by day she was forced to give up her body to anyone with the money to pay.

After a few years she tried to run away on her own. When she was caught, they whipped and beat her. Additionally, she was given more men each day. Bruised and breaking on the inside and outside, she had finally given up. She ran away again and when she was caught, she fought against the boy whom she'd loved and his friends.

With the loss of consciousness, multiple broken ribs, and a body as purple as a plum, they finally took her to the hospital. She remained in a coma for three weeks and when she awoke she met a woman named Nicollete who cared for her. Each night as she came to clean her wounds and check her vitals, she'd sing old worship hymns, or she'd whisper prayers and words of encouragement. Mirari's eyes tear up as she speaks.

"She told me of a love I couldn't imagine. Someone who didn't care how broken I was or how much I'd done wrong. She said when God created the world he wanted a relationship with us, and even after we messed up and sinned he still wanted us and still chose us. When she said that God himself came to Earth I couldn't believe it. But she said that Jesus is God and he came and lived a perfect life and paid the debt for all we had done because we aren't good enough. All I had to do was believe, and boy did I want to believe. I finally had hope that someone loved me, God, my creator, loved me, unconditionally. I felt shame for so many things and he wiped that away, and Nicollete told me that some of my shame wasn't justified because what happened to me wasn't my fault."

After another two weeks, Nicollete realized the pattern when Severo would come to check on her or send his men to keep watch.

Mirari's face twists into a restricted smile as she continues, "Every Tuesday evening there were twenty-three minutes when no one was there. To this day, I don't know what happened, but before I knew it, I was being lifted into the back of a car." Her voice trails off briefly with sadness. "I couldn't thank her. As I looked out the window, I saw Nicollete watching me drive away with her hand over her mouth. Whether it was a look of hope or fear, I'll never know." Mirari finishes her story by telling me how lucky she was. It's not common for people to escape. "I had wanted them to kill me. Instead, Nicollete helped me find new life." She smiles now, genuinely and without shackled memories. "That is why I work here. I hope to do that for these women."

I smile at her and she hands me a tissue to wipe the few tears that have broken free. "Let us go meet some of them now, shall we?" She asks with pure joy and gusto.

As we walk, she tells me all about the new home they'd built and how it received its support. It's meant to house around twenty girls from ages thirteen to eighteen who have faced exploitation and have fallen victim to trafficking.

I look around the living room and quickly realize it is probably the size of my bedroom back home. I'm immediately reminded of how privileged I am and how much God has blessed me.

Mirari quickly rattles off the various activities and schedules that take place in the room, and then she ushers me back out. As we move to a hallway that branches off into various rooms, I feel my palms clamming up, and my stomach turns in anxiousness. I've never actually engaged with victims before; what if I say or do something wrong?

Mirari turns her friendly smile to me and nods. "There are only two girls here right now because the others are all at a program in the city. Sorry I didn't plan your visit very well, though this may be less overwhelming for them and you.

"Emilia is one of our older girls and she's been here for a little while. Kiara is younger and newer. We try to partner girls in this manner sometimes because it helps create a mentorship. There are four women to each room, two younger or newer girls and two that are older and more adjusted." She knocks quickly on the door and waits for them to open it, wanting to respect their space and comfort.

A smaller girl opens the door. She must be about fourteen despite her size and stature, which remind me of Jo's. I assume this must be

Kiara. Her smile is pulled tight across her face in greeting, but her eyes still hold an aura of caution and distrust, an unwillingness to let me in, both physically through the door and emotionally.

An older girl who's maybe seventeen peers above her and opens the door up wider, greeting us softly. I stand in silence for a moment, taking in the room and the girls before me. The room is small, with two bunk beds and two dressers, which the girls must share. Each young woman's hair is similar to Mirari's (long and dark), though Emilia's has red highlights running through. They are each the essence of stereotypical Latin beauty.

Mirari introduces me, and I smile gently in response, greeting them both with as much warmth as I can muster. Mirari then steps forward, ushering me farther into the room, and takes a seat on the bottom of one of the bunk beds. I join her hesitantly and the girls take their seats across from us.

Emilia is much more open and inviting, sharing about her hobbies here in the home and how she feels about school. Her sincerity shows me how much a facility like this can work to break down the girls' self-protective walls.

Kiara sits quietly twirling her hair, nodding along as Emilia shares bits and pieces of her story with me. She speaks up boldly once in a while to fill in other details and scenarios girls can experience. I bite back tears again as they speak, thanking them quietly as Mirari excuses us to finish the rest of our tour.

There is a physical weight dragging my heart toward my knees, and my stomach is knotted like fishing wire. I pause outside the door to regain my breath and my composure. I've never felt this weight or this sorrow. I've also never felt so inspired or so hopeful.

Mirari waits patiently with me until I rise up from the wall I'd just sunk onto as a support. As she begins walking us down the hall farther, she speaks softly but with purpose.

"You won't be here super long, so it's hard to put you in an advocacy role where you'd work as a liaison between the girls, courts, investigators, and their families. The most helpful thing would be for you to come and just become friends with the women. Come hang out, make them feel known, listen to their stories, and show them the love God has to offer them. Then in the evenings, if you're available, you can come with us to the streets to connect with people, pray over them, and talk to them about God."

Her words are soft and kind, informing me what my role could look like as she guides me through the rest of the home.

When we get back to the front door, I'm hesitant to leave and I tell her I'll be back as soon as I can. I then tell her that I'd love to specifically mentor Emilia and Kiara if possible.

She agrees readily with her radiant smile reaching her eyes, and before I can think, she hugs me strongly before reminding me how to get back to the bus stop.

As I walk to the stop and then take my seat, my mind is still reeling. I'm contemplating everything I've just heard and witnessed, and I'm wishing I could come every day.

The bus bumps along and I stare out the window pondering my own life. Only God knows what's coming and I want to push toward him to the fullest until I can't anymore. I don't want to live in fear of myself or little things when there are bigger things in the world that people have to deal with.

I pull the postcard out from my bag again and twirl it between my fingers. I'm surprised by the reality that hits me as I watch the fox flash in and out of sight. *I may have just as many walls around my heart as these women.* Hopefully I can learn from them and teach them to trust and receive love as God gives me new wisdom.

As the bus pulls back into Puntarenas, I leap down the steps and jog home. I need Wi-Fi, and I need to text Xander. I can't ignore my feelings and what God could be trying to encourage me into anymore. Right?

# 18

"Hola, Doña Isabel, gracias por permitirme venir—" I tune out the rest of the exchange between Xander and Isabel as the reverberation of my heart thumping in my chest hits my ears and deafens me.

I still can't believe I agreed to join him tonight. After all, it did take me more than a weekend to finally get a message back to him, and then another four days before we actually decided to meet up. That was probably my fault too. Well, definitely my fault. But what was I supposed to do when he was so vague? I recite his postcard message back to myself, having it memorized from staring at the words for so long.

> *You're a mystery to me and everyone else. I'd like to reverse the roles for a night. Will you let me?*

Umm…what? Like what is that even supposed to mean? I'm a mystery? What does he mean, 'reverse the roles'? I'm completely out of my element, but I told the girls I was possibly ready to try stepping into a new role or maybe attempt this whole *trusting* thing. I told them I'd try to run the race.

As I stand in the outfit the girls compiled at the mall for me, I contemplate changing my mind. "Te ves increíble."

Elena and Luci have made a habit of coming in unannounced more often since that first time and I've found that I really appreciate it, especially in this moment as their compliment brings reassurance. "¿Estás lista?" Luci asks giddily, reminding me of the situation I'm in.

I smile reluctantly at them and they encourage me again. When I hear Isabel tell Xander that I'll be right out, I am forced to move my feet—I can't back out now. I breathe slowly and deeply as I shuffle down the short hallway. I pause briefly at the end before hesitantly entering the kitchen.

I catch a soft quirk at the side of Xander's mouth when he looks at me, and Isabel's eyes turn up. "¡Qué hermosa, mija!" Xander nods shyly in agreement as he finally turns his eyes from my face and to her, thanking her again and wishing her a good night.

I walk in front of him out the door. He steps in line beside me, bending his head as he speaks gently, "She's right Adelina, you look beautiful—stunning actually." He glances down at himself and frowns. "I wish I'd dressed up more."

I try to slow my steps discreetly as I take in his appearance. I can't help but vehemently disagree. The long, wavy strands of hair which reached his eyes are now cut a bit shorter—and they're styled up—creating a wispy fauxhawk. He also has a faint stretch of facial hair along his jaw line. That's definitely new, but not unwelcome. I notice the small black hoops in his ears he'd worn previously have been replaced by small black studs.

Switching my attention again, in the fading light of the sunset, I see the gold around his pupils shines as purely as the stars that will soon come out. They contrast warmly against the pair of dark gray slacks he's wearing, and of course he's still wearing the same shoes as most every other time I've seen him—I'd expect nothing less. When I glance at his shirt, I'm pretty sure that it also may be the gray shirt he wore the first day I ever saw him, rolled to his forearms yet again. The memory of that day, almost two months ago, brings a smile to my face.

He nudges me softly with his elbow. "¿Qué pasa?" he asks as a bashful smirk tugs at his lips.

I shake my head to finally signal that I disagree with his previous statement. "I think you look great: your hair, the five o'clock shadow, your eyes, the outfit, all of it," I stammer out embarrassingly. "I'm smiling because I was reminded of the first day I saw you. When you were reading, you were wearing that same shirt," I continue, sharing more information than what's necessary... again.

His eyes shine brighter as I ramble on, and his smile continues to stretch across his face, bringing the beloved dimple with it.

"Well, you certainly stared blankly at us long enough." He chuckles. "I didn't realize you'd actually been paying that much attention, you looked like you were zoning out."

I smile knowingly. I had been zoned out—he'd distracted me.

"Anyway, thank you," he concludes.

I nod my head and start walking again, unable to address his appearance further for fear of saying too much or embarrassing myself more.

His motorcycle sits shining on the street, ready to take us on an adventure. He swiftly throws one leg over the bike while passing me the helmet. I get on cautiously, frustrated that I wore this outfit. My Converse were for convenience, but I'd temporarily forgotten about the bike. Luckily, I can still straddle the bike without much problem; I just have to be careful with all of these sequins.

As I tuck my hair back and pull the helmet on, I'm immediately cast into complete darkness.

Confused, I tug it back off and quirk my eyebrow as I look at Xander.

He's smiling at me again, a dare resting in his eyes. "Like I said, tonight's a mystery, you don't get to see where we're going—not that you'd really know your way around anyway. Go with it, it's nothing, I've just put something in the lens to black it out. Can you trust me?" he asks jokingly, as though that's not a real issue I'm facing. The smirk tugs at his lips but his eyes are soft and cautious, pleading for me to agree to the secrecy.

I purse my lips briefly in consideration as my head screams to get off the bike and go back inside. Instead, I pull the helmet back on and am alarmed as the engine rumbles to life.

Not having the visual awareness of what's coming, I cling tightly to the sides of his shirt to keep myself from losing balance. When he pulls my arms around his waist, I startle briefly from the closeness and the unexpected touch but quickly gain comfort in the stability of him.

After we stop, I remove my helmet and my sight returns. The sun has set farther, and it illuminates a beautiful building arrayed with stone and glass walls.

The host greets Xander warmly, smiling between the two of us before we're seated at a back window overlooking the rainforest treetops.

I feel as though I could leap out the window wall and land lightly among the vines and leaves.

Making the experience better is the fact that the top half of the window is open. The cry of howler monkeys and a broad range of calls from various birds settling in for the night fill the air and create a replacement for the music which would normally be playing through hidden speakers.

"What do you think?" Xander speaks to me while we continue admiring the view.

"I love it! We can see so much of the forest up here. I even think you could surf atop those trees."

He chuckles, "Of course! I'd maybe even pull a few tricks, so long as some crazy American girl didn't fly out of the trees in front of me." His eyes light up in remembrance and I smile sheepishly in return.

"Señor Dash, Señorita Adelina." The host returns and greets

us, bringing glasses of colorful juice and informing us that our food will be out shortly. Why am I not surprised he knows my name, my *first* name nonetheless?

I suddenly realize we haven't received menus, and when Xander—or should I say Señor Dash—recognizes my confusion he smiles.

His mouth opens as though he may speak but I quickly interrupt, "Tonight's a mystery, I get it." He gives a hearty laugh and I feel heat rise up my cheeks.

Thankfully, in that moment, the gentleman brings us two plates of food. "Sus casados, buen provecho." Our what? Weddings?

I imagine Dash must've seen the alarm on my face and anticipated my confusion because he quickly explains. "It's what the meal is called, because it's a mix of multiple things together. I really hope you'll enjoy it!"

I now look wide-eyed at the array of food filling the plate: rice, beans, salad, tortillas, and something else that's unknown to me. Then I smell the fish and notice the tail extending from the line of meat. I purse my lips tightly, not wanting to disappoint him but knowing that I won't even be able to enjoy the main part of the dish.

Without hesitation he notices my change in demeanor and his face falls to a frown that matches my own. He looks down at my plate, hoping to find the problem. "Perdón, Jerry accidentally switched our plates. The fish is mine. I realized down at the dock that you probably don't like it much. You scrunched your nose so high and pulled your brow down like this." He pauses, trying to mimic my look of disgust. "I must admit, it was quite cute!"

I look down at my plate, sure I'm blushing yet again. I don't know why I always react this way around him. Actually, who am I kidding, of course I react this way around him.

We unlock our eyes abruptly and turn to eat our food. Yet again I'm surprised by how much I like the meal he's picked for

169

me. He looks at me intently and I assume he's trying to be sure I'm enjoying everything. I smile and watch him for an extra second, capturing an image of his face for when I return home; I'd better take it in now because I know this won't last forever.

There's a slight flutter outside the window beside us and we both jump, startled by the arrival of our new dinner guest. The bird's head shifts from me to Xander for a few moments and then stops to stare at me. As I notice the bare white stomach, the black and white face, the piercing blue back and long tail, a memory flashes in my mind. I peer over at Xander. Trying to put pieces together, I lean forward to get a better glimpse of the tattoo above his collar. I look between the two in comparison; while the bird pictured on Xander's neck is in flight and the one beside us isn't, I'm almost positive they're the same.

"La urraca. A magpie-jay. They're fairly common throughout Costa Rica," Xander says, catching the bird's and my attention.

I look at Xander intently, not sure if I should ask my next question or not. He looks back at me expectantly, knowing I'm not saying something I want to. How does he keep catching my thoughts and questions before I've voiced them?

I speak up finally. "It's the same as the bird on your neck." This is a comment rather than a question, because I'm almost positive I'm right. He nods in agreement. "Why?" I probe.

His eyes turn down almost in sadness. Is it because I should already know the answer, or for some other reason?

I hear the subtle sigh escape from his chest before he speaks. "You're not the one to be asking questions tonight, remember? I'm supposed to be learning more about you." His eyes stay fixated on his plate.

I glare in slight frustration, knowing he can't see me, but my tone remains light, "We never said that, you merely said the roles were reversing and tonight I was experiencing the surprises." His eyes flick up to meet mine, and I watch him quietly as he ponders my response.

170

The bird hops down onto the table beside my glass and eyes my food, distracting me briefly from my goal. "Can't you answer this one question?" I prod gently, looking up into his still soft eyes.

"Urraca, it's my last name," he responds simply, shrugging his shoulders.

So maybe I should've remembered the connection, is that why he seems upset?

He pauses again. "All of the men in my family have this tattoo. My brother and dad have it, my uncles had it, everyone. It's kind of like a trademark." He goes quiet and I almost miss his next comment, "Or a branding."

He's mentioned his father twice now and Violetta brought him up at the mall. It seems to really bother him, but I'm afraid to ask what happened. "We can save the family stories for another night I suppose, yeah?" I ask, trying to be a bit cheerful to draw him back to the present and away from old memories.

He looks up at me and grins. "Right, I'm the interrogator tonight!" The bird beside me frightens at the exclamation and flies away. His attitude has shifted abruptly and it makes me feel better, but I'm also saddened by how easily he can push aside his hurt, though I guess I'm no different.

My eyes widen a bit as I begin to grow anxious. Whenever we've hung out before, he's asked me simple questions and I easily diverted them or manipulated the answers to be very surface level, but I don't feel like either of those strategies are going to fly tonight.

He looks at me but says nothing; I'm beginning to think he might not ask anything when he suddenly inhales as though he's been as nervous as I am. "Have you enjoyed your time in Costa Rica?" He begins slowly, making the mistake of asking a simple question that can be answered with one word.

I give a bit more, trying to cooperate, but only provide a few extra words, "Yes, I've really enjoyed it. I can't believe it's already been a little more than two months!" He smiles but I can see the slight disapproval.

"Really? That's certainly a good amount of time. Would you say there have been things that have challenged you here so far?"

I don't know if he wants me to answer. I assume he does, so I nod my head and say, "Yeah, I guess a couple." He nods in acknowledgment, urging me to continue. "Nothing too drastic I guess." *Aside from the fact that I think God's trying to use you to teach me something.*

"Anything you're gaining progress in?" It's an odd question but I guess valid.

"I mean, yeah. Obviously my internship with the girls is going so well! Better than I'd imagined. The language is so much easier now, and there are a few things I think God's been trying to nudge me toward. I'm working on taking the steps to get there, at least kinda, I think." My hesitation and wishy-washy answer may not be enough, but it should be, right? It kind of addresses the big issue without actually mentioning it.

He notices that I'm not giving details so he switches his angle. "What do you think you've been learning? What has God been teaching you so far?"

I pause a moment, taking time to gather my thoughts so I can decently genuine. "I guess he's trying to show me that I have to be present, even when I know my situation is temporary. I can't hold back from trusting, or run away just because I think I see the finish line already. I have to allow people to race beside me sometimes." I realize that I've veered toward the race analogies Jo and I have used but he may not understand, so I redirect my thoughts. "The key is to take risks and trust no matter what, to step out of comfort."

His eyes trace mine tenderly yet inquisitively, waiting to see if I'll continue—trying to connect unknown dots in my story and read between the lines. I could probably stare into his eyes forever, or maybe not, but a really long time, at least.

I don't really want to make things awkward by staring too much, so I glance down while waiting for his next question.

Xander hums lightly to himself, "Are there places where you've seen yourself doing that successfully?"

*Yes. Me being here with you right now is example numero uno.* I keep this thought to myself and nod my head. "Well, with Jo and Violetta I guess. I don't usually open up super easily, but I've been trying to do that with them. Usually I'd just rely on myself in a situation so temporary but I've been trying to talk to them and engage with them on a deeper level."

He smiles knowingly. "They both really seem to enjoy being around you. Even Luc says Violetta raves about you."

I feel my cheeks redden. "Thank you. I know they're both kind of frustrated with me, but they're giving me grace. I'm not great at making friends or opening up in relationships, so I hope they can see I'm trying. I just feel like I can't make a commitment of fully and completely opening up to them when I know I'll be leaving so soon."

I pause briefly to sort my thoughts and then continue rambling. "I once watched a TED Talk by Brené Brown where she talked about vulnerability and how it's this huge thing in relationships, incredibly valuable. I couldn't help thinking, 'Hmm, no wonder I suck so bad.' Ya know?"

I just rambled more than I meant to, and my question was rhetorical, but I see him pondering his own relationships and how this applies in his own life.

I think he's trying to take some of the pressure off while also demonstrating the truth of how positive vulnerability can be. He gives an answer even though I wasn't directly asking him to. "I feel like it definitely depends on who I'm talking to. I can tell Luc anything now and some of the other guys, too. I used to be a lot like that though—like you—private and restricted, not knowing who to trust or who to allow into my life."

I'm sure my eyes widen at this last statement, not because

he said he used to be like this, but because it so accurately describes the reasons behind my hesitance. I guess I'm maybe also a bit surprised that he was this way. He hasn't been super open about his personal life either, though, now that I think about it. He's talked a decent amount about family memories but not deep ones, and nothing specifically about himself.

"What do you think has changed?" I ask, trying to go deeper.

He shrugs. "I think I just realized at some point that I was inhibiting those around me from knowing me and that I wasn't allowing them to live into who God had called them to be. I wasn't allowing them to challenge me, hold me accountable, or encourage me. I mean, how could they if they didn't know what was going on in my life?"

He looks at me again with a teasing smile and looks like he's going to ask another question, but I interrupt him. I'm going crazy and I have to have answers. "Is that why you ask me so many questions? And why you don't just let me brush them off when I try to skirt around them? To know me? Because it's insanely frustrating."

His eyes squint at me while he seems to be contemplating the right answer, as though I've asked him a trick question. His hand shifts forward on the table toward mine but then he stops, our fingers now only centimeters apart.

My chest is pounding and my eyes are flitting from our fingers to his eyes at the same pace as my heartbeat. Oh, no. I didn't mean to start whatever I just started. Whatever I think he's about to do, whatever he might say, he should just stop. Nope, nope, nope.

I glance at his face once again, still horrified by the silence. "Umm, actually, do you by chance know where the bathroom is?"

He pulls his hand back and nods his head. "Uhh, yeah, just back toward the front doors and take a left, then all the way down the hall."

"Cool, thanks, one sec," I say as I nearly jump out of my seat and rush toward the bathroom. I'm a little embarrassed because he now either knows I'm freaking out or thinks I've just had a major bladder malfunction, neither of which is really a good thing.

Once the door shuts behind me I decide to pee, cause ya know, I'm already in here. When I reach the sink I wash my hands quickly and splash water on my face. I take multiple deep breaths and pull out my phone just to distract myself for a few seconds, maybe to see if Jo or Vi have somehow had an emergency and need me to leave right away.

The screen lights up and I see our group chat highlighted. Yes, maybe something happened. Well, hopefully not something too bad, I guess. I swipe it open quickly and find two messages, one from Jo and one from Vi.

Jo's reads:

> *Adelina, Cariño, look to the Lord.*

The message from Violetta is less serious as she adds:

> *And have a little fun while you're at it.*

So much for an emergency.

I know I've been in here a few minutes too long, so I try to prep myself to head out. Before leaving I swipe out of the messenger app and am sent back to my home screen.

The verse I've set as my background now blinds me and permeates my thoughts. I know this verse better than I know my name. I mean, it's been my favorite for as long as I can remember. But why did I have to be reminded of it now?

> *Have I not commanded you? Be strong and courageous.*
> *Do not be frightened, and do not be dismayed, for the*
> *Lord your God is with you wherever you go.*

Nothing like good ol' Joshua 1:9 to clear me of my anxieties and remind me why I'm here and what I'm aiming for this summer. Except I'm in freaking Costa Rica! I know it says 'wherever you go,' but I find it hard to trust when I'll only be here for a few more months.

# 19

I'm totally mumbling to myself as I walk back to the table, and I probably look crazy. *Wherever you go. Do not be frightened. Even in Costa Rica. Even as you sit across from this guy. God is with you.* I repeat this last phrase over in my head as I sit back down.

Xander raises his head as I pull my chair in and accidentally knock his knee with mine. He appears to have been in deep thought as well, maybe he was even praying. I find some comfort in the fact that I may not be the only one in this situation who is freaking out right now.

I sit quietly, hoping he'll possibly change the direction of our conversation—hoping he's either forgotten my questions and minor breakdown or is choosing to ignore it.

When I look in his eyes I'm surprised. There is a tenderness in them but behind that there is an undeniable strength. He's not about to ignore what I said before.

I watch his chest and shoulders rise as he inhales deeply. I breathe in, too, and remind myself to exhale even though I'm not sure what's about to happen. If I had any food left I'd try to shovel it into my mouth, but sadly, I have no distraction. His eyes hold mine and I find myself grounded to the chair and feeling wholly present in this moment.

"Kit." He shakes his head at himself, already having started wrong. "Adelina." Another pause for a breath. "Adelina, we've talked a lot over the past few months and we've had the opportunity of hanging out in groups and by ourselves. First, I want to apologize for any reservation or confusion that you may have received from me. I, umm, I'm kind of new to this. I mean—" He clears his throat and sits up a bit straighter.

As he speaks again there is no reluctance or doubt in his voice. "I don't know if you know this, but you are quite intimidating. It's making it hard for me to talk and that's part of why I haven't done this well. That's not on you though, that's on me."

I think of what my mom's told me so often. You're too intimidating, honey. It scares guys away.

My usual response back to her flits into my mind next. Well, I guess I'm just going to have to find someone who can see it and be strong enough in themselves and God to overcome that.

Is that what's happening right now?

I come back to the present and he continues speaking. "Anyway, I've enjoyed the past few months far more than I was ever expecting. I anticipated a smooth and normal summer but so far it's been anything but that.

"It started from the moment I saw you journaling on the beach, when I realized the book you were taking notes from wasn't just any book but rather it was the Bible. Then, when I thought I was going to run you over. When you fought to keep yourself so strong during the movie when it showed forced prostitution. The moment you spoke of Ruth. The way you listened to me so intently at the aquarium. The nights hanging out with Violetta, Luc, and Jo as you constantly serve us. The mud fight at the falls when I was able to see you let loose. Catching pieces of you teaching the young women at the church. In every moment I'm astounded by who you are and feel as though I'm seeing new sides of you.

"The best way I can describe it is that you are like the inside of a kaleidoscope; when I turn the nob the picture changes, but the pieces are all still the same on the inside, combining in different lights and forms to produce a variety of beautiful images."

My heart is pounding so heavily. My stomach is constricting and twisting on itself. My thoughts are pinging around in my mind. Somehow, I think each of these things are actually all positive.

I notice myself cocking my head slightly sideways in anticipation as he continues, and I chew in anxiousness on the inside of my lip.

"The Lord has revealed himself to me already in so many ways through you. Your desire to learn, to teach, to love, to challenge yourself, to suffer and sacrifice, all for obedience in the light of grace is astounding. I haven't been a believer for long, but I would hope—and I say this in the humblest manner—I would hope I'd be wise enough to listen to God and say yes when he provides me with new opportunities to trust and grow in him."

He swallows suddenly and takes a drink of water. "I'm rambling. Am I rambling?"

I gently shake my head to signify that he isn't.

"No, I'm—" he pauses, "I need to say all of this. Adelina, I've messed up big in my life. Before Jesus, well, let's just say I hurt a lot of people. Surprisingly, I'd even say you know less about me than what I know about you. Because while I talk, it's about my family and friends. You don't talk, but your actions say enough about you to tell me so much of what I need to know."

His mouth quirks up in a smile as his confidence only continues to build. He's hit his rhythm and I couldn't stop this even if I wanted to. *Surprisingly, I'm not sure if I would want to.*

"I know you're leaving. Leaving probably way too soon, but I've been praying for a while and I've talked to many men in my life. I've talked to Jo and Violetta also, and I think God is showing me a beautiful path that he's asking me to walk with him.

"My question for you, Cachorra, is 'Will you walk it with me?' I haven't met anyone like you and I believe that you will help push me toward God. I pray that together we could show other people his love and glory. I would love, more than anything in this moment, the opportunity to continue to learn about you. I want you to learn more about me, also. And I want us both to learn about the Lord together.

"I guess in this overly elaborate and possibly boring and overdone way, I'm asking if you'd allow me to take you on another date. Not a trip to the aquarium or dinner or whatever else. Well maybe, but not as friends this time. Adelina, for however long God leads us to stay together, quieres ser mi novia?"

Why did he have to switch languages? Can I pretend I didn't understand him? *Do I want to be his girlfriend?*

His eyes are bold and courageous, and his smile is all dimples. Looking at him I know I want this, but there are still so many uncertainties. Like, should I ask him what we'd do when I leave? Or should I ask him what he meant earlier when he said he'd hurt a lot of people?

*Risk and trust. Risk and trust.* My eyelids flutter closed briefly as I prepare myself for what I'm about to say. What I'm about to commit myself to.

As I begin to speak, I find it hard to imagine I was ever intimidating because I'm sure he can see me shaking in nervousness and anticipation. "I think it's only fair I tell you outright that I'm freaking out a bit right now," I start slowly.

"First off, I don't trust people easily and I don't know how to open up well in relationships. Secondly, I haven't ever dated anyone. Ever, like not even one of those little-kid, flirty, hit-each-other-and-chase-each-other-around relationships. I'm 100 percent new to this idea." He merely bats his eyes at these few statements, so I continue.

"I think you're incredible. Your thirst for adventure and your ability to go with the flow is admirable. Then, the way you're able to sit down and be so serious and so intentional, seeking to know others and me far beyond surface level, well, it actually scares me, but it's so powerful. Finally, your ability to look to the Lord first and the way you worship him and attribute who you are to him is encouraging."

As I speak, the smile only grows across his face. I know my words aren't nearly as beautiful or crafted as his, but hopefully the simplicity will express my thoughts well.

He's looking at me with hope, eagerly awaiting the answer I haven't yet given to him. Regretfully, I have one more thing to add before I can give him an answer.

"However," the corner of his eye twitches as I imagine he tries to prepare himself for the worst. "I am incredibly terrified." I take a deep breath to contain my shaky words. "I'm afraid of you hurting me." As I finish these words I stop, letting the reality of that simple thought settle in my heart and his.

"I'm even afraid that I'll hurt you. In all honesty, the phrase 'It's better to have loved and lost than to have never loved at all' is probably the antithesis of my motto in life."

The smile fades from his face and he looks at me warily. I continue anyway, wishing to bring the smile back. "On the other hand, in my walk with the Lord, as I accept his love, I've committed to trusting him. This means I'm meant for more than an easy and painless life, because sometimes we're brought closer to him through hardship. So, while this may be temporary, as all things are in life, I do believe that right now I'm being led to trust and to take a risk." His mouth is now the one to twitch as a smirk tries to creep onto his face. "In all honesty, this is the most authentic answer to your previous question. My being here with you now, my speaking like this, and my attempt at vulnerability, this is all me trying to grow toward Christ."

As I finish this last sentence, I realize that this makes it sound like I'd only say yes to be obedient, and he looks at me with hesitance.

"Not that it's only for obedience. Sorry, I think that's part of what is making me feel more at ease in this but it's totally not the only thing. In all honesty, while I'm fairly nervous, I'm also excited. Weird as it is, I kinda like you. Maybe even a bit more than kinda." I say this while smirking at him. "So, I guess, with all that being said, if your question still stands, then con mucha alegría, sí," I agree with eagerness.

He's now beaming at me, surprisingly even more than earlier. He quickly picks up my hand and kisses it to his lips before exclaiming, "Yes, of course the question still stands!"

I blush deeply at the sweet gesture but slowly slip my hand from his, not wanting to jump all in at this very second. That's not quite what I committed to yet. The touch and vulnerability still need to be developed, I think.

He chuckles softly. "Sorry, I got carried away. Honestly, I'm surprised you said yes. You've been so closed off. Plus, Luc has told me repeatedly that you're too good for me and that I wouldn't stand a chance, which I'll admit is true in ways, so I can't help it if I'm a little excited."

Now I laugh. Everything he's said in the last hour is more than enough flattery to last me quite a long time.

As I go quiet, we sit staring at each other for a bit. I don't know what's going through his head but I'm busy trying to figure out what this means from here on out. I don't feel awkward, but I definitely feel out of my element.

Should I say something or ask what is supposed to happen now? Do I just stay quiet? Maybe I do feel a bit awkward. Ugh.

I'm about to speak up when he smiles at me and begins to speak instead. "How would you feel about one more surprise?"

I look at him with a question in my eyes, but I know I'm going to say yes. This has to be the best night here so far, and maybe one of the best nights ever, so I'm not about to make it come to an end.

"As my girlfriend?" he speaks again. The courage in his eyes masks the hesitation he may be feeling at my lack of response.

I scrunch my nose and tilt my head at him. "I'm just gonna say that it had better be good because if date one goes wrong, that's definitely not a positive sign." I smile but his lip twitches slightly.

Oh no, I hope I didn't just make him second guess himself. "Xander, I'm kidding, you're fine. I'm sure I'll love whatever it is!"

He laughs at my flustered response. "Well then, even if the first date doesn't go well, I'm going to take you on a second and then a third until we get it right, so just be prepared." His eyebrow quirks up at me as he throws my joking right back.

All jokes aside, though, I have a feeling I'd like anything at this point because, well, I'm now officially on the newest and most uncertain adventure of my life.

# 20

Before I pull my helmet off, Xander instructs me to close my eyes. While I'm not totally confident in my ability to walk wherever we're going, let alone get off the bike without stumbling or completely falling, I close them.

I reach out my arm and his hand finds mine. It's warm and steady as he bears my weight so I can step off the bike. When I'm off he lets go and places his arm around me instead. Surprisingly, I'm a bit disappointed at the sudden weightlessness of my hand.

Ignoring this, I listen for clues that may let me know where I am. I hear a gate open and, after a few more steps, a door. "You can open your eyes now," Xander whispers in my ear.

I'd forgotten how close he was and the sudden bristle of his breath on my skin causes me to flinch away slightly. I guess labels don't really change old habits. 'Boyfriend' or not, his nearness still gives me chills.

As I open my eyes and step forward, I find myself in the unfamiliar hallway of a quaint home. Echoing behind the sounds of our footsteps are the soft words of a group of people.

Xander rests his hand on my upper back and leans in toward me.

"Tranquila, chica, I'm not stupid enough to throw a party or anything. It's not that big of a deal." He winks at me as he finishes this last sentence, letting me know that the first part was true and he isn't throwing a party, but at the same time, it really is a big deal to him.

As we turn the corner I find three heads huddled over a game in the middle of the dining room table. Immediately the flaming red hair floods me with relief and I send a quick elbow into Xander's side for freaking me out for a second. He smiles bashfully and continues walking us forward, his hand now radiating heat across my spine.

Jo turns to face us while the other two are busy debating some key detail of the game. This feels weird. I know they all know. And while this may not be a party, it's still really obvious. Will we all act different now? What the heck, why didn't I ever ask people more questions about what this would look like?

"¡Kit! ¡Dash! ¡Vengan! We're playing, well actually I don't know what we're playing. Luc is trying to teach us some new game he just found online and it's not making a lot of sense. Violetta thinks he has the rules wrong. Maybe you guys can come help figure it out, or at least you can chat with me while they hash it out."

Her infectious giggle fills the room and the other two finally turn to see us. They each smile and give a warm greeting but then return to discussing the game. So far nothing seems different.

Xander looks at me encouragingly and asks if he can get me anything. I shake my head no—I think I just need him to stay beside me for the next little bit.

Why do I feel so skittish? *God, is this what's supposed to be happening?* I feel so out of my element.

"We can go if this is too much. I just thought you'd maybe like to hang out with everyone, have a chill night." Jo has turned her attention back to the debate in front of her so Xander is only speaking to me now.

His comment makes me annoyed. Not at him, but at myself. This isn't a big deal; nothing's really changed, I don't need to freak out.

I shake my head again. "No, sorry, I really do want to be here. I'm just new to this and I don't know what the particular unspoken rules are." I feel even more like an idiot saying this out loud, and when he chuckles it only makes it worse.

He gently moves his arm from my back to around my shoulder and tucks me into his side, giving me a gentle squeeze. "Ah, Cachorra, there are no rules. Just be you."

His hug and his words reassure me as I move to take a seat between Jo and Luc. She looks at me briefly with curiosity but then refocuses her attention. Xander sits on the other side of Luc and smiles at me reassuringly.

"Umm hello, Dash, can't you see that you just divided me and my girl? Get your butt up," Luc teases as he and Xander switch seats. I can't help but share an eye roll with Jo and Violetta. That was so not subtle.

"So, did you guys figure it out?" Jo says, redirecting our attention.

Luc looks at her with confusion. "Figure out wh—"

"No. No we didn't. Does anyone have any other options?" Violetta interrupts with a hint of frustration but mostly just a plea for someone to save her from whatever confusion they were previously discussing.

Everyone stares around the table back and forth. I've gathered that games aren't super popular here, so I'm not surprised that no one speaks up.

"Well, I may know a few different games that I used to play with my family," I suggest hesitantly.

Luc chimes in, "Are there teams? I want you on my team without a doubt."

"That's so cheating, mae," Jo intercedes.

"No way Luc. Anyway, I think I get first dibs if there are teams," Xander finally interjects, smiling widely at me.

Moving on, I shake my head and laugh. "No dibs. Luc, do you own playing cards?" He immediately jumps from his seat and returns with two decks.

I introduce them to a few random games my grandma taught me, and we play for a while. Growing tired, I decide to switch up the pace. I stand from my chair and look around the kitchen. "Spoons?" I ask Luc as I walk toward the various drawers. He points to one on my right and I grab four of them before returning to the table.

Immediately hands are flying and words are being hurtled at one another rapidly in Spanish. In the last round it's Xander and I against one another. Of course.

He flits his gaze between the cards in front of him and my face. I'm trying to play my hand but find myself distracted by his glances.

"Cachorra," he finally says with gentleness as he stops moving cards.

I catch Jo's eye as she looks at him with wonder and then at me with curiosity. I'm wanting her to translate but she clearly doesn't realize it.

When I redirect my attention, he looks at me and then at his cards before laying them down gracefully to reveal four kings. The spoon is gone.

I cock my head a little and look at him in astonishment as he reveals it from beneath the table. "When?" I ask simply.

"About five minutes ago, dude! And you just kept going." Luc laughs harmlessly.

*How?* I think to myself before rescinding that question. Duh, I spent more time staring into his eyes than at my cards and the rest of the game!

I blush at the realization. Could they all tell that's what was happening too? Probably.

Xander simply shrugs. "It was a good game." He smiles at everyone and then hides his mouth with his hand as it transitions to a yawn. "One worth replaying another night," he says again as he looks at me for confirmation.

I nod my head and get up, still a little stunned that I was so distracted. We say hurried goodbyes and walk toward the door.

Xander is walking close beside me again, giving me the chance to poke him quickly in the ribs. "I so want a rematch," I say, positive that only he can hear me now.

"Deal!" he says without hesitation. "If you watch me the way you did tonight, it'll be another win no doubt." He smirks and I dip my chin in embarrassment at his words. Of course he noticed me staring. Ugh. "Or maybe we can switch roles next game; you'll win, but I'll get the better view," he chimes again cheekily.

Is it cute when my face glows red like a stoplight? I certainly hope so, because I swear that's what happens at his words. At his presence. At the mere thought of him.

"Let's just go, you cheater!" I say, gently bumping his hip with mine as we head out the gate.

His eyes flash amusement at my signal to keep moving but I'm freaking out a bit. *Too much. Too much flirting. No more hip bumps. What was that?*

I try to recover, "And can you take that black thing out of the helmet? I want to see the stars as we head back."

He nods his head in agreement and chews on his bottom lip gently while he works the plastic piece out of the lens.

The drive home is relatively short, and sadly I don't have much time to look at the stars. When we stop, I pause to glance at them for a few more minutes.

At home I used to walk for hours in the middle of the night just staring at the sky, but that's not really an option here. I mean it wasn't really the smartest thing to do at home either, but I certainly can't risk it here.

Xander kicks a small rock near his foot. I come back down to Earth and catch him staring at me with the same peaceful intensity that I imagine was across my face when I was looking to the skies.

I inhale a deep breath. I don't know how to react when he looks at me like he is now, but I'd say the flitting of my heart is worth the stunned thoughts.

We each step around the bike and into sync as we walk through my gate and to the door again. Suddenly I'm reminded that this was a date. Dates end with a kiss. Or at least they do in many movies. I can't handle that yet.

The stir of his fingers beside his leg catches my attention and I get the urge to grab his hand in mine. I don't. I can't.

The solidness to his stance and certainty in his face tells me that he's confident. He doesn't move because he's choosing not to, whereas I'm not moving because I'm nervous and unsure.

He steps toward me and his fingers stop twitching briefly. "Thank you for tonight," he finally says as his gaze pierces my heart with a deep sincerity. "And thank you for saying yes."

He steps forward again, placing us right in front of one another. In the same step, his arms slide around my back and he tucks me into a hug against him. It isn't needy, possessive, or perverted. It's comfortable, and I can feel the gratitude of his words in this small but perfect gesture.

He pulls away slightly and I raise my head to look up at him just as he softly kisses my forehead. My eyes close involuntarily, and immediately the inner battle of fear and faith flashes behind my eyelids.

The tenderness of his gaze when I open my eyes decides the winner for me. "I'd have been an idiot to say no."

# 21

"¡Aye, Cachorra, felicidades!" Jo congratulates me the moment I walk into her house. Violetta is peering from behind her with the same ecstatic smile plastered on her face but she pinches Jo on the arm as a signal to be more discreet.

I smile in response but shield my face with my hands as I feel myself blushing. Only Xander's called me that; she must've heard him. Plus, the way she says it and congratulates me makes my insides twist. "¡Felicidades, hermosa!" I say in return, moving past last night's events and on to the more important event of today—Jo's new job.

I push my way past them and walk myself back to Jo's room before flopping down on her bed. The white ceiling above me provides enough distraction as I search for cracks or patterns in the texture.

"So, remind me the details of this again? What are you doing specifically?" I ask to keep the conversation off of me.

She flops down beside me, with Violetta following suit beside her, before she dives into an explanation. By the end I'm still confused, but supposedly this position is the next step toward a greater role in advocacy against drugs and alcohol abuse. She reminds us of how the teens line down 'el paseo' each week to drink and how the bars frequently have problems with violence as well.

"We should all just be able to talk, and dance, and party without all of that! ¿Por qué nos escondemos detrás de esas cosas?" She proclaims, frustrated by how we all hide and bury ourselves in various substances.

"Speaking of," Violetta interjects "didn't you say you wanted to go dancing tonight?"

"Claro que sí, mamita. Y comida, quiero comida." She twists her head toward each of us while agreeing and adding the obvious need for food. Her eyebrows wag obnoxiously.

I laugh softly and of course we agree; it's her day, so the least we can do is provide food.

Jo rattles off a few more key things she's hoping for today, but my mind keeps wandering to yesterday. Suddenly, my memory highlights a detail I'd missed in my embarrassment.

"Jo, hold up. Sorry, wow, I feel bad for interrupting, but I've been meaning to ask this for so long and I'm afraid I may forget again."

She looks at me and her eyes grow wide in anticipation. Even Violetta turns to her side and props herself on an elbow to pay better attention.

"You said something when I walked in and it caught me off guard. I always forget to look it up and I have no idea what it means." I'm taking the long way to get to my point since I'm a little hesitant to actually find out.

The point between her eyes scrunches delicately for a moment as she debates what I'm talking about. Then, it releases as her eyes turn up at the outer corners in remembrance and recognition.

"Ah, Cachorra. But what would cause you such difficulty?" she replies lackadaisically. A quick twitch peaks up the corner of Vi's mouth as she recognizes it as well.

I roll my eyes at them in feigned irritation then just stare, hoping she'll see my interest and keep talking.

She smiles to herself briefly and lets out a large sigh as though this will take all her energy. "You, my darling, have got yourself a little pet name."

I turn my head slightly and think I must be misunderstanding, but Violetta nods her head on her hand in affirmation.

"It's quite cute in my opinion. I don't think I'd have ever thought of it. It makes sense, and yet it has just enough variance to make it even more perfect—"

"¡Jo, más rápido que me muero!"

Obviously she's not killing me, so Jo rolls her eyes and continues in her overly dramatic fashion. "He's essentially calling you by your name. Kit. Cachorra is a phrase that's used to refer to young animals, so in this case, a baby fox, a pup."

"He's calling you his little fox! It's seriously the cutest, Adelina!"

Jo shoots Violetta a small glare for stealing her thunder but then breaks into a smile of agreement.

I don't like nicknames. Right? And I don't really like overly cutesy and cheesy things either. Yeah? Yet somehow I feel a warmth flood through me. It's a feeling of comfort and security, one that roots my feet to the ground and settles my mind.

I push this from my thoughts as Violetta and I work frantically to contact the guys and gather the necessities for the remainder of the night. Now my mind and heart stir again as we sit in Jo's living room, waiting for them to get here to walk with us to Búho's to dance.

My leg shakes in anticipation and my eyes pop away from the commercials that flash across the TV screen as soon as I hear the door open.

As he comes into sight my heart flutters again and I'm reminded of the last time we went dancing. The hair, the eyes, the dimple, and the faint birthmark. Even those stupid shoes make my heart soar. When his eyes catch mine, his smile reflects the one I imagine he sees growing across my face.

Somehow in the past hour, talking and hanging out with the girls—and learning new definitions—I find myself further emboldened in his presence. I hop off the couch without reservation and without much thought find myself in front of him and wrapping my arms around his slender but muscular waist.

As I tighten my arms, I feel him tense in what must be surprise or misunderstanding and I let go quickly, stepping back and smiling at him sheepishly. "Thanks," I say, before quickly following up with an apology. "Sorry."

His eyes hold tenderness and pleasant encouragement. "What for?" he asks.

I've confused him; heck, I've confused myself. "The thanks, or the apology?" I question back.

"Both?" He laughs and steps closer.

My mind goes blank, what did I mean?

I shrug my shoulders. "Thanks for being you, and sorry that I won't fully meet your expectations." The last part I say with hesitance, and I feel his eyes shift over my face as he searches to understand.

I haven't noticed him come closer again but suddenly his arms are around me and I'm tucked delicately against his chest. "Thanks," he whispers into the top of my head, "and sorry," he says in the same gentleness as he pulls away.

He keeps one arm wrapped around my shoulders as we walk outside to join everyone. It shifts to around my waist as we walk the rest of the way to the bar and, remarkably, I don't shudder away from the affection.

As we approach I'm immediately surrounded by the thrumming of music and bodies once again, and my heart soars to catch up with the tempo. Jo immediately ushers us inside and pulls Vi and me with her. The smiles slide across our faces as easily as our bodies move around each other on the floor.

As the familiarity of Romeo Santos starts beating through the speakers, the energy in the room lifts to the ceiling. The bodies glide around one another and sway as I've only ever seen in videos.

The girls and I rush around one another circling, and our laughs glide along the wavelengths of the music.

The beats shift and flex as the hours pass, and the guys join us eventually, though they keep their distance a bit to allow us to celebrate Jo on our own.

Finally, I have to step out to breathe for a moment and am awed watching my friends.

Xander has an arm above his head, hand clasped with Jo's. Her eyes are brilliant, and she squeals with delight. Violetta and Luc are in their own world. A warm and heavy beat floats through the air but they sway to a slower rhythm of their own.

I'm overwhelmed by how grateful I am and how joyous I feel. Yet in a moment, that feeling is replaced by the dread of the upcoming future when I have to leave. I close my eyes and inhale deeply to stabilize myself.

My eyes flick open as I commit to fighting back, fighting against my fears.

My gaze is met by a tender smile and beckoning eyes. I bow my head meekly, embarrassed that he's just seen me wrestling within my mind and heart. I regather my courage and smile at him but he's already sweeping around the bodies in front of him, parting the wave of people to reach me.

His mouth opens and closes again without making a sound. The edge of his eyes tilt down and I know as soon as his eyes meet mine that he's thinking about me leaving as well. I step toward him and he reaches out for me. I'm swept into his embrace softly, but he holds me tightly against him as though willing me to stay with him right now, in this moment and in Costa Rica forever.

I constrict my arms once more, closing my eyes and inscribing this to memory as well. Then, in an instant, I twirl under his arm, catching his hand behind me and dragging him toward the dance floor. As I trudge forward into the crowd, I feel him loosen his grip in acceptance before guiding me away from him in a flourish of circles.

As he pulls me back, he runs his hand down his face as though to temporarily sweep away the sorrow from the past moments. As his hand comes back to rest along my shoulder and his thumb grazes along my collarbone, it's as though he didn't have to come rescue me at all; we've simply been here all along, matching each other's movements with the music caressing us. We're all smiles and swaying bodies beside the flurry of movement around us, and I soak in this feeling.

As we spin and move, I'm not so afraid of him as I was the first night and I'm less reluctant to flee his presence. When I catch Jo's eyes with mine, I can see she's thinking of that day also and the message she's sending me is clear, *Como la primera vez.* Then the corner of her lip tilts up and she hurtles a wink at me. *Don't mess it up and run away this time*, she's telling me. I send a quick wink back in agreement before I'm twirled away from her line of sight.

It's a little after 2:30 in the morning when we arrive at Luc's house. The house is dark and empty until our laughter spills through the walls. Luckily, his parents are on vacation for the weekend in Jacó and his sister is at a friend's house for the evening.

Although yesterday was the first and only other time I've been here, it's small and begins to feel comfortable quickly as we gather together tightly on the two loveseat couches, Luc and Violetta on one and Jo perched to my left while Xander is settled on my right.

With all the other activities happening this summer, we haven't been able to finish our Harry Potter movie education quite yet. So, tonight, or rather this morning, Jo decided we should watch the last two. If we can all stay awake that long.

I attempt to focus intently while Jo points out key details now and then, but as time progresses I become more and more aware of the heat radiating beside me from Xander.

My leg shakes incessantly, and Jo keeps giving me a subtly obvious glare every few minutes before directing her eyes at my jackhammer knee and then back to the screen. Finally, I tuck my legs up beneath me, managing to still my legs. It's left them overlapping Jo and Xander's legs slightly with my own, but the nearness only freaks me out more. I attempt to shift nonchalantly toward Jo.

She does nothing so I stay like this for a while—watching as Harry and his friends rush to find the final Horcruxes—until my legs go numb and I have to shift again. As I attempt to untangle my legs from one another I bump Xander. He gives me a slight smile before centering his attention back on the TV. Jo, on the other hand, slides off the couch and onto the floor, stealing the blanket and pillow with her to create a makeshift bed below us.

As Ron lights up the screen in front of Hermione, I feel Xander shifting his weight beside me and lean away to allow him to move his arm. It comes to rest behind me on top of the couch, and a light shiver runs through me. He didn't fake a yawn or sneeze or anything; he moved swiftly and intentionally. I look up at him curiously, and his eyes meet mine before he wraps his arm assuredly around my shoulder and tucks me into his side.

I feel awkward and look to the other couch to see if anyone has noticed this change. Luc is passed out with his head on the back of the couch and his mouth open, and Violetta lies with her feet tucked in his lap and her head on a pillow facing the inside of the couch away from the TV; she's no doubt sleeping as well. Below us I see Jo's eyelids drooping slowly and snapping open in uneven increments as she attempts to stay awake. She'll be out in less than five minutes.

The sudden awareness of how quiet and dark it is fills my mind and sends a surge through my senses. I know I could very easily forget it isn't just the two of us here right now.

"Are you watching?" I whisper as quietly as I can, hoping not to stir the others.

"Kinda. I, umm, I've never seen all of the others so I'm a little bit lost." He says this shyly, as though I'll shun him for not knowing what's happening.

I smile up at him playfully. "You'd better not tell Jo that, or we'll have to start the series all over! This is my second introduction into the Harry Potter world and I'm not in a rush to start again any time soon. Just don't tell her that, either." He smiles down at me and the screen is just bright enough to highlight the faint marks that circulate his eye. Somehow, they are refined and elusive, but they bring out a strength and regality in his appearance.

"What are you thinking?" he asks quietly, his breath brushing across my face.

"Your birthmarks," I say, reaching up to trail my finger along the curve of his hairline, careful not to brush them, "they're beautiful." His eye crinkles at my touch and I pull my hand away quickly. "Sorry."

"Don't apologize," he says reassuringly before continuing. "What's something about you I don't know yet? And you can't say nothing, because I know there's a lot to still discover."

I ponder this for a moment. What's something I love, or hate, that he doesn't know? "Umm, well I love watching the stars," I say simply, not knowing what else to say.

"I already know that," he says tenderly. "You made me take the screen from the helmet so you could watch them, remember? Plus, you kept gazing out at the sky during dinner all night as they started to fleck the sky." I fall silent, stunned by his awareness. "Sorry, I don't mean to shut you off," he says, trying to recover and nudging me to continue speaking.

"Well, sometimes I try to make images out of them that aren't the typical constellations, like people do with clouds. Or sometimes

I just stare at them for hours, watching them shift through the sky slowly. I used to walk late at night by myself and sometimes I'd just stop somewhere in a park slide or on a swing set, sometimes just on a random patch of grass, and I'd watch them until I felt myself growing cold or until I started to drift to sleep."

I shiver at the memory and he rubs his hand along my arm, causing goosebumps to prickle at his touch rather than from the cold memories. It catches me off guard to have him this close. At the same time I feel at peace, relieved.

"You shouldn't go by yourself, Cachorra." The plea in his voice pinches my heart. "No one would be able to help you."

Of course I know this. I've been told a million times by others and it never takes root in my heart. Yet somehow, with the caution flooding his voice and the worry that turns down his eyes, I feel a prick and know that when I go home, I'll try to listen. "I know. I, I won't. Okay?" I respond, knowing he needs to hear me tell him this.

He nods his head, but the fear and sadness still seep through his eyes when he looks at me. I nudge his leg and smile at him. "Your turn. What's something I don't know about you?" I whisper way too loudly. Jo shifts below us, and Xander laughs quietly before turning to the screen to think.

I watch him. The hardness of his jaw in contrast to the tenderness in his eyes makes me want to reach out again. He turns suddenly. "I've never read the books either," he says, glancing toward the TV.

I hit him on the arm. "I could guess that!"

"Yeah sure, but you didn't know it for certain!" he says back.

I roll my eyes at him and sit quietly. "I used to read to escape what was happening around me with my family, or school, whatever." He struggles to speak a little, as though it's too hard to explain. "I'd make myself read dystopian novels over and over, telling myself that this world was gone and that I lived in the new world, whatever it was. It worked for a while, probably until I was

197

about eleven. Then life became too real and I became someone else." The muscles flex at the back of his jaw and his eyes are distant, cloudy.

"I've always enjoyed dystopian books as well. It always amazed me how creative people were to develop these new realities." I whisper, hoping to distract him from whatever thoughts have taken him from this room. I reach over and squeeze his hand firmly—reminding him that I'm here—before letting go and returning my hand to my lap.

He brushes the memory away while his fingers comb through his hair. He sighs deeply. A smile comes slowly to his face. "They always had just enough romance and adventure to keep you on your toes, huh?" he questions. *Yes, that's pretty much exactly right.* He's more observant than I've realized. I smirk and nod my head begrudgingly.

We fall silent for a little while, but as the night goes on we continue to ask each other questions and our attention flicks to the TV in the lapses of silence. His hand brushes up and down my arm yet again, and the movie becomes only background noise.

With my hands folded in my lap I tap my fingers to match the rhythm in my head. It's partially from habit, but right now I'm also trying to distract myself. After a while he must realize what I'm doing because he begins to tap out a pattern of his own along my arm. The warmth from his fingers and the brief panic I feel cause a rush across my skin in a shiver. He peeks down at me and smiles.

"The spots, umm las pecas, across your nose and under your cheeks have gotten darker through the summer. They're incredibly cute," he speaks quietly of my freckles, before redirecting his attention to the movie again as though he'd said nothing. The curious quirk on the side of my lips shifts a little to admiration.

As the action of the movie comes to an end I shift restlessly. We have another to watch, but should we just wake everyone and go home?

My question is answered as Jo stirs awake and crawls to the DVD player to switch out the disks. I look to Xander and he shrugs his shoulders before resting his head on the hand that's propped up on the armrest. His eyelids look as though they're growing heavy as well and I begin to feel the weight of my own as my vision shifts between the dark colors on the screen and the dark backs of my eyelids.

I straighten up, to wake myself more, and shift slightly away from Xander to ensure I'm not squishing him into the side of the couch.

Outside the window, the light is beginning to illuminate a golden shade on the streets. I blink my eyes rapidly while staring out at the light to wake myself more and then shift my eyes back to the final movie. I can't fall asleep now or I'll have to start over.

I'm honestly getting into the movies more than I'd thought, but I still can't bring myself to read the books. It's too much commitment and would take so much time and energy. Why go through all the trouble?

As I feel a twitch beside me, I notice Xander's hand resting delicately beside his leg. My hand is tucked tightly under my own leg, putting it in close proximity now to his. My heart starts pounding and the sound of blood rushes through my ears.

I look at the movie again and then back down at his hand, remembering the conversation I'd had with Jo. We run beside someone, even temporarily, for the positive things they bring to our lives. It brings joy, lessons, and adventure in the little moments, even though it is a huge commitment and expenditure of time and energy.

I can now feel the light, pulsing heat waves from his fingers and I draw mine closer. The overwhelming knowledge of how close we are to touching flares in my mind and I imagine it must be the same for him because slowly but knowingly he wraps my hand in his. I don't need to look at him to know he's smiling. My heart pounds and I know his does too as I feel his pulse beneath my fingers.

I shiver and he unclasps our hands and leaves the couch, returning with a blanket since he must imagine that I'm cold. I don't reach for his hand again because I feel guilty and begin to think that maybe it was just me who wanted that, that I shouldn't have moved toward him. To my relief and surprise, he quickly finds my hand again and holds it between us.

With his fingers intwined with mine he slowly drifts off to sleep and I shift slightly, careful not to stir him. I watch the sun creep higher and listen to the birds sing to one another.

Sometimes I look at how peaceful Xander looks and how peaceful everyone else is. I notice the slight wave in his hair and the pronounced, yet smooth, line of his jaw. I notice his gorgeous brown eyes hiding behind his stunningly long eyelashes.

I think about the joy that fills them when he laughs, and the fear and sorrow that seem to cloud over them when he talks about his life before. I wonder what haunts his memories and when he will trust me enough to tell me. Then again, when will I be confident enough to ask?

# 22

When I pull up to Hogar de la Esperanza after the long bus ride, the idea of Xander's haunted memories keeps running through my mind. I wonder what it will take for Xander and I to be more open with each other. Trust is crucial in relationships and so often in our lives it is broken down.

Emilia and Kiara come out and, while Kiara is still quiet and bashful, they both smile at me, which I take as a good sign. We walk a few blocks down to the bus station and hop on to go to our favorite little coffee shop in the area. One of the walls is lined with shelves littered with books, and long wooden tables fill the center of the room. We take a seat at a taller round table near the windows at the back so we have some privacy.

As usual, we start by holding hands and bowing our heads to pray together. I ask God to open our hearts to each other in vulnerability and to him in obedience and trust.

"I went to the mall the other day with a group of friends, Adelina! I was nervous to be out so much in the open, and there were some guys in our group, but it wasn't bad. One of the guys was really friendly, though, and I don't know what he wanted so I kind of avoided him," Emilia starts off immediately.

"Which sucks, because you said he was cute," Kiara offers in her soft voice.

"Yeah, that's why I was even more hesitant, he seemed like he actually could have been good," Emilia says, shaking her head disappointedly.

Their distrust is evident in their words, though it doesn't come out in bitterness or anger as much now. It's displaced in fear and sadness.

Last week the girls finally told me their stories, and as I sit here with them now I understand more of where they're coming from. I even criticize myself a bit for being so distrusting when I don't really have an excuse.

When Emilia was thirteen she met Leo. He was handsome and sweet, only a few years older than her. They went on dates and she hung out with him often; she never wanted to be at home with her mom and younger siblings. In a matter of weeks she believed she loved him, and he told her the same. Since she was never home to help, her mom threatened to kick her out, but instead, she went willingly. She ran to Leo's home for a place to stay and she gave him her heart and her virginity on the same night. Despite the conflict with her mom she still thought she was the luckiest girl in the world, and she was willing to go anywhere and do anything for Leo because of all he'd given her.

The next week he told her he was in trouble and he asked her to earn him money through prostituting herself. She refused and tried to run away but he caught her by the hair and beat her as punishment. His dad came not long after and helped drive her to their family-run brothel, where she stayed for the next three and a half years of her life. The first time Leo returned, she was almost fifteen and she thought he'd come to rescue her. The second time he came, she was so fearful from what he'd done the first time that she tried to hide under the bed.

Kiara's experience was similar but different, more like Mirari's.

Just after she turned twelve her mom's new boyfriend told her how beautiful she was. He said he had a friend at a modeling agency who would love to work with her, and she couldn't have been more excited about the opportunity. Her mom had been single for many years and was struggling to make a living. Her older brother worked as a bartender trying to help support the family and Kiara wanted to help in whatever way possible.

When the agent came to her house he said he wanted to talk to her in private about all of her possibilities. That was the first night she was ever forced to be with a man.

As he left, he told her mom that he was looking forward to working with her and that he'd be back in the next week to take her with him for a while to do some shoots. She begged her mom and brother not to let her go, saying she'd changed her mind and would work to find another job. They thought she was just nervous about the job, when really she was terrified about the man.

The day he came back for her she went to a friend's house, but her brother went looking for her and brought her back. She hasn't seen her family since, and it's been a little over a year and a half.

Day in and day out they were both forced to sleep with many men, sometimes more than ten in a day, each of which were often violent or aggressive. They were beaten, strangled, and starved without any form of assistance or signs of a way out. Through their experiences, they each lost all hope and trust in loved ones, especially men.

Kiara found rescue when a man, pretending to be a customer, came in and offered her a way out. He promised a better life and said he would come back until she went with him. She refused the first two times, but in those times he never touched her and she saw this as a comfort and hoped that if anything he would put her in a slightly better environment than the one she was in.

Mirari met Emilia a few months ago on the street one evening while she and her partners were doing outreach. She offered a cookie, coffee, and a safe home. Emilia feared for her life but trusted this woman more than the man who'd taken her.

Now I tune back in as they talk about some of the other girls and what's going on in the house. One girl has started dating again and it's got everyone in a ruckus.

"What about you, Kit? Is that going well so far?" Kiara asks pointedly.

"Honestly ladies, it's hard. I've told you before that sometimes I feel silly for being so distrusting of everyone but nonetheless I can't just flip a switch. Xander has been so kind and wonderful but that doesn't mean it couldn't end in an instant. The only thing that helps me keep trusting and hoping right now is the fact that God hasn't shown me anything else. I keep praying he'll tell me when to run away or he'll give me an easy way out, but he hasn't."

"Why did you say yes in the first place if you knew you'd leave? How is it worth the risk?" This comes from Emilia.

"I think I'm learning that every piece of our journey points to God, whether it makes us sad or happy. It's all for our good, remember, and sometimes our idea of what is good is different from his. And more importantly, what we do reflects God and his glory to the world, that's what matters most, and that's what I believe Xander and I do better together," I remind them.

They both stare at me in silence for a bit, allowing the entrance of some boys to distract us all. "Do you think we'll ever trust like that again? Even with a guy?" Emilia asks, gazing toward the group that just sat a few tables from us.

I smile at her, catching her line of thought. "Of course, Emi! I think you both will, even though it's hard. And I'm not promising you'll never doubt, or retreat, or even close yourself off again for a while, but hopefully in those times you'll try again. It's about the little steps toward progress. I mean, look, you've known me for what, a little over two weeks, and you already have opened up to me more than I would have hoped for or imagined."

She smiles bashfully. "Somehow it's easier with you; you're not a threat, really."

A pang of sadness washes through me at my immediate thought. "That's where you could be partially wrong. I'm leaving soon and we can keep in touch, but things will be different. So even though it's really different, this relationship still brings a degree of hurt with it. Though, in my opinion, and I hope you'll both agree with me, it's worth it!" I emphasize this last point, "We trust each other despite the roadblocks and risks because they lead to a destination we can't imagine."

# 23

I wake up to the buzzing of my phone on the small dresser beside me. Groggily I accept the FaceTime call, and the slightly crackly speakers ring out with my dad's voice. "Na na na na na na, they say it's your birthday! Na na na na na na, it's my birthday too, yeah!" Immediately I'm flooded with joy at the familiar sound of the Beatles remix that my dad has sung for me each year for as long as I can remember. It may be a bit off-key, and some of the verses may be a mixed with one another, but it's tradition, and I'm so grateful he remembered and that he even called while I was away.

"Happy birthday baby, we love you and miss you so so so much!" I hear my mom's joyous voice ringing through.

"Have a wonderful day, beautiful," Dad says after finishing the song. "We just wanted to call and tell you we love you but now we've got to run to church. Hope you feel celebrated."

"Bye, babes!" Mom chimes in at the last minute.

Shoot, that reminds me—Jo and Violetta said they were going to stop by before church so we could go to breakfast. I quickly pull on a pair of dark, high-waisted shorts and a gray and white off-the-shoulder top. I slip on my sandals and touch a bit of mascara to my eyelashes. I can't even remember when I wore mascara last, but why not dress up a little extra for my birthday?

I feel a bit guilty as the girls arrive. They don't say anything about my birthday, and neither do I. I still never told any of them when it was. Really, though, while I love being celebrated, I still don't want to risk it. I hope they'd all know me well enough at this point to make it something I'd enjoy, but in case they don't, I just want it all to be normal. I want a beautifully simple day with the people I'm closest to here.

We walk a few blocks to YellowFin, one of our favorite cafes, to grab drinks. David greets us warmly as we enter and take a seat at one of our normal tables. Again, the familiarity and normalcy reminds me how blessed I am. How many people get this opportunity every day: the chance to be woken up by loving parents, share breakfast with friends, and be in a different country nonetheless?

Jo and Violetta quickly order us food. It's become a fun habit since that first day with Xander; they'll order food for me and I get to try something new and unexpected. When my breakfast comes there are multiple pineapples atop a pancake, and sweetened condensed milk flows abundantly down the edges and pools on the plate. They really love their sweets here, too, and it makes my heart happy.

"You still don't really have plans today, Kit?" Violetta asks around a mouthful of eggs and beans.

I shrug, feeling bad again about not telling them, "This and then church. I hung out with Emilia and Kiara a few days ago, so I won't see them for another few days. It's crazy how they've been starting to open up to me more and more, even in just the past three weeks. Anyway, after I get back we're having lunch and hanging out as a family for a while, but I don't really have plans after that. Maybe we could just go to your house and watch movies or something? Try playing some games again?"

207

"Yes, it definitely sounds like you need a few more things to do, we're on it!" Jo interjects, and it's true, so I nod my head. I didn't want to sit around doing nothing on my birthday; I just also didn't want some grand and crazy event.

Breakfast ends fairly quickly after discussing some of my favorite memories here so far and some of my hopes for the rest of my time. I think they're starting to realize that things are going to start flying by.

My heart halts for a second as a horn sounds outside. "I thought it'd be nice if Luc came to get us this morning instead of walking. Plus, it gave us a little extra time to eat and chat," Violetta says, waving at Luc while ushering the two of us outside. My heart sinks a bit when I see the empty front seat but then elevates again when Xander hops out of the back door and holds it open for me and then Jo before walking around to the other side. We're sitting in the same seats as when we went to the horse ride and waterfalls a little over a month ago. The memory makes me shiver. I was still fairly unsure about Xander at that point, thinking I could like him but not wanting to.

He twines his fingers with mine on the seats between us and I'm reminded of how far God's taken me already.

At the church we gather at the front like normal, with Jo on my left and Xander on my right. Just as in that first time, his voice bellows out during the worship, rising to the ceiling with his arms lifted in surrender as his eyelids drift closed. This time I'm able to refocus again on the worship with ease.

In taking our seats I pray to myself that I'll hear the message this morning and it will be something I'm able to cling to for this twenty-first year of life.

As the pastor states we'll be reading out of 1 Corinthians 13, I know without a doubt that my prayer is being answered. For the next thirty minutes, he focuses on love and Paul's assurance that in love we do all things, and without love nothing of any worth will be done. It is a Scripture I've heard many times, but one that also pierces my heart with new truths each time.

Verse seven is the one that so clearly convicts me this morning: Love bears all things, believes all things, hopes all things, endures all things.

Love remains under the weight of trial, and love causes us to trust even when we may not want to; love leads us to seek for hope and the best futures, and love lasts beyond separation or death.

I think of my dad who called this morning and the rest of my family. I think of Daisy and my other friends back home. I look to my left and right.

Love lasts no matter the distance. It isn't a fleeting wind that comes and goes with changing weather, but it is like the consistency of the air that we breath, always there and always available. It's able to bring life and renewal; we need only inhale.

Lunch goes by quickly. Isabel fixes me pineapple chicken with our usual sides of rice and beans and then we walk to the heladería near the beach to get some ice cream. "Eres una gordita, Adi," Axel says, calling me a fatty as I finish my large cup of sorbet.

Elena quickly reaches across the table and rubs a bit of ice cream down his nose in my defense. We all start laughing and I shove him playfully. I love how close we have become. I'm further amazed by how much the girls have opened up after that day at the beach and how they engage with their family more rather than just sitting around them.

After a while, Violetta meets me at the ice cream shop and for a moment I'm afraid the family will blow it and she'll find out it's my birthday. But then Isabel simply wishes me a wonderful day and we say goodbye.

The two of us walk to the point of the peninsula and Jo is waiting for us on one of the concrete benches near the lighthouse.

I think we're headed to Isla Cocos, the bar we've found to be one of the best, but instead they lead me down a small dock to an awaiting boat. The guys aren't there and I'm honestly grateful to have time with just the three of us again.

Jo introduces me quickly to Dennis, our guide, and the boat pulls out, heading east down the opposite side of the peninsula. We pull up near a sand bar and he points out a crocodile on the bank. I'd heard there were some in the estuary, but up until now I hadn't made it to see them.

We move on and he begins describing the four types of mangrove trees in the forest here. "¡Mira, mira, Kit!" Violetta exclaims while pointing high into the tree beside us. I look hard toward where she's pointing and see a small monkey atop one of the branches. It's a white-faced capuchin, she tells me, and I can see the color differentiation from here.

As we pull toward the shore, Dennis grabs a bulbous fruit from a tree. He splits it easily and lets us try the sugary paste within, which is a common delicacy for the monkeys. I'm not too impressed by the flavor.

We continue coasting through the shallow water. Between the times when we make him take our pictures, he points out various birds. As the sun begins to sink, we start back. Another croc passes beside us in the water and various pelicans dive and soar around us as well.

The sky fades into a feathery orange and then begins to darken, casting a deep pink and vibrant purple across the sky. We round the point past where we entered, and the length of the peninsula becomes visible. My heart is content in this moment and already I know this day is a success.

The boat docks and Dennis wishes us a good evening. We walk back, passing various Ticos on benches, most of whom are soaking in the sunset as well. We join them, walking out on one of the small piers jutting into the water. Rather than sit on the bench we sit on the piled boulders, trying to be as close to the waves as possible without getting wet from the backsplash.

None of us speak and the waves crash around us, mingling with the voices of families that rattle in our ears. One by one, a multitude of stray cats start to peek out from the boulders piled beneath us, though they hide again quickly if we shift or try to approach.

As we continue walking, we leave the path and near the edge of the water. We carry our shoes in our hands and allow the foam tips to chase up our legs every so often when a large wave rolls in. The sound of the crashing and the rush of the water consume all of my attention.

"Hey baby, you're so beautiful. ¿Quieres casarte conmigo, mami?" I shiver as the words of a flippant marriage proposal flood my ears and tear me out of the moment.

I roll my eyes at the typical display of machismo and try not to look toward the perpetrator who's just trampled on my good mood. I take a few more steps and a whistle piercingly calls to me through the air.

Geez, what's with this guy? Usually it's just once and they move on, but he's not letting up as I hear him trying to say something else in English, as though he assumes I wouldn't understand his gross comments in Spanish. Violetta and Jo sway their heads toward him now as I do the same.

"Que preciosa, mami." I read the words as they fall off his lips and mingle in the air with the sound of laughter. Not his laughter, though, it's Luc's.

"¡Xander! ¡Te odio tanto!" I cry out my frustration as he rushes up to me and lifts me in a circle. He's trying to make up for the joke and I'm not going to let him see that it's working. Not just yet, anyway.

I mask the sliver of a smile that's crept onto my face and look at him seriously, waiting to see if he'll explain, catch onto my façade, or drop it all together.

"You don't hate me, Cachorra, not anymore at least," he says, winking at me and kissing me on the cheek. My mind again flashes back to our first times interacting. I drop the mask of irritation so he can see my sincerity.

"I never hated you, Xander, I was just afraid." My words are quiet so I know the others didn't hear me. I'm not even sure he heard me until he pulls me into a hug and whispers into my hair, "I'm glad you're taking the risk anyway."

He says it as though he knows it wasn't just then that I was afraid, but that it was also when I said 'yes,' and his words cover the strands of fear that linger even still as we stand holding one another in this space. Instinctively I lean up on my toes and before I realize what's happening, my lips meet his with all the thanks I want to express. It's quick and gentle but as I step back I see the surprise catch fire in the gold of his eyes. I guess I just needed a special birthday gift for myself, even if he doesn't know.

I see him tuck his lower lip into his mouth in curiosity or revelation of what just happened, but he says nothing; he just turns and wraps me against his side like usual before walking me up to where he'd been before with Luc—where the others wait now. I don't know if they just witnessed our first kiss but if so, they show nothing and stay engaged in their own conversation until we join them.

My mind is a little hazy at the perfection of the moment and his simple appreciation. It wasn't fireworks like they all say, but rather, it was like when you light a match perfectly on the first try and even after you blow it out the smoke and smell linger a while lazily in the air.

We're sitting in the inside of what must have been the bow of a broken ship that's washed ashore sometime recently. It's mossy and a little dank from corrosion, but the guys have laid out towels we're all able to sit on.

Xander is so close to me I can feel the heat radiating from him that contrasts with the gentle cool breeze in the air. Luc and

Violetta are just across from us and Jo sits to my right, finishing off our horseshoe that opens to the ocean.

I close my eyes quickly, trying to take all of this in. The mind-halting smell of Xander mingles with the damp, earthy smell of the beach and the hint of rain floating in the air. The sound of the waves comes back, and now I can also hear a faint rustling from various clam shells as they shuffle through the pull of water and sand.

The sky around us is balancing between a deep orange and a fuller tint that would match a blackberry. In each streak of the sky there are a multitude of colors combining to cast their alluring hues as the sun fades behind the ocean. My friends, these incredible people around me, chatter and laugh. They remind me that they're the blessing I never knew I needed for this journey.

"Okay, Kit," Jo reaches over, touching my shoulder to get my attention. She pulls bowls and spoons from behind her and hands me two of each. I pass one to Xander, slightly confused, but he smiles and accepts easily as the others get theirs from her as well. Then, as though she's just remembered something, she asks us to give the bowls back and laughs to herself. When she's got them all again, she reaches back into the box and pulls out a carton of ice cream, which she smoothly dishes out into the bowls before passing them back again to each of us.

"Butter Pecan. Xander said it was your favorite," she says, shrugging. I smile slowly and shake my head in appreciation. Though I had some with my family earlier, I finish my bowl quickly and accept without hesitation when Xander offers me some of his.

As soon as I pull the spoon from my mouth he leans over to my ear. "That's three times now you've forgotten about my nasty microhomes," he jokes. I turn my head in confusion and hold up two fingers, reminding him that we've only shared ice cream once before this.

He gently taps his finger to his lips and winks at me. Without saying anything I know he's referencing the brief kiss just minutes ago, and my cheeks flare with embarrassment as I shove my shoulder against his. He just laughs to himself and I can't help but join him.

"Kit, you know you're one of us now, right? An adopted Tica," Luc says over his mouthful of ice cream while the others all nod their heads in agreement.

"Thanks Luc," I tell him simply, though it doesn't fully quantify the warmth flooding my heart.

"Nah, mae, thank you, you've made this kid more alive than I've ever seen him, and my girl loves you too." I quietly soak in the value of his words, and even the simplicity of their colloquial word for 'dude' fills me with more joy than I could imagine.

"Remember the one day you made us go night swimming for a minute, even though we told you there's sometimes crocs in the water? Your heart seeks the rawest unknowns, whether that's in an adventure or in my life, and I'm so grateful for that part of who you are," Vi tells me as a smile radiates across her face.

"You're a badass, Kit," Jo chimes in, giggling. I've never really heard the words from her and realize that this must truly be the best way she can express herself, as she never says something without sincerity. "As much as you fight against us sometimes, you also fight for us incessantly and with your whole being."

Tears prick the corners of my eyes as they each jump in over each other in true Tico fashion to list my other quirks and qualities they love. After a while they go quiet again and I let my heart rest in their words.

What an incomparable way to start year twenty-one.

As I think this, Xander wraps his arm around me in his typical side hug. When he releases, he leaves his arm and I remain snuggled against him. He looks at the others and there's an unspoken question in his eyes that I can't decipher. Jo smirks and Violetta nods her head subtly. In response he looks over to me and puts his other hand on the side of my face.

"Feliz cumpleaños, Adelina. Te amo, mi amor," he says gently before tipping my chin up lightly and meeting my mouth with his again. This kiss is longer, sweeter, and deeper than before and when he pulls away my mind is spinning. So many things just caught me so off guard.

They know it's my birthday? Wow, that kiss. Did Xander just say he loved me, but for real? In front of all of our friends. The kiss. He said he loves me. They've known all day. They made my birthday more perfect than I could've even imagined…I think I love you too.

Tears are now slowly sliding down my face. My heart constricts and tightens on itself, overwhelmed by the immediacy and weight of all of this—by their affection and effort.

I don't say anything; I wouldn't know what to say even if I had breath to give voice to my words. How do I adequately respond to what was just said and all that happened, what they did for me all day and even these past few months?

I'm shaking and their bodies slowly envelop mine in a tender group embrace. We sit like this until I've run out of tears to cry. I laugh once to myself. I usually only have my breakdowns about twice a year when I finally allow myself to feel my emotions, and I guess I must've been due.

"Thank you. I can't begin to express how much you each mean to me and how much I love you." I also can't begin to imagine the heartache I know I'll face in a few more months when I leave them all, but I forcefully push this thought away to the farthest part of my mind.

Instead, I'm concentrating on Xander's hand wrapped over mine as it rests on his knee. I tune in to Jo's joyous giggle as Violetta commends their skilled secrecy. I sit in the here and now, as Luc kicks my shoe and smiles fully at me. This is where I am now. In this moment, with these people, there is joy.

# 24

*Spontaneous date night. Just wear something comfy and casual but maybe bring something warm in case it's windy. I'll be there in an hour.*

His message lights up the dim room as it rests on the screen. An instant flutter passes through my heart. It's odd to me that even just the thought of spending time together can still do that after four and a half months. I mean, I guess maybe it's not that crazy, it's just new to me. I think I'm also extra excited because today was a long one with Kiara and Emilia, and I just want some of the comfort he can bring. Plus, he's usually pretty good when it comes to the spontaneous and surprising.

I look at the book resting in front of me and the analytics Mirari has me examining. I'm struggling to find the motivation to work through it, and my excitement falters.

*Well, mae, there's a small problem. You see, I've got work. So, it looks like we may have to postpone.*

I respond, knowing full well that he won't go for it, but wanting to see his response. It comes quickly: *Luckily for you, you've got a little over an hour to get your stuff done.*

After a half hour my phone lights up with an hourglass emoji, and I sift through my material to see how much further I have to go. The next message comes at ten 'til with an image of his bike, which I take as a sign that he's on his way or will be in just a second.

I shut the book that I'd only just gotten to and run to pull on a pair of pants instead of the shorts I was wearing. I leave the tank top on but grab a light jacket and the hummingbird tapestry I bought from one of the street vendors. I do nothing with my face or hair because it's all hopeless with the humidity and, well, he doesn't mind the difference.

I rush quickly to say bye to the boys and to tell Isabel where I'm going, then rush out the door to wait for him. It feels like I'm waiting forever as I merely stand and shift from foot to foot. He should've been here six minutes ago, and from the picture I would've assumed he'd be on time. Then again, he's a Tico, and they always run on their own clock.

He shows up thirteen minutes past when he'd originally said— enough time that I could've read another decent chunk of my book— but the spark that hits his eye when he sees me after removing his helmet reminds me I'd rather make Mirari's project wait.

He gives me a quick peck on the cheek and a cheerful "¡Buenas!" before handing me my helmet and telling me to watch my foot so I don't kick the cooler he's jerry-rigged to the tail and back edge of the seat. With my hands full of both jacket and tapestry, it's more difficult to get my leg over. I also have no way of holding on as we drive.

When we stop, I shove both items under my arm and grab Xander's shoulder to balance myself but still end up hopping a bit to regain my balance on the exit. He glides off smoothly and gracefully, of course, and then helps me get my helmet off before grabbing my jacket in one hand and my now-free hand in his other. The trip was really short, so this seems like a lot of work, but I'm excited nonetheless.

217

He first walks us in front of the tiled "Puntarenas" letters that I've seen what feels like a hundred times now. At this time in the evening, there aren't many tourists piled around waiting to get a picture. He sets my jacket on a bench and grabs the tapestry, placing it down as well. He then leads us to a couple who's just finished getting their picture taken and boldly asks if they'll take one for us, telling them to "just keep clicking."

When they agree he hands his phone to the woman and then collects my hand again, walking us back to the center. We turn to face the camera, and he wraps his arm around me in a hug and leaves the pose for a moment. He's such a natural, and his confidence must seep into me as well because with him beside me I feel confident and beautiful enough that my smile comes easily.

After a moment he places me between the 'R' and 'E' before he goes to stand between the 'T' and 'A' on my right. I know this picture won't look as good because I feel off again and don't know how to pose.

Luckily, he comes back quickly, and as I go to step down he quickly whisks me up and spins us to the center again. A squeal of laughter escapes my mouth and the dimple in his cheek hollows deeply in response. *The lady taking our picture better have just gotten that image.*

He gives me a soft kiss on the forehead and then sets me back down before sauntering back to his phone to look at the pictures.

He thanks the woman and then waits for me before he starts scrolling through. The first set is of our backside, hands clasped, with the letters and a faint lavender sky before us. In the next few I'm tucked perfectly beside him and our smiles are bold and bright.

The next ones, as I'd assumed, aren't nearly as cute. He stands strongly and confidently with a stern but gentle look in his eyes. Power radiates from the image until you look at my side where I appear small between the letters and my attempted smile leaves an awkward quirk on my face. He chuckles lightly and I shove his shoulder with my own.

As he shifts through the next few images, we watch the progression of him lifting and spinning me and the joy on our faces grows profoundly with each new frame. *Thank goodness she got it.*

The final image, while simple and unexpected, is my favorite. My smile still rests faintly on my lips and our eyes are closed as his lips brush my forehead. The laughter, joy, and love are captured in refined perfection.

"This one's my favorite," he says with quiet certainty after assessing it thoroughly. I smile and nod my head in agreement as a warmth of appreciation weaves through my heart. This night is beautiful.

I assume we'll maybe walk along the beach or down the pier since we're in the area, but then he starts walking back to the bike. When I look at him he can see the confusion flash across my face, but he merely swings a leg over the seat and directs a nod toward me, inviting me to do the same.

I follow his lead and pull my helmet back on but then startle when his leg brushes back across mine as he pulls it back over and hops off the bike. Of course I left all of my stuff. He rushes back shortly and passes everything to me before he gets back on with a quiet laugh, acknowledging my forgetfulness.

This trip isn't long either, as I suppose none of them really are, given the size of the peninsula, but I'm more confused now when we stop in front of the expanse of grass that unfurls before us. On either end I see simple goal posts indicating that he's brought me to a soccer field, and I'm surprised because somehow I haven't been here before.

He seems sure of what he's doing as he grabs everything from me and walks to the center before laying out the tapestry and placing the cooler in the middle. He sits in front of it and begins to empty its contents onto the ground as I walk over and sit across from him, putting the goodies between us.

I'm surprised when I see the four cans set out neatly in a diamond. Two are the popular rum and coke mixes, which many of the Ticos drink, especially on their Saturday night beach get-togethers. The other two I assume must be mine because one is a mixed berry and the other is a sort of mojito—they're sweet drinks with practically zero taste and effect of alcohol.

I'm pleased that he's remembered my preference but more eager when I see the rolls of cookies and a few packages of assorted gummy candies that I'm so fond of.

It's quiet around us and we merely sit in the calm of the night, saying nothing, just resting in the presence of one another. In time I open a drink and a bag of gummy rings, scarfing through half of them before I think to offer any to Xander.

The quirk to his lips, the slight squint of his right eye and the lighter skin around it, and the laugh he gives at my panicked last-minute offer signals amusement at my behavior and lets me know he's not upset at all. I smile sheepishly as he takes two and then pushes the bag back to let me know the rest are mine. Maybe I'll remember sooner with the bag of sour gummy worms, though honestly, I don't foresee that happening.

As the last drop of my first drink glides swiftly down my throat I look around and realize the lights which normally illuminate most of the streets, and the ones on the corners of the field, are turned off. This leaves the area fairly dark, but more than that, it leaves no light to contrast with the stars that are beginning to pop out as the clouds roll away overhead.

I ball my jacket up and lay it on the ground before lying back and shuffling down so my head rests on it. Xander moves a bag of gummies to my other side where I can easily access them and pulls my second drink and the cookies the other way before lying beside me.

His arm rests along mine, and it doesn't take long for our fingers to find each other. We stare up in silence for an eternity before he begins to point out various shapes in the clusters. I can't help but laugh, as I'm sure the Easter Island head and Mushu from *Mulan* are not recognized constellations.

We keep searching the skies and find a palm tree, a frying pan, and what he assures me is the outline of Thailand among other less defined images before I feel the rush of a shiver run through Xander's body beside me.

Without the clouds trapping the heat in, and with the rainy weather we've been having, it's a bit colder than usual, but Ticos aren't as acclimated to lower temperatures as us Idahoans, so he's probably more than slightly chilly. It's somewhat amusing, since it really is still pretty warm, but I'm grateful for the opportunity to inch closer. He sighs in relief as I also wrap the excess edges of the tapestry over us to capture whatever heat we can.

His shivering lessens, but opposingly, a shiver runs through my body. I know I'm not cold. No, my shiver is from mere proximity and nerves.

"What are you thinking about?" he asks in just the wrong moment.

"Well, I think it's funny that you get so cold when for me this is still pretty warm," I say, swerving to my previous thoughts. He gives an exaggerated, short laugh that signals he doesn't think it's so funny.

"Do you know the word 'friolento?'"

I rack through my Spanish vocab that's grown exponentially since arriving but still come up short. "Hmm nope, I don't think so."

"It means I'm sensitive to the cold, so stop making fun of me or I'll take you home so I can go be in my warm house rather than out here," he threatens jokingly and I scoot closer, giving his hand a quick squeeze to let him know he's not allowed to leave.

"How was your day?" he asks after a period of silence. I pause hesitantly, still not always comfortable with telling him when things weren't so good. Then I remember that in this relationship we're fighting for each other. We as humans aren't meant to live on our own strength and power, no matter how hard we try.

He waits patiently for me to begin, and eventually I tell him about my day with the girls. I guess Emilia caught Kiara cutting herself a few weeks ago but didn't say anything because Kiara promised she'd stop. When Emilia found a razor blade in their room with fairly fresh blood, she took it to Mirari immediately. Kiara has been on self-harm watch since then and isn't on good terms with Emilia. They were both still encouraged to talk to me today and luckily, they reluctantly agreed.

While we were at the plaza a huge argument broke out between them about privacy versus the need to be open with each other and safety. At one point, Emilia left completely. I freaked out for a minute, but Kiara reassured me that she'd come back. So, in the fifteen or so minutes while we were waiting, I got to talk to Kiara on a deeper level about what she was feeling.

I guess she reached the part in the program where they let her have a phone, and she immediately contacted her brother. He began to tell her how horrible she was to leave the modeling agency and he didn't believe her when she tried to tell him all that she faced. She thought that if her family couldn't care even now, and if they didn't trust her, then she had no one left to care—no one to go back to even if she did finish the program.

"Xander, I just held her as she cried and cried. I stroked her hair and tried to hug her hard enough that the sobs would stop racking through her body, but they kept going. Emilia found us like that and joined us. Then the three of us sat in the middle of the square crying together. I didn't know what else to do. I told her we love her and that there is a reason to keep fighting. I told her about how God's created her for something bigger, but no matter what I said, I couldn't fill the hole that man and her family ripped through her." I'm crying now as I finish telling the story and Xander has rolled over to tuck me more directly into his chest.

"She'll see it, Adelina. There's no way she won't see his love if you keep pouring into her and if you keep showing her his love." He seeks to reassure me, but I reject his words and pull away again.

"How, Xander? I barely have two months left. What can I do in that time to fix all that she's been through and make it all right?" The words choke out through my tightened throat.

"Cariño, you can't. You're forgetting that's not your job. That's God's job and you're the one who is pointing the way to him. You are planting seeds for him to water, and believe me when I say that fruit will grow, even in these two months."

His voice is calm and the wisdom penetrates my disrupted thoughts and my heart. "I only have two months left, Xander. Then this is all over." I whisper now, turning more to my own fears rather than Kiara's.

"Yes, this is one season in your life that will come to an end," he says confidently, "but the fruit from this season doesn't all have to die if you keep nourishing it." He leans over and kisses the top of my forehead again softly before tucking the tapestry around me, scooting in close, and leaving the air silent.

# 25

"Please tell me your day went better than mine. Por favor." I eventually plead, breaking the quiet. His body doesn't move, he doesn't nod in agreement, and he doesn't say anything in confirmation, which in its own way confirms the opposite.

I'm trying to decide if I'm ready to hear his hardships while I'm still thinking through my own. "Will you tell me what happened?" I ask after a bit of time elapses.

He releases a large sigh, but when he speaks there's still tension in his words.

"Visité a mi papá."

Immediately I sit up and face him. He still hasn't told me much, but I do know his last visit with his dad was roughly five years ago, when he was nineteen, so for him to have gone is big.

I don't know how to target the emotions of this situation yet, so I don't ask how he's feeling—he's clearly not feeling great about it all. "Why did you choose to go today?" I ask, treading carefully. He sits up slowly, thinking.

"I guess there were a lot of little things," he says easily. I stay quiet, waiting for him to elaborate. "It's the seventh anniversary since my mom passed away." He says this simply as though I should've known it was the anniversary, and as if he visits his dad every year, except we both know he doesn't. "And I guess I just decided it was a good day to stop running."

The weight in the air is heavy, but I don't say anything to lessen it. I'm so confused. Seeing the grief and weight of today now helps me understand why he needed this date.

This is something he needs to talk about, something that's been swallowing him for a while now.

He clears his throat and it sounds like it's strained from holding back tears.

"I went to apologize. I apologized for not coming to visit the last five years, and I asked him to forgive me for leaving him so alone. I asked him to forgive me for hating him and what he taught me, and for despising who he was. Reversely, I went to get closure and to tell him I've forgiven him for all he made me do and for who he encouraged me become. I went to finally share with him who I've become now and to tell him all God has done in my life despite the environment we were in. I went to tell him who God can be for him. I guess today I finally decided to listen to all God's been asking of me for multiple years now."

He takes a deep breath as though relieved to have been able to express so much, but I'm still lost in the fog of his ambiguity. My mind is reeling with questions and searching for solutions.

In my surprise, I let go of his hand when I sat up. I reach over for it again now, hoping to provide comfort however I can as my words fail me.

I look up at the stars and say a quick prayer asking that he'll trust me enough to open up and speak when he's ready. Then I merely sit in the quiet, staring at our hands linked together. My eyes follow the few highlighted veins that trace across the back of his hand. I allow my fingers to run across them as I attempt to distract myself from overthinking and analyzing what could be going on in his head.

"Cachorra," he finally speaks in a voice below a whisper.

I watch his chest rise and fall with the next wave of breaths as he tries to drag the air into his body. He squeezes my hand. "Adelina," he says clearly but with reservation. "I've been praying for so long about the right way to tell you these things I want and feel like I need to say, and somehow I still can't think of how to do it, at least not in a way that'll make it better somehow, because I can't really make it better. I know you'll be hurt in the end and you may even hate me, and I don't know how I'll be able to ease the truth or your response even though I want to."

He goes quiet again and closes his eyes in an attempt to block me out or to process, I'm not sure which. His eyes stay sealed shut, but his words begin to fill the air.

"Lo siento mucho, mi reina," he apologizes gently and a shudder runs through his body. He opens his eyes and the pain in them shoots through every nerve in my body.

"When I was ten, eleven, twelve, I don't think I really knew what I was doing or getting myself into. Like any guy my age I started to pay more and more attention to the girls in my classes, and I'd come home with a story of Sofia or Alicia, the girls with the shy but brilliant smiles, and I couldn't wait to tell my dad about them.

"He'd always told me that one of the greatest experiences in life is having a beautiful and bold woman to call your own. He told me of the pride a man feels to love her, care for her, and make her feel seen as no other man could. So when I started to see these girls, immediately my feeble mind wondered if they could be my one. Of course I didn't realize, but my dad was already grooming me."

His sentence hangs in the air and my question rests on my face. *Grooming you for what?*

"I was always drawn to the quiet ones. They were reserved and seemed shy, but they lit up and became bright when complimented or given a quick wink. He told me this demeanor could help because the soft-spoken were often the ones that wanted love the most, they were just less likely to show it.

"'Good, good, make them feel special mijo, show them you care for them even more than their parents. Make them think that you will give them the world because they are *your* whole world.' He whispered these affirmations into my heart the first night I came home and told him I'd kissed a girl.

"'They want you, and they need you, they just haven't realized it yet. Don't be afraid to show them what they lack,' he said, patting me on the shoulder after I copped a feel and felt the first tongue sliding through my mouth."

My stomach is starting to roll at his descriptors. He was so young. I only just experienced my first kiss, *with him* nonetheless, mere weeks ago.

He continues, "'I want you to help me with something,' my dad announced proudly after I'd finally slipped my hand under a girl's skirt the first time. His words, and the heat that rushed through my veins with each experience, encouraged and emboldened me.

"At thirteen and a half years old I fell in love for the first time. Or I thought I had. Our age didn't matter, we had each other, and we wanted everything from each other."

His eyes fill with sorrow as he whispers his next words. "She was my first."

Blood is pounding like subwoofer speakers in my ears and I'm struggling to hear, though I know I need to keep listening, even if I don't want to.

He speaks next of how easy it was to convince her he needed her help. His family was in trouble and they needed money. She would've done anything for him. And she did.

His dad warped his son's desires and dreams into demons and darkness.

When he finally realized what he'd convinced her to do it was too late. His dad had already given her away twice. She was his, now she wasn't, and he didn't know what to do. So he sought another.

His dad told him it didn't mean anything and that there was another 'one.' But time after time, and girl after girl, he felt hope again and pushed back. But the fist of his dad's disapproval fell hard if he didn't respond as planned. "'See how they made you feel? Don't be selfish Xander, she could do that for someone else too!'"

So he led them to his father time and time again.

By the time he was fifteen he was teaching his brother and taking the blows of the belt when anything went wrong. It was 'conveniently perfect' timing he said, as his dad was arrested a few months later.

To commemorate their father and show they would carry on the legacy, the two boys went and got their family tattoo, just as all the other men had before them. He rubs it hard now in frustration, wishing he could tear it off, I'm sure.

He tells me how this cycle continued for the next five or so years. Only when Luc decided to stop living in that life and began attending church with Violetta did Dash really start to question himself and all his dad had taught him. He couldn't believe yet, but he didn't know if he wanted to be living the same way anymore.

"I stopped visiting my dad because I didn't want him to convince me to stay in it. I saw how joyful Luc was, and I wanted that. He and Violetta had some problems for a while obviously, but then God reformed them both. I wanted that so bad." He's crying now as he says these things and the pieces from Violetta's story are beginning to click.

"My brother didn't understand why I was starting to hate our style of life, especially since I was the one who taught him all I knew." He's quiet as he speaks. "He got out a few years ago, but that's because he found his one and got married. I haven't been able to reconnect with them well because I'd been jealous. Of course he got his girl. I was the one who had messed up after all: disappointing my dad, teaching my brother a life no one should learn, not being secure enough in anything to say no."

"I didn't sleep with any of those women for money and I didn't beat any of them. Then again, I never had to. They all trusted me enough to give themselves up. I stole their lives from them." He's finally said it, clearly and in deep sincerity and sorrow, but I'm rejecting it all. My stomach is eating itself and I'm about to puke. How did we go from such serenity and beauty in the events of my birthday and the following week or so, to now?

He must not see it on my face because he continues, "Girls like Kiara and Emilia, these women you care about and this evil you hate so much. I contributed to that, Cachorra."

That name snaps everything in my mind that is stirring to complete stillness and I pull my hand from his and scoot back. I pulled my hand from him once before, when I'd tried to pet the shark, and now in this moment I realize that maybe he really was dangerous and my fear was justified.

He sits staring at me and is silent. The horror is clear in his story. The apology is evident. And I know my next step should be to comfort him. But I can't. No, he didn't do this to me. But he did it. Yes, he's been redeemed. But that doesn't make it hurt less. Yes, he's telling me now. But he never mentioned any of this before.

It's too much.

"Es demasiado, no puedo, Dash," I say, voicing my thought. Deep hurt scrunches his face as I use this name for the first time in so long. "I, I'm sorry," I say with sincerity—sorry for his past, sorry that in this moment I am not responding well, sorry for everything. "I just…give me a minute, I need to think," I say as I scramble to my feet.

He nods his head and I take that as my signal. It's the gun at the track meet that tells me to go, and immediately my legs take off underneath me. I don't know where I'm going but I've got to go somewhere else. I need the pain that is raking through my heart and mind to carve deep into my body as well. Maybe if it's in my body I won't feel it so much anywhere else.

I left all of my things, but I don't care. I watch as gate after gate goes by. I'm on the beach now and the sand kicks up behind me. It slows me down and I go back to the street. I kick my sandals off and feel the gravel beneath my feet. I chase my thoughts away, willing the last twenty minutes to be a dream.

I can barely hear as cars go by and a few clusters of men holler their disgusting compliments at me. The times I do hear them, my blood boils hotter and my feet kick faster. The pier is long gone by now, and I'm heading into the neighboring barrios.

I pass the University of Costa Rica in Cocal and keep going. Eventually, I'm on the stretch of road that has water on both sides. I keep going. I only stop when I reach the cemetery. I feel like this place represents what I'm feeling. It's a representation of beautiful lives and people lost.

I feel like I've lost him. How do I trust him now? I don't know if I'm strong enough to look past all of this. I know I should, but can I? I should've known it wouldn't last. Actually, I did know, and I went in like a blind fool anyway. I kick the gate outside and then realize that probably isn't the best move.

My mind floods with irritation at myself and I take off running back home. All I can hope for now is to just outrun myself and my ignorance. This was the first time I decided to open my heart after protecting it for so long, and it turned out exactly as I'd feared it would. I'm frustrated because I knew and didn't put up bigger walls.

I'm exhausted. Physically, emotionally, mentally. Crushed. I start walking when I'm a few blocks away from my house. I don't know how long I've been running but I need a break. When I reach the street in front of my gate I don't even look, I just rush to the large metal trash bin and finally puke, maybe from his words, maybe from the exhaustion, probably from both.

I jump when a hand comes to rest on my back and gentle fingers pull my hair farther from my face. I should've known it'd be him, but I don't, and I have to hold my scream back with everything in me as I clasp my chest and seek deep breaths to regain my stability.

I spit a few more times before turning around to face him. When my eyes meet his, my heart both constricts with affection and sinks in disappointment. His eyes are regretful and numb from his past, affectionate and soft as he gently helps me. Immediate feelings of hurt and frustration wash over me. Feelings of anger, betrayal, and annoyance overwhelm the physical elements again.

He reaches out and clasps my hands, pulling me slowly and gently toward him. My feet don't move forward so he steps closer instead. When his arms encircle me I remain stiff for a moment, but then the familiar scent of his cologne and the sudden rush of his warmth begin to break through my negative thoughts.

When I feel him crying, I realize this may have been a hug to comfort him more than to comfort me, but I'll take it right now. I'm not crying, but my chest feels like there is a bag of rocks in it. My breathing is strained and I can't get the air into my lungs fast enough.

I know he's going to allow me to speak first. I'm the one who ran away, after all, so I'm the one who needs to explain or at a minimum express my thoughts. I still don't know if I can, though. The plus side of running is that I'm distracted and don't really think about the issue that made me want to run away, and the downside is that I'm distracted and don't really think about the issue, so I'm left to process through it later.

I don't know if now is that time, but I can tell him a few things for certain. I know there's nothing technically to forgive about his past because he didn't do any of that to me and God has forgiven him already. I know my head will make this all bigger and worse than it is because still in my subconscious I'm searching for an excuse and a reason to run from the relationship itself. Whether that part is true or not, this is the moment when I have to reanalyze and reevaluate. It's the first bump in our road, possibly the first of many, possibly the first and last.

"I already feel myself pushing you away piece by piece. It's what my mind says is smart and safe," I say, trying to wrap up all of these thoughts. "Dash, I don't even know how to address any of what you said. It hurts to know this is what you went through, and it hurts to also think of what you made those girls go through. I know your pain is worse than mine and the weight is yours not mine, but I feel it right now and I want to help you, but it's a weight I don't know if I'm ready to carry."

"Cuando soy débil, entonces soy fuerte." His words are sure and steady as though he's recited them hundreds of times. I pull away slightly and hold his left arm in my hands, reading the ink that marks these same words into his skin. I run my fingers across the letters and goosebumps prickle on his arm. This is the first time I've ever really looked at this tattoo, and I definitely haven't asked about it before.

"I couldn't carry the weight, either. I still can't. I'm not strong enough," he says confidently and without shame. "It's not your weight to carry, Cariño, not directly at least, not in this time of life. But if we are together it is something you have to live knowing and something you have to face whether it's pretty or not. Yes, we would face it together, but that's your decision."

Dash's words slow in my mind, and I really have to concentrate to take them in. "I wanted to wait because I needed you to see who God has made me to be now. I hoped you'd learn to trust me and find me worth it despite my past. I didn't finish earlier, but I want you to know that if you have to say no, I understand. I've loved this time and this journey, but I want what is best for you. If my past breaks you too much, I don't want that." His words dig the knife deeper.

"Remember at the marine park when I told you that you were like a turtle—beautiful and strong?" I nod my head slowly so he knows I'm actually listening. "Well, I still believe that's true, and if this is something you want to fight for, I know you're strong enough to do it in a manner that is elegant and full of grace. But I don't want you to be in this if you don't want it, or if you decide you can't. Your heart and your pursuit of God are what matter most in this, and if I'm going to inhibit that then I need you to tell me, even if it's not what I want to hear."

I nod my head again and he gives me a tight hug.

He quietly whispers his final words into my hair, then lets me go and walks to his motorcycle. Kickstart, engine, throttle. The noises all ring in my ears. Yet somehow, the words he whispered play louder: Cuando eres débil, entonces eres fuerte.

# 26

The first day after Dash's declaration, Axel and Manny knocked gently and then peeked into my door. When I merely shook my head, they got the message and disappeared. Isabel brought me food around lunchtime when she realized I wasn't coming out for anything.

The boys came back a little later and just stood with their soft eyes blinking at me. This time my nod invited them in, and the three of us curled up on my twin bed together in silence. They just wanted to sit with me, but I couldn't torture them, so I turned on the newest Spiderman movie.

My eyes brimmed with tears in various moments and I felt bad that they both chose to stay with me anyway. Stupid superheroes. What a load of crap. After the final credits rolled through, they finally left, giving me a tight hug together before scurrying back to their room where they didn't have to be surrounded by as much sadness.

The next few hours I read and read and read, trying to distract myself. I pressed the heels of my hands deeply into my eye sockets until I saw sparkles fleck across my vision. Desperately I tried to wipe away the tiredness, but really, I was trying to compress the pressure that flowed from my heart all the way to my head and back through every part of my body.

When my eyes couldn't hold themselves up any longer, I set my alarm and allowed myself to sink into sleep.

That day was the worst. It's been better since, though not great. I haven't seen Dash in a week and a half. In fact, I haven't seen anyone, really. Luciana and Elena have been trying to invite me out with them more, which is sweet, and the boys and I have been playing soccer again like when I first arrived.

Mostly I've resorted to walking the back half of the peninsula. I explicitly avoid the beach, the bars, and all their houses. Who knew that I'd end up back at square one after being here four and a half months? Jo is the only one I've seen—very briefly when I stopped for a cheap meal last week. I didn't speak at all but she was encouraging, telling me I have time, even though I know I don't really.

But, most importantly, she reminded me to remember the cross and to remember God sending himself to Earth to die for all we've done, to forgive us. The tiniest things like lies or jealousy, even those are worth punishment against the creator and God of all. Yet he forgives everything when we ask. She reminded me to forgive, as God forgave, and to seek love.

I want to, but I'd need his help. Just as he has helped lift the veil to make me see Xander and all he is now. Just as he's redeemed me and is transforming me to trust more and have more hope and faith. He would have to transform me, to help me forgive. He is strong, and I am weak. I don't even know if I really want to be transformed. This is safer, easier, more comfortable.

Her words were nice, but I feel my own brokenness fighting back right now. I'm at the park across from the church; there are bigger benches and fewer people walking around. Moments ago a woman walked by me and needed some of my paper to write something down. Before she left, she looked me up and down and told me quickly, "Cuídate, Cariño."

Like thanks, señora, but I should have watched out for myself better months ago, from the moment I rode home with the guys in the Jeep and Vicente warned me to do so.

This thought rushes through my mind and I scribble it hurriedly and sloppily across my journal. I can only imagine what I look like sitting here: an abnormally tan gringa on her own, with tears starting to drip down her face and an assassination planned for the pages on her lap.

How did I miss so much? Both of his tattoos were summed up in that one conversation. His history with Luc, why he's weird around girls, his relationship with his brother and his dad, all of it makes sense now. It's all too clear, if I'm being honest.

I even understand more about his job at the youth center now. He said he wants to keep the guys off the streets and give them a future that wasn't reflective of his past. One of the things I loved most about him—how well he loves those most at risk—flows from his stained past.

Oh man. I don't even know how to go forward at this point. I'm so stupid for diving into this relationship. I knew I should keep my walls up but no, I ignored it all—I trusted my heart over my head. Didn't I always tell myself that logic should win over feelings.

It's fairly late when I decide to go back to the house. I weave my way through the brightest and safest streets, away from those that hold poor reputations. I remember now how Axel had warned me not to go down certain streets. "Es el área de prostitutas, no es seguro para mujeres." I'm still uneasy about the fact that there are unsafe areas where prostitution is common.

I quicken my pace, trying to outrun the uneasy feeling in my stomach. It's no use, because when I get to our gate my insides lurch. A postcard is nestled among the bars above the lock.

*The girls really miss you, and Luc's gringa jokes just aren't the same without you around to direct them at. I'd love to talk soon, or see you, but if you can't do that, my only ask is that you reconnect with them.*

*+506 2629 1417*

*Your move.*

The message is short and to the point, I don't know if I should be upset by it or if I should be grateful. I think I'm a bit of both. It's signed just like the first one with the phone number and the fox drawing. This time I'm more conflicted about responding; the giddiness is gone. I know more this time, which means I'm really the only one to blame for whatever goes wrong.

What he shared is horrific and deeply saddening. But it was also his past, and he has been redeemed. This new person is the man I've given my heart to. But dang, that's a lot to step into.

I read the card again and again, taking it inside with me and sitting on the couch with it held in my hands. "Me alegro que la encontraste," Isabel says from behind me. *What if I hadn't found it?* I wonder at her question. She must have seen it on the gate, or maybe he came by while she was here.

I look at her silently for a few moments. The Spanish conversation floods around my ears as Isabel and the kids now give their inputs. They weren't surprised when I told them what Dash revealed. His family was known on the peninsula for decades. Isabel didn't think to mention it before because she assumed Dash had, or would in the right time, and because she'd also seen him come out of it and change. The boys now even play soccer with Dash's nephews.

"¿Qué piensas?" Isabel asks me, pulling me back into the conversation.

"What would you think if you were her, Mom, she's hopeful but nervous, obviously," Axel replies as he walks from the hallway.

I'm surprised by how wise he is in his words, especially for being only thirteen. Curiously, I nod my head in agreement. Does the whole family know it all?

"Ay, mija, I used to know his mama. She was a good woman, and his dad was good too. Sometimes life happens to people and it leads them into bad circumstances. What matters is what we choose to do afterward. Will we continue to live from what we've experienced and have been taught, or can we step into new paths if it's what is better?" She stares at me intently again and waits, though I don't respond. I see her mentality, but I think I can actually see more hope and freedom because I see it from a perspective that includes God's grace and how he reforms us.

"I think he did the best he could given the influence he had, and now he's found a new life and he's running with it," Axel speaks up again. "You have shown him grace and you've taught him what it means to be in a sacrificial relationship. It's so different from what he grew up with. And think of all he taught you. You were so afraid of people when you got here; you didn't even invest in us as much as you have now. You've let your guard down, and none of us would say that's a bad thing."

Isabel smiles proudly at her son and I can't help but do the same. He's so right, and so is she. It's at least enough to motivate me toward another conversation or two. I'm not saying this will be anything official again, because maybe it's not worth it as I'm about to leave, but I do want to talk to him. I don't really know what to hope for beyond that yet.

It's past midnight by the time I get up the nerve to message. In seconds I see the tiny blue checkmarks. His reply is immediate as he invites me to lunch tomorrow.

I don't know if I want to, but I tell him yes. Then, in my nervousness, I toss the phone away from me on the bed. I can't bear to keep texting right now, so I pick up *Redeeming Love* and start reading it again on chapter one. Maybe I'll learn something different this time.

# 27

Dash is resting outside of Isla Coco's already when I arrive. When he sees me and gives me a timid but beautiful smile, the knot in my stomach flips.

I didn't expect myself to lose feelings automatically, obviously, but I'm surprised by how much I'd grown accustomed to his presence and his alluring smile.

"Te extrané," he says quietly when I'm right in front of him. I can't help but roll my eyes at the cliché of this statement. How can you miss someone so significantly after only a week and a half, like honestly?

"I mean that I've noticed the lack of you being around. I've felt a difference in the days we haven't spoken or seen each other," he emphasizes. These words sound so much better than 'I missed you.' Why didn't he just start there?

He catches my hand and links his fingers with mine. My heart is fluttering but I don't want it to. I want to let go, yet I don't.

I think he knows I'm not eager to speak; he understands that I want to listen and try to understand. Rather than speaking immediately, he begins walking down the street. "We're not eating here," he says, acknowledging my confusion. "I wanted to take you on one last adventure, if it's all you'll allow me."

I can't help but smile as I agree. He really does know my love language.

He leads us a little past the restaurant and takes a left unexpectedly. I should've imagined this is where we'd go, but I haven't been on the ferry before and I'm a bit surprised when he hands off two tickets and I follow him on.

We wind up to the primary seating decks and make our way to the food area. He watches me hesitantly, trying to decide if he should order my food or if I'll speak up. I decide to let him continue with the game we've played so often and let him pick for me while I take a seat at one of the benches near the front windows.

He joins me shortly and we eat our simple meals silently. When we've finished, he stands up and waits again. I get up, assuming that's what he's wanting, and follow him to the outside where we can feel the light breeze as we lean over the side rails. He takes a seat and puts his legs through the railings, so I follow suit.

The conversation he starts is basic as he asks how I've been doing. I tell him about my walks and how I've been able to hang out with my family more again. I leave out the part about my furious journaling and frustration—I'm sure he already knows. Then I courteously ask him the same and learn that he's been working on a bigger community event for the youth in his program.

He's been put in charge of a skate competition and show for the guys and girls. At the park along the beach the guys can do their tricks, and the girls can use their roller skates on the basketball course nearby. Hopefully a lot of the community will be involved.

Man, I missed how excited he gets when he's talking about his guys and how they really seem to be pursuing positive things— unlike himself at that age.

My head sticks on that thought for a little while longer as he keeps talking, and I miss some of the details to what he's saying.

While he's leading these kids away from what he did and who he was, that doesn't reverse or take back his past.

"Lo siento, Adelina." His words break through my wrestling thoughts. He knows I'm tripped up on his confession still and he doesn't know how to fix it. As some sort of solution, he stands up and walks away.

I don't know if that's what I was hoping for, but I don't go after him. I sit staring at the water for a long time as I think through it all. Time seems to pass slowly, and it only enhances my awareness of how long he's been gone.

I'm surprised when his voice resounds from the wall behind me. "Una tortuga." I'm startled as well as confused until he steps forward and points below us to the right.

It's the first turtle I've ever seen in the wild and I'm awestruck. As I watch it over the next few moments, I'm distracted by the realization that Dash must've been standing behind me for a while, watching the water or watching me.

He's standing beside me now and he voices my previous thought, "It really is magnificent."

I want to rest here and now. I want to act like nothing happened, but I can't keep waiting. "Why didn't you tell me earlier?" I ask, breaking the peace of the moment. I don't need him going on again about turtles, and certainly not about how I'm strong and beautiful and blah blah blah. I just want to understand.

The smell of him drifts around us as he takes a seat and settles facing me. His voice is steady and sure as he speaks, because he has no doubt about what he wants to say.

"The main thing my family has ever been known for is the one thing you most fight against. From the first day we spoke, I could tell you didn't put up with crap. You stand for truth and justice, and you seek to protect yourself and others from anyone or anything against that. I'm part of the problem, well, I was. I contributed to the things you're fighting against with Kiara and Emilia.

"I wanted to protect you from myself. I mean, it took me months just to ask you on a date because I kept battling myself. Meses, mi amor. Never in my life have I waited so long. I guess for you it doesn't sound like much, but I knew so early on that you were the one my dad had talked about. At least, I hoped you would be, but I had to take my time to give you space, and also let you see who I am now—to let you see the man God is shaping me into."

I process his words quietly as they roll to a lull and only the sound of the ferry surrounds us. It's starting to pull into the loading area and people are shuffling to get off. I criticize myself for the poorly timed initiation of the conversation.

We pack ourselves onto various busses too crowded to talk properly and let each bus carry us across the peninsula to a city called Montezuma. As we get off, Dash looks at me eagerly, pushing aside the conversation and focusing on the moment before us.

"Are you ready for an adventure?" he asks with a daring smile.

My head stops thinking for a slight moment and my soul kicks into gear. While this isn't the best situation, it would take a lot for me to resist.

I respond with enthusiasm and a smirk, challenging him to give me the best he's got.

He nods readily and takes an abrupt turn off the road we've been walking to direct us along a small river channel. As we continue, he begins to weave us farther from the illuminated path and onto a masked trail that weaves along the trees.

We go over roots and rocks and stop short as a bustle of people appear before us. They're all gazing at a thin waterfall that cascades from a few stories above us. More specifically, I realize, they're gaping at a man who clambers surefootedly down the rock face toward the mouth of the falls before leaping over.

We each catch our breath at the feat and stand in awe as he

emerges seemingly unharmed from such a long drop.

"That's where we're headed," Dash says nonchalantly as he continues forward again and begins to head up the side of the mountain. As we cling to root after root and shuffle upward, my mind spins at how ludicrous this is. He can't be serious, right? I'm certainly not jumping from that. Even I have my limits.

He checks on me from time to time and extends a hand as he situates himself on another small path above us. We wander briefly and finally I see it. There is another fall, and also a cascade of rocks traced by the river. "Okay, more specifically we're headed here. Only the locos jump the big one."

Dash's voice trails back to me and instantly some of the knots in my stomach release themselves. "This one should be no trouble," he proclaims excitedly while shuffling off his shoes and shirt.

Immediately I blush. It's not from the sight of him—well, at least not completely—but rather at the recognition that I don't have a swimsuit. And no way am I going to strip down to my underwear.

I sit nonchalantly and observe around me for a while. I feel deeply at peace, but after his seventh jump in Dash saunters over. His hair has grown slightly longer again and drips water on my legs crossed before me. He stares at me intently, analyzing his options.

I don't know how many he runs through, but he soon grabs my phone off my lap and lays it on his towel a few feet away. My irritation rises a bit, and even though I know what I'm sure to face, I stand abruptly to retrieve the phone. Swiftly he steps in front of me and the glimmer in his eyes leaves me with no doubt of his intentions.

I'm pulled tightly against him and for a moment I'm surprised by the hug and quick kiss on the forehead, but he shifts quickly and in the next moment he simultaneously scoops me up and jumps into the water before us.

I emerge beside him and my emotions are uncertain. He collects a mouthful of water and spits it gracefully toward me. Seconds later he's choking on whatever he didn't manage to spit out, and a smile tugs across my lips. I guess I'm in it now, no going back.

Hoping that he'll follow, I rush out of the water and along the ropes that guide me up the rocks. He's quick behind me, and when we get to the top of the falls he extends his hand. I grasp it and pull as I launch off, taking him along beside me.

This is what I feel like alongside him: he fits comfortably, tangled into my life. Each time we jump into the next moment I'm faced with a rush of panic and exhilaration. It's a feeling I long to experience frequently and ceaselessly.

# 28

I slide my phone open to Vi and Jo's gleaming faces. "Eek, it's good to see you again," Vi squeals. Jo laughs beside her.

"I just saw you yesterday," I tell them both with an exaggerated eyeroll.

"Es cierto. But you disappeared for like two weeks and we have to take all the face time we can get, in case it happens again," Jo pipes up with a tone of concern at the end of her statement.

I want to roll my eyes but restrain when I think of how much my retreat actually hurt them. "We're at the announcer's stand, just make your way up when you get here," I tell them instead, before ending the call.

There are teen girls gliding backwards and spinning off to our left while the guys practice their various tricks on the rails and ramps. Dash looks over at me as though he thinks I'll go into hiding again right this moment. Even after our conversation the night in Montezuma, he's being extra cautious.

We talked over grace and forgiveness, freedom and trust. Moment by moment I was drawn toward peace and contentedness. Hours drifted by as our conversation shifted to thoughts of the future, what it could mean to stay together, and even what it would look like if we were together and I moved back home.

"¿Quién es Dios para ti?" It was the first of three questions which carried our conversation deeper into the night and into feelings of hope and security.

Who do I believe God to be? How does that change my life? What will I do in response for him? These things seem so simple, yet in the context of self-analysis—and definitely when aligning futures—I found myself more hopeful and eager for what potential lies between us.

Xander stands just to my left, and I know that in this moment he is responding to all God has done in him and for him. He finds joy in this. He's burdened by the fates of these youth, but his joy is made complete in living alongside them and showing them a way out through Jesus.

As I watch him greet the new contestants and run around to check on each of his kids, a dream forms inside me. It's a desire I think I've had for a while without being confident enough to admit it.

Even in the face of inevitable trials, I desire to serve the Lord side by side with someone. I long to walk hand in hand with someone into the depths of ministry as we each use our gifts and passions to serve God.

He rushes by me, carrying his own skateboard to give to a kid who has just broken his own. I catch the wink he flashes at me deep inside my heart and know that Xander is the one whom I want to walk hand in hand with. Through the brokenness of current struggles, through the pain of past hurt and fears, he is the only one I could imagine myself fighting alongside, and he's the only person I know who could fight for me as God intends.

Vi, Luc, Jo, and even Kiara and Emilia each gather together beside me as the competition starts. My family is alongside the rest of the crowds and they're eagerly watching as Xander collects the teens together to pray before the event starts.

I'm trying to stay engaged, but my mind flashes back to a conversation that I had with my parents after I learned all about his past. My dad's face grew serious in the screen as his question passed through my headphones. "Alongside his faith, because you've talked about that a lot, what do you love most about him? We want you to be head over heels for this guy."

I think to my answer, remembering how stunned I was by the question. The whole scene plays in my mind as if it were happening now.

What do I love about Xander? *Que profunda es esa pregunta.*

I sat chewing on my bottom lip and their faces were staring at me intently, waiting for a response. I was slow to answer, wanting to give him the most true and honest response that I could. I didn't want to just throw something out; I needed to answer with certainty.

Of course. I spoke without hesitance, conviction and clarity guiding my words. "Day after day he shows me grace upon grace." My dad's head cocked to the side, encouraging me to explain.

"When we first met, he was bold, pursuing me despite my hesitation. He could see how nervous I was and continued with delicacy, but with confidence. He knew I was pushing back because I just didn't want to get hurt, and because I didn't think I could trust him, when all he ever did was show me the opposite. But he waited and he prayed, seeking God's wisdom and displaying God's grace. He reflected to me what Christ continuously does for each of us on Earth in his pursuit and love despite how we reject him and choose our own way."

But, I told them he made me question my trust in him. This was the first time; the other times I really just distrusted myself. But this last time— "This time it broke me. It showed me that my original fears could prove to be real. So I ran away."

Their eyes widened at that and I laughed. "Literally guys, I literally ran away from him, for hours." A smile quirked on my mom's lips but she stayed quiet, knowing I needed to work through my thoughts.

I think through it all now, though, the rest of my answer to them. He never gave up on me. He saw how scared I was, how hesitant and how closed off, and he just fought harder. I gave up. In a matter of ten minutes with one story I gave up. The truth of what he did was too much for me to look past. I forgot to give grace. Still, I'm hesitant to give grace.

I stare out at him in the huddle. It's definitely easier to run away than to stand and fight. It's easier to be wary and guarded rather than to give him my trust so fully.

My mom's last comment before the call ended hit me hard when I talked about running away. "Isn't it more painful? Isn't it actually more difficult in the end when you have to deny your heart and your mind? Aren't you trying to walk through thorn bushes to get off the path you think God has put you on?"

She paused for a moment. "You're putting yourself back in the trap," she concluded confidently.

I looked at her quizzically.

"What trap?" I asked forcefully.

"Whatever trap he and God had to work so faithfully to free you from."

This statement runs through my mind as he removes himself and approaches the podium where I'm currently standing, where he'll continue running the event.

I quickly rush down the stairs to meet him as he comes around the back of the stand. When I approach, I can tell he doesn't know what I'm thinking.

I'm slow and purposeful as I get closer to him, and when he stands just before me I delicately place my hands on either side of his face and look at him intently. I want him to feel my sincerity.

When the gold in his eyes finally catches on my mossy hazel irises, I inch up just a bit on my toes and place my lips over the mark on his neck—his branding. In that moment I can feel the tension release from his body, and though he hadn't moved before, he now envelops me in his arms and holds me tightly against him. This is us again, back to almost normal. A new normal.

The most important thing is that now he knows. He knows his past is not going to inhibit our future, and he knows that I'm choosing to keep fighting despite the resistance I've had since the beginning.

# Epilogue

When I arrived back in Costa Rica a few months ago I didn't know what to expect.

The last bit of my internship had flown by and I went home with the promise that Xander and I would continue trying to make things work. I mean, how could we not after my grand revelation?

Mirari and I stayed in contact throughout my time back in Idaho, and she continuously reiterated to me that I'd have a job if I ever wished to return. My final courses ended quickly and my work through the summer was fruitful, but I longed to go back to Costa Rica. I couldn't be in a distant relationship anymore, and I had to either stop and find a new path or go forward—toward him.

So, after months of deep prayer I finally accepted her offer. At that point Xander didn't even know I'd been considering coming back. We talked every day yet this was something I couldn't tell him, in case it wouldn't happen.

Now, I stand across from him at the front of a church. Jo is beside me and two of our best friends stand before us, hand in hand, declaring their love and covenant to one another. I look up at him and see his eyes glittering with the haze of joyful tears. His *dashing* smile meets mine.

While it's not particularly common here, Luc and Violetta exchange rings with one another to visibly demonstrate this connection they're making. I look down habitually at the delicate diamond triangle that now rests on my ring finger in place of the purity ring that's held its place for so many years.

In five months we'll be in their place—Xander and I—and they'll be standing behind us in support, confirming that they are confident in God's plan for us together.

I'm caught in his smile and that dimple as I listen to the words of the preacher. He clings so dearly to these words of promise and commitment. I cling to them as well, though it's taken me a while to get to this place.

When Vi and Luc kiss and the ceremony is complete, there is an uproar of joy. The reception that follows is also full of excitement and celebration and love; it is full of contentment and peace—assurance of the future.

Jo's piercing squeal surrounds me quickly as the dancing starts to wrap up. She grabs my hand in a spin and then pulls it to her face before reminding me again of how she's partly responsible for the ring on my finger. We laugh knowingly but chat only quickly because we want to wish Vi well. Plus, I'll see her when we get back to our new apartment later.

When the bride and groom finally leave and everything has been cleaned, Xander grabs my hand and drags me away. When he hands me his helmet I'm plunged into darkness.

I shake my head and laugh. Again? He did this for our first date, the proposal, and now, but I can't think of what would be so special in this moment. It wasn't our day.

The motorcycle rumbles to life below us and it takes a while before we arrive at our unknown destination. Knowing the drill, I keep my eyes closed as I take the helmet off and follow as his hand pulls me close behind him.

The building he leads me into has a faint chemical smell, and a faint buzzing is buried beneath the radio that pounds music through the air. Immediately I'm more cautious, but his words in my ear are reassuring.

At his direction, I open my eyes. He tells me that this is really more for him than me, he just liked the idea of the surprise. All the markings of a tattoo parlor surround me and I'm thoroughly confused, to say the least.

The man at the front greets Xander warmly, as though he's been here before, so I assume he has. He eagerly turns to greet me as well and then without hesitation pulls a beautiful sketch out from under his desk. The style is almost that of watercolor, but it is simple and the colors are bold yet refined.

Tears prick my eyes as recognition hits. The gift is for him, he said, yet I feel like it really is also for me. He doesn't ask my permission to see if the design is acceptable; he already knew that I'd appreciate it.

I sit with him the next few hours as he gets this delicate image inked into his right forearm. As I sit there, I think and debate with myself, but really I know I've made my decision.

He finishes and pays the artist. "¿Lista?" he asks as he turns to head toward the door. I give myself one last pep talk and then shake my head no, I'm not ready. It catches him off guard.

I walk confidently back up to the tattoo artist and whisper quietly to him, asking if he can do a piece for me as well, even without previous notice. A smirk tugs up the side of his mouth in understanding and he nods gleefully.

I make Xander wait at the front for the next hour or so while my piece is completed. Mine is on my left arm, in the same place he has his mantra, though mine is not words. Oddly enough, I always thought my first tattoo would be words.

When I finish, I tell him to close his eyes. Delicately I grab his right hand in my left. There's a slight sting of pressure from my muscles when I loop my fingers through his. It's oddly comforting.

He squeezes my hand, asking permission to see if he can finally open his eyes. "You can open them," I say softly, nervously, not knowing what he'll think.

We both look down at these two images together. The fox that rests upon his arm is exquisite, displaying a perfect representation of the one so delicately drawn on the postcard that started all of this over a year ago. Seated gracefully, it appears beautiful and delicate with its orange and red shaded fur. In its golden, sharp eyes, it appears strong and powerful. Beautiful and strong, the attributes he's given me time and time again.

His question follows his finger as it traces delicately over my arm. Under his touch, the brilliant blue and white of the feathers appear to shift colors. A tear drop falls to my skin and I look up at him. He shakes his head and I think he's frustrated.

I pull my arm back, worried I've messed up, but he grabs it again and his question pricks my heart. "Why?"

His voice breaks on this one word, and I can see the confusion and the hurt. Hidden behind it, however, there lingers a hint of potential hope.

Why would I put this symbol of destruction and hurt on my body? Why would I want to remember that side of him? Why would I brand myself by choice, knowing the story line?

I'm silent and a tear comes to my eye as well, falling toward where his fingers still delicately grasp my arm. I smile up at him. "This bird is now a symbol of redemption and of restoration. A reminder that no matter the circumstances or environment we're in, we can break free; when we seek God, he sets us free. You've helped show me that, Xander. You've shown me that I can risk trusting and loving; you've shown me grace and you've shown me faithfulness. You've shown me my God. This, for me, represents all of that."

His dimple becomes more profound with each sentence as conviction rolls from my tongue. "I love you, Xander Urraca," I say with finality, making sure to include his last name—this label of his that I am eagerly willing to wear.

He squeezes my hand tightly. "Te amo, Adelina," he says as his smile brushes a kiss atop my knuckles. The weight of his words and our future now swims in my heart completely as we stride joyfully out of the parlor with our newly painted arms entwined between us.

## THE END

# Author's Note

It was late one evening in my junior year of college when I began to write this novel. My relationship with God was feeling very flat, I felt numb and disconnected and I wanted a way to reignite this relationship. Writing, specifically journaling, has always been a way for me to communicate with God when I've felt I don't have the words or keep getting too distracted in prayer. So, I thought, why not write? This time was different. I wanted to engage my own heart in a new way to express some of my thoughts, but as a story with a conclusion I myself hadn't experienced yet.

When I was younger I always loved reading romance but I didn't particularly love some of the more adult styles romance books could get into. I wanted to see these beautiful and fun stories from a different perspective, so that was the direction I wanted to write from.

Adelina's character blossomed so much from my own heart and my own story. Yes, I was also 20 when I started writing, and I was to be heading to Costa Rica for my next semester of school, which is where I ended up completing my first copy after tweaking the pieces to fit the area better. More than that though, Adelina's fears and doubts about love were something I found myself wrestling God about. I loved my singleness and the freedom it provided me to do what I wanted and also to serve God. While I didn't find my love in Costa Rica, I believe this book served to open so much of my heart to finally see all the things I'd hidden away. In it God prepared me for the year to come, when I met Peter, who would come to be my husband (reach out to hear more of that story, because in my mind, it was better than any novel that could have been written!).

The details related to human trafficking are based upon research that I did while in high school and university. Tragically, due to the highly touristic nature of Costa Rica, it is a prime place for this to flourish. While I myself have never worked at a restoration home or spoken with a victim, I've had the opportunity to interview workers in this field from other parts of the globe as well as to speak with the local Costa Ricans about some of the effects they see. I in no way intend to state facts within the novel, but the stories represented were meant to depict some of the most common stories of those who are trafficked globally. If this in any way touched your heart, please research the global effects of human trafficking and find ways to get involved or reach out for some of the resources I have!

# Acknowledgments

As a new author, it has been such a joy to receive so much encouragement and help in this novel. First and foremost I can only praise God for his help in this book. I was constantly astounded by the scripture he would bring to mind or even pieces of the plot when I felt like I couldn't go any further.

I want to thank you, mom and dad, for all of the love and encouragement you have given me through life. With your help during school, with my hobbies, and even as I began to venture out into farther places and to risk not only my own heart but yours. Mamma, thank you for being my first reader and for all the help since. Daddy, thank you for each and every time you've told me you wanted to see this book published and that we'd do anything to make that happen, here it is.

Ryden, thank you for your love as we grew up, for being the sibling who always had my back, and for the fact that I know you definitely would've been willing to beat up any guy who needed it if he messed with my heart. I'm so proud of how much you've grown in these last years and for how you've trusted God more with your heart as well.

To my grandparents, thank you all for showing me the intentionality of time with loved ones. Nana and Grandpa, thank you for all the times you invited us over or out for walks because you wanted to be invested in our lives. Grams, thank you for the many stories that bred this love of storytelling in me and Gramps, thank you for showing me that it's okay to step out of your comfort zone to talk to people and show them the love of Jesus.

To my wonderful husband Peter, thank you for being the one to see the deepest walls around my heart and to push me toward God for healing. Thank you for your patience and love and for how much you have shown me that romantic love is really worth it as we are able to work together for the Lord.

To all of my girls, thank you for the ways you have challenged me and loved me with the utmost patience and grace (at least most of the time). Specifically my ladies from the Underground, I love you so much; thank you for pushing me closer to God and for sharing my love for the nations and dancing! Alanna Kay, thank you for always being the one to share even the hardest truths with me, even if no one else will. Ameena, thank you for our adventures and for being willing to challenge me with the perfect balance of grace and truth. Meg, thank you for all of those road trips where you asked the best questions and made it clear you were trustworthy from the start. Mimi, thank you for your gentleness, for your constant reminder of God's mercy. Annarose, thank you for being mi media naranja, the one who understands my love for Latin America, for practicing Spanish with me, and for all of our explorations. Kayla Jo, thank you for being my fellow introvert and book lover, and thank you for being the one who always calls out my crap. A huge thanks also to the guys in the Foxhole for welcoming me and for the ways you challenged me to open up in friendships and to pursue the Lord in community.

Thank you to the ladies from Theta. Jay, thank you for your encouragement and for partnering with me in the depths of ministry. Mads, thank you for being raw and for showing me what it means to embrace our emotions and be vulnerable with others. Yajaira, thank you for your encouragement to let down my walls and for always having faith that I would find love one day.

For my girls on the Logos Hope, thank you so much for helping me in my own journey of unwinding my heart, specifically when it came to Peter. Keila, thank you for meeting me in the middle of the night when I was emotional or any time I needed an adventure. Talita, thank you for letting me come to your 'office' so many times, for being so understanding of all my fears, and for showing me incredible compassion. Fi, thank you for being real with me and for being bold enough to speak from your heart, whether regarding your life or mine. Noomi, thank you for coming alongside me in the end and for being the sweet but quirky spirit my heart needed when I felt so alone.

For the lovely ladies in the Inner Pentagram, thank you so much for exploring Costa Rica with me and for making it a temporary home. Rae, Kiks, Caeli, and Maggie, I'm so grateful for how each of you made our time so unique and memorable.

I want to say a huge thank you to my editor Rachel Rant at Bluebird Writing and Editing Solutions. Thank you for all of the time you've put into this, for encouraging me that it could actually be something that people would want to read. Thank you for helping me rearrange my plot and for making the story really demonstrate Adelina and Xander in the best way. Thank you for all of the long-distance communications and the few times we've connected in person!

Agata, thank you for sitting with me in the depths of drydock to work out the best translations for each situation according to a Tica's perspective.

Steph, thank you so much for your work on the cover! I'm incredibly grateful for the time and details you put into it. It reflects Adelina and Xander's story and I couldn't have asked for more!

I want to thank every one of you who has heard about this book and has shown interest or excitement. It's been such an encouragement. And for those who have read it, thank you for taking the time to dive into Adelina's heart and for sticking with her even through all the internal strife. I'm so grateful for the love and support in this journey!

# About the Author

Payton E. Carrigan is a new author in the YA and Contemporary Christian scenes and her first novel, *Unbound*, has attracted readers around the globe. She has degrees in Psychology, Sociology, and Spanish, all of which played into the writing of this novel. Payton was born in Idaho but now finds herself living in Ireland with her husband. They are currently living out their passions through serving alongside the church and investing in international community development. Payton continues to seek the depths of love and writes about these profound mysteries in her spare time.

If you loved this book, don't forget to leave a review on Amazon and Goodreads. For more information about Payton and her writing, visit her on Instagram.
@author.paytonecarrigan

Printed in Great Britain
by Amazon